Jon Rance writes novels about love, family, relationship, and all the messy bits in between. His novels have been described as hilarious, romantic, and perfect for fans of Mike Gayle and Beth O'Leary. His first book *This Thirtysomething Life* was a self-published Amazon top-ten bestseller and subsequently published by Hodder and Stoughton. Jon grew up in England, but now lives in California.

Also by Jon Rance

One Hundred Moments of Us
Not Moving Out

JON RANCE

NOT MOVING OUT

hera

First published in the United Kingdom in 2025 by

Hera Books, an imprint of
Canelo Digital Publishing Limited,
20 Vauxhall Bridge Road,
London SW1V 2SA
United Kingdom

A Penguin Random House Company
The authorised representative in the EEA is Dorling Kindersley Verlag GmbH.
Arnulfstr. 124, 80636 Munich, Germany

A CIP catalogue record for this book is available from the British Library.

Print ISBN 978 1 80436 858 9
Ebook ISBN 978 1 80436 863 3

Printed and bound in Great Britain by Clays Ltd, Elcograf S.p.A.

Look for more great books at
www.herabooks.com | www.dk.com

1

To Charlotte and Jack

Chapter One

Joe

Freya and I agreed to meet at Pelicano Coffee Co in The Lanes, which we had been to before during happier times and it was one of our favourites. We could have held the meeting in the comfortable surroundings of home, but we thought a neutral venue like the Paris Peace Conference after the First World War was probably better. Paris seemed a little far, and so we decided on one of the best coffee spots in Brighton instead. We were meeting to discuss the terms of our separation, write a manifesto of a way forward, while sipping coffees and nibbling on pastries on a damp morning in late March. It was a thoroughly depressing occasion, but at least the coffee would be on point.

'I see a table back there,' said Freya tentatively, looking towards the rear of the coffee shop.

'Right, I'll get the coffees. The usual?'

'The usual,' said Freya, with a nostalgic glance towards me that sated both of our needs for something meaningful in a morning that had, until that point, felt unwaveringly practical and devoid of the emotion it deserved. It was like watching one of the royal family lay a wreath on Remembrance Day. You knew there were emotions beneath the surface, but they were so focused on doing a good job, and not falling over in front of the nation, it always came across as a bit robotic. I ordered Freya her usual oat milk latte, and my flat white, plus a couple of pastries, and waited for those before I walked across and sat opposite my wife. It felt like a strange term considering she hadn't felt like my wife or done anything a bit 'wifey' for quite a while, but until all of this played out, she was still my other half. Better half? Probably.

Freya Jane Wallace was forty-five, and still beautiful in the same way she had always been beautiful to me. Strawberry-blonde hair, cornflower-blue eyes and pale skin she usually applied make-up to, to render her darker than she actually was, and to cover up the freckles she didn't like but that I adored. On family holidays in years gone by, she would go the entire week make-up free, and I would get to see that gorgeous face in its natural state, and it was always my favourite version of her. Today she had on a layer of make-up and her hair was pulled into a high ponytail exposing her ears with the two small earrings in each. She was also wearing her tortoiseshell framed glasses, which I preferred over her contact lenses. In essence, Freya, the woman I was about to discuss breaking up from after almost nineteen years of marriage, looked fucking gorgeous, and I knew that whatever happened going forward, it was highly unlikely I would find a partner I would find physically more attractive. This fact cast a shadow over the whole affair and had me questioning why we were even there. I also knew the answer to that very question like the easiest question on *University Challenge* that literally everyone got right. Our marriage that had once upon a time felt perfect, destined to last a lifetime and perhaps beyond if you believed in that sort of thing, had come to a grinding fucking halt.

'Thanks for the coffee,' said Freya with a tentative, uneven smile.

I hated the awkwardness and the stilted small talk. It was like an uncomfortable first date but without any of the sexual tension.

'Right, well, I suppose we should, you know, crack on,' I replied, stumbling over my words in an effort to get the ball rolling so we could get this over and done with as quickly as possible.

'Right,' said Freya, reaching down and grabbing a small handful of the Danish she had wanted, breaking it off and popping it delicately into her mouth. I noticed she had dark nail varnish like the sort you might wear at a funeral or on Halloween, which reflected something of the mood: sad and scary. 'It was me who wanted this meeting, so I guess I should start.'

I took a sip of my flat white, and then I crossed my legs.

'Joe, you and I are broken. Our marriage hasn't felt like a marriage for probably eighteen months if we're honest.'

'It hasn't been that long, Freya.'

'It has, Joe. It's been gradually getting worse and worse, and I can't take it any more. It feels like we're just going through the motions, but we aren't happy, are we?'

I looked at Freya, and at the small crease between her eyes that always appeared when she asked a serious question, the way her forehead wrinkled, and her eyes looked at me longingly – not that sort of longing because she was fucking right about that – but more with a need for me to get on board with the separation idea.

'No, I suppose we're not particularly happy,' I replied.

'It's time we ripped the plaster off, get it over with so we can both move on with our lives or at least try something different because just blindly staying together feels like it's hurting us more than helping us, and we have to think about Dolly. I can't keep living in limbo, Joe. It's fucking killing me. Something has to change.'

Talk about a dagger to the heart. She wasn't pulling any punches, although I couldn't disagree with her. We both knew why we were there. We had seen the trailer multiple times, read the reviews and knew exactly what was going to happen when we sat down with our popcorn.

'Understood.'

'You agree we need to officially separate?'

The words, although expected, said out loud felt like a swift punch to the gut. Almost nineteen years of marriage, and it all came down to two fucking words, and they weren't 'I do'.

'I mean, yes, I suppose. I'm just not sure how we officially separate. What's the protocol?'

'It means we have to tell people. Dolly first, obviously, but then family and friends.'

'So, saying it out loud makes it official? Perhaps something in the newspaper, too? *The Telegraph* has a lovely announcements section,' I said, realising I was being a facetious knob, but the whole fucking thing was making me feel like a bit of a prick. It was easier for me to resort to childish banter than actually dealing with it like a proper grown-up.

The truth was, I hated that my marriage was dead, that I had to somehow move on, make new arrangements, and I had to tell people about it. It all sounded like a bunch of work I didn't want to do, and I already had enough work with actual work, and now I was adding to it by officially separating from my wife. I had a sudden pang of nostalgia for days gone by when couples stuck together through thick or thin, no matter how thin it got. You married for life whether you were happy about it or not, because there wasn't another fucking choice. You signed the contract and it definitely said 'till death do you part', so from a legal standpoint there was no getting out of it until you drew your last breath. What was so wrong with that?

'I suppose saying it out loud does make it official,' said Freya, coolly. She wasn't falling for my usual prickly self when it came to discussing us, or anything vaguely serious or important. She also knew sarcasm and humour were my first line of defence.

'So, we tell Dolly, and then what?'

'That's what today is about, Joe. It's about sorting out the practical stuff, like where we are going to live, what our day-to-day lives will look like, finances, and how we deal with other things like potentially dating going forward?'

'Woah, what? Dating?' I asked incredulously, shocked how she had just casually dropped that in there, like tossing a grenade into a library, and wondering how long until anyone noticed. *Fuck, what's that small metal object that looks suspiciously like a grenade doing in the reference section?* 'What do you mean, dating?'

'I mean that eventually we're going to date other people, and it's something we need to discuss,' said Freya, casually. She had obviously already thought about this. Perhaps she had a date in mind or was already dating someone else. 'And before you say anything, no, I'm not dating anyone, Joe, and I don't have any intentions of dating anyone soon, but eventually it might happen.'

'Eventually, yes, I suppose it might.'

'But more pressing, Joe, is our living situation and money. You know we can't afford for either of us to move out, and I love our house. I don't want to end up living in a shit one-bed flat just because our marriage doesn't work any more.'

'Okay, I wondered when this would come up,' I said, feeling a flash of heat around the back of my neck. The burst of anger and frustration that got to me when the chips were down – and the chips were really fucking down. Of course, this came back to me and my inability to contribute financially to our marriage. The slow death of my writing career had contributed to the slow death of our marriage, and we both knew it. If there was a graph, and you could pinpoint when my career tanked on the y-axis, and how that correlated to the decline in my relationship with Freya on the x-axis, I think it would be quite illuminating. Especially if you were into graphs.

'What?' said Freya, taking a quick sip of her coffee.

'Money, and the fact I don't make any.'

'This isn't about that. I have never given you a hard time about how much money you make.'

'Or don't make, right?'

For the first time, I saw a flash of frustration on her face. 'For fuck's sake, can this please not be about you and your career for once.'

'I'm just saying, Freya, my career is a part of the problem.'

'Fine, obviously you want me to say it. Yes, your career is one of the reasons our marriage has failed, and yes, the fact you make barely any money has put a large financial strain on us that has contributed to the breakdown, but knowing that and acknowledging it doesn't actually change it. We need to deal with facts, and the facts are—'

'We can't afford to move out because of me, and so we're stuck together in the house?'

She looked at me, closed her eyes for a second, took a deep breath in and then slowly released it before she opened them again. 'All I'm saying, Joe, is at the moment because of our financial situation, neither of us can afford to move out.'

'Which is my fault.'

'For fuck's sake, really?'

We each took a moment. A pause to take a breath. A lady with a dog opposite gave us a look, and then stood up to leave. Even the dog looked a little uncomfortable. We had created an atmosphere.

'Fine, sorry, go on,' I said after a minute.

'I've been thinking about it, and I think I have a workable solution.'

I nodded, but I was already frustrated, and increasingly angry at this whole thing. This was all my fault. This was what Freya was trying to say in the politest way possible. We were trapped under the same roof because my career had imploded, and I hadn't made enough money in the last decade. Despite the lack of love in our relationship, we both loved the house we lived in, couldn't afford to leave it, and selling it wouldn't help because we had remortgaged it to pay off debts, and so now even if we sold it, it wouldn't be enough for either of us to restart our lives properly – not in Brighton or London, anyway. We were officially stuck in a marriage that didn't work any more but at least we had a gorgeous roof over our heads.

Freya worked at a solicitors' as a paralegal, and I couldn't help but think that the legal environment had rubbed off on her. She was being remarkably professional about all of this, when all I wanted to do was make snide remarks, and increasingly petty jokes about our fraught relationship. Freya, on the other hand, was revelling in her role of secretary, researcher and general all-round legal problem solver. She had already used the phrase 'workable solution'. How long before we were 'blue-sky thinking it', 'circling back' and 'putting a pin in it'?

'What's this "workable solution"?' I asked.

'Dolly will be off to university at the end of September, and I don't want to unsettle her during this important time with her exams coming up.'

'Neither do I,' I added quickly.

'So, for the next six months, we will keep living together—'

'You want to keep sharing a bed with me for the next six months?'

'No, Joe. One of us will move into the spare room, obviously.'

'By one of us, I assume you mean me?'

'We can toss a coin for it if you like?'

'No, it's fine, I'll go. It's already my office, so it's easier.'

'Right, thanks.'

'So, we keep living together for the next six months until Dolly leaves, and then what? You want to keep sharing like we're back at university? A couple of housemates, and I'll put a sock on my bedroom door when I get lucky? If you see a Marks and Spencer striped crew on the doorknob, don't come a-knocking!'

I looked across at Freya, and she looked back at me with an expression she had worn countless times before. It said something like: *Why do you always have to act like a total prick when it comes to anything vaguely uncomfortable, you ridiculous child?*

'It's six months, Joe. I think we can manage it.'

'But then what? Just because Dolly leaves for university, it won't change our financial situation. We still can't afford to sell the house, and living together but broken up will just be fucking weird and depressing like a sitcom but with literally zero laughs.'

I was waiting for her to say something about my last failed sitcom, but she wasn't that petty.

'We'll deal with that when Dolly is gone, but can we, for the next six months at least, try and get along?' said Freya, and then she added, 'For Dolly.'

She was right, of course, as she generally was. We had to make the next six months work for Dolly's sake, and then once she was gone, we would somehow try to sort out the rest of our lives, untangle the complicated web of our marriage, like unbuilding IKEA furniture without the instructions. It was only six months. How bad could it possibly be?

'For Dolly,' I replied, feeling a lump of sadness slide down my throat and into my chest, heading for the knot in my stomach because, despite my need to defend myself with immature retorts, I couldn't help but feel the agony of grief at the break-up of my marriage.

Chapter Two

Freya

When I first met Joe he was a ball of creative energy, excitement and ambition. He was filled with an effervescence that made me feel more alive than I ever thought possible. It was as if he was the half of me I didn't even know was missing. I realise this is obviously how the beginning of most good relationships start, but I genuinely thought for so long that Joe and I were one of 'those' couples. We had both found 'The One' – our soulmate. While other friends broke up with partners, moved on, were single and happy to stay that way or stuck in seemingly doomed relationships with partners they clearly weren't well matched with, we had struck relationship gold. Freya and Joe – as Rick Astley sang – together forever.

'I guess I'll move into the spare room today,' said Joe after what felt like an hour of silence, when it was probably more like two minutes.

'I'll make up the bed for you when I get home.'

'You don't have to do that.'

'I mean, changing the bed sheets has always fallen to me.'

'Not fallen, you're just better at it than me. You always get it so tight. I'm better with the bins.'

'Bins?'

'That's right. You do the bed and I do the bins. It's how it's always been.'

'Is this how we're going to delegate housework going forward?' I asked because I knew this was one of the practical things we needed to discuss. 'Who has always done them?'

'What do you mean? Wait, if we're going to get into housework, I think I need another coffee. Fancy another?'

'I'm good,' I replied, and Joe stood up and walked off towards the front of the coffee shop again.

While he was there, ordering himself another coffee, I took the opportunity to have a good look at my husband. He was still very handsome, and whereas other men his age had started to let themselves go a little, he definitely hadn't. He was still in decent shape, his dark hair was thinning with age but that wasn't something that worried me, and he had the same kind, soft eyes that had always pulled me in. I had no problem admitting I still fancied him – although I hadn't told Joe in a long time and probably wouldn't confide in him again – and any problems in our sex life hadn't stemmed from the physical, but were always to do with how I felt about him. We had lost that closeness, the emotional connection we'd always had, and it was that which was the fly in the relationship ointment. From a purely aesthetic perspective, Joe Wallace still had it as far as I was concerned, but it was hard to jump into bed with a man you'd just spent an hour arguing with about the cost of a writers' retreat in Cornwall, or why after almost twenty years of marriage he still insisted on waiting for everyone to get into the car and ready to go out, before he decided it was time to hoover up the mess that had been on the kitchen floor all morning.

Joe soon returned with another coffee, and sat down.

'Right. Where were we?' he said.

'Housework,' I replied. 'And who's doing what.'

'I mean, can't we just keep everything the same? Why do we need to suddenly start designating housework just because we're separated?'

'For that very reason. Case study. You're in charge of cleaning the bathroom.'

'Which I have done for years without a fuss.'

'Agreed, but what if you start slacking and I have to mention it or do it myself? Then it becomes a problem, and it's just something else for us to potentially argue about. I'm trying to make everything as easy as possible, Joe, so we don't have any reason to bicker or cause a scene in front of Dolly.'

I looked at Joe, and I knew he didn't want to be having this conversation and would, in fact, rather be anywhere else in the world than at that table with me. He didn't want to organise housework, discuss the finer points of our new reality, but I couldn't let him off the hook because I had been doing that for far too long. Joe's avoidance tactics and lack of desire to actually sit down and fix things was one of the reasons why we were in this position at all. He had flatly refused to see a marriage counsellor when I had asked, and his continued habit of placing his head firmly in the sand and refusing to acknowledge reality was one of the biggest stumbling blocks when we had both realised our marriage was in serious fucking trouble. Joe's tactic of repeatedly saying 'I'm sure it will be fine' obviously hadn't had the desired effect.

'You're suggesting some sort of housework schedule, I assume?' he finally said.

'Something like that, and we also need to discuss money.'

'Do we have to?'

'We can't ignore it, Joe. Right now we have a joint bank account, joint credit cards, and our finances are so intertwined, we need to talk about what we're going to do about it.'

I looked at Joe, and he sighed.

'I mean, you've always been in charge of money, Freya.'

'So you don't care what we do?' I said.

'Honestly?'

'Please.'

'Just do what you have to do. Rearrange our finances however works best. I just, I don't know, it's all a bit much for me at the moment. I trust you, and I'll do whatever you think is best to make this work.'

I looked at Joe and if there was one word I would have used to describe him it was resigned. He looked resigned to defeat, and it made me sad. I suppose a part of me had still held out hope that maybe he would have turned up today full of determination to fix us. Maybe he would have suggested counselling, and when faced with the reality that we were actually separating, he might have panicked and begged me to give him another chance. I worked for a solicitors' in Hove, who specialised in family and divorce law, and I had seen my fair share of couples who, after some tough reality checks and some professional mediation, decided that, yes, their marriages were worth saving – especially when faced with the reality of a single life at almost fifty. The thing was, I needed Joe to care and want to put in the effort, and at that moment, neither seemed to be true.

'Even if it means giving you a fixed weekly budget?' I said, and I waited for his reaction.

'Sorry, what do you mean, a fixed weekly budget?'

'At the moment, all our money funnels into the joint account and we both spend whatever we want and we pay bills from that account too, but if we're separated, I think it makes sense if we budget ourselves.'

'And because you bring in more money, I assume you're suggesting you get a bigger budget than me?'

'I think that's fair, don't you?' I said. Perhaps this was the thing that was going to elicit a response and make him care. However, after a moment, he just looked at me and smiled.

'I suppose it does. How much pocket money will I get?' I detected the sarcasm in his voice, and I knew he didn't love the idea, but he would accept it because he wasn't up for the fight, and also when it came to finances he knew he didn't have a leg to stand on. We existed almost exclusively on my wage.

'We can discuss the details later. Shall we move on?'

'Suppose I'd better enjoy this coffee now, while I can still afford it,' said Joe, before his face broke and he added, 'I'm only joking.' Although it was clear he definitely wasn't.

We discussed the finer points of our separation, and what would happen after Joe had moved into the spare room. We would disclose any dates to the other person, and no dates would be brought back to the marital home, obviously. Although we both acknowledged that neither of us were expecting anything to happen on that front anytime soon. We would, as much as possible, try to keep eating together, mainly for Dolly's sake, but as our lives separated further, alternative shopping and eating schedules would emerge. Flexibility would be needed, I stressed like a politician discussing difficult policy changes. The main thing, we both emphasised, was that no matter what happened over the next six months, Dolly always came first. She was the greatest thing we had created, and she was at a pivotal point in her education, and we weren't going to fuck that up just because we didn't want to be married any more.

Eventually, after almost two hours of talking, we stood outside the coffee shop, about to say goodbye. Opposite was a florist: Joe had bought me flowers there once on his way home from London after a successful meeting and had good news to share. It felt like a lifetime ago now, and was another reminder of the complete and utter failure of our marriage. We had agreed upon our 'Manifesto of Separation' without arguing or raising our voices – much – which felt like a bit of a triumph. But was it too easy? Shouldn't Joe have argued his corner just that bit harder? Joe had never been one to fight and, over the course of our marriage, I could count the amount of times we had shouted at each other on one hand, but that part of us that I used to think was a positive was now suddenly a giant red flag.

'I'll see you later then?' I said to Joe.

'Okay. We can talk with Dolly.'

'Should we order a takeaway? Stress that, despite our break-up, we can still do normal things together.'

'Good idea. Perhaps an Indian?'

'Sounds great.'

'Right then.'

'Off to see your mum?'

'Said I'd pop in after. You?'

'Just home to work.'

'Right.'

Joe smiled, and then I turned around to leave.

'Freya?'

'Yes,' I said, pivoting back towards him.

'Are we giving up too soon?' he said, and I noticed subtle notes of desperation in his voice like key changes in a song. Maybe he cared more than I thought.

I looked at him with a blank face, and then I smiled. I knew what he meant, but the truth was I didn't know the answer. It wasn't like we had decided on a whim. It had taken eighteen months of gradual decline to arrive at this point. We had fallen into this hole and despite some attempts to clamber out of it, we appeared stuck, resigned to our fate, and neither of us knew of another solution, and so I said the only thing I could think of.

'I don't know. Maybe. Maybe not.'

I looked at Joe, and he smiled a sad sort of smile. He was still so handsome, but it was hidden underneath a veil of all his disappointments.

'Okay. I just…'

'Just what, Joe?'

A pause. Was he going to say something to alter the course of our lives?

'It's nothing. See you later?'

'Okay. Bye then.'

'Bye.'

Then I turned around, and walked away through The Lanes towards Mum's house, but as soon as Joe was out of sight, I turned down a quieter lane, and then I stopped. I closed my eyes, squeezing them tightly together, and then I let the tears come. The tears I had been holding in all morning. There had been so many tears shed over the last eighteen months, and all of them had been because I wanted to save my marriage and the thought that it might be over scared the living shit out of me. But these tears felt different. They felt like the tears you shed not when you were afraid your marriage was over, but the tears that came when you knew it was.

Chapter Three

Freya

I was standing outside of Mum's house in Preston Park. The ominous gunmetal clouds that had been gathering all morning had finally relented, and it had started to spit with rain. A full stop on what had already been a pretty shit morning. After crying in The Lanes, I pulled myself together and dragged myself there for a cup of tea with Mum, or in reality probably something a little stronger. She had texted on the way over.

> Are you coming over this morning? Martin has a doctor's appointment. Haemorrhoids. I have a hair appointment with Angela at two. Hope everything is ok. Mum x

After Mum and Dad got divorced and Dad disappeared to Jersey, Mum moved down from Surrey and bought this house to be nearer to me and Dolly, where she had lived alone until Martin entered our lives. They met in Waitrose and, according to Mum, they both reached for the same jar of marmalade and the rest as they say is history. After hearing that story, Joe and I had given him the nickname Marmalade Martin or more commonly just Marmalade.

I suppose I had always known my parents weren't the happiest of couples, but I was still shocked when they finally announced the break-up of their marriage. I was eighteen and had just left home for university when it happened and my biggest takeaway from their split was how it made me feel. They had clearly been waiting for me to finish sixth form, and so all I could think was that they had obviously been unhappy for years and I was the only thing keeping them together. If that was the case – and they insisted it wasn't – surely they would have been better off breaking up and being happy much earlier. I also made a pact with myself that I would never do that to my own child, and yet here I was doing the same fucking thing. I hated myself for it. Joe and I were no better than my own parents, which was a thoroughly depressing thought because they had set a pretty low bar.

I pressed the shrill doorbell, waited, and then after a moment the door opened and Mum appeared.

'Oh, Freya, darling, there you are, you poor thing, come in, and you can tell me everything over a glass of wine,' said Mum, who despite being home alone was dressed in a gorgeous sequined dress, had her blonde hair styled as if she was going out somewhere nice and a full face of make-up. Mum lived her life by one simple rule: Always be ready to go out!

Mum knew why Joe and I were meeting. She was the only person I had confessed everything to because, well, she was my mum and it was impossible to hide it from her. She could see the cracks in our marriage, the stunningly low disappointments, the long silences when she would come over for a Sunday roast, and the obvious air of tension between Joe and me that had become increasingly tense. She had lived that life, knew the signs to look out for and recognised exactly what was happening. She had questioned me over and over again when I had insisted my marriage was fine, and she made me tell her everything. Mum was many things, but persistent and nosy were definitely in the top five. At least with Mum, I knew that however intrusive she was, it was all wrapped up in love and good intentions.

'Oh God, Mum, it was awful,' I said, walking in and falling into her arms for a hug. The moment I felt her body pressed against mine, I felt a few tears loosen, escape and then slide down my face and onto Mum's dress, but I quickly pulled myself together. Mum wasn't much of a crier. She was solid, strong and always in a positive mood. Growing up, I hardly ever saw her cry. It felt like she didn't believe in sadness in the same way that some people didn't believe in God or election results. If only I had her classic English stoicism, and point-blank refusal to mope no matter what. Her upper lip was perfectly stiff, while mine often wobbled and waned.

'Come in, sit down, and tell me all about it. I have two glasses of wine, chilled and ready to go. There's nothing in life that can't be sorted out with a good chat and a nice glass of Chardonnay, darling.'

I laughed. 'I'm not sure that's true, Mum,' I said, walking along the hallway with the refinished oak flooring, and then into the vast glass-and-brick extension at the back of the house that contained the kitchen and dining room. After her parents had passed away, Mum had inherited some money, which she had ploughed into the house.

'Remember Gloria Parker? Drives a Range Rover and has two cocker spaniels? She found her husband, Roger, trousers around his ankles behind a Pizza Hut with a girl half his age. A Pizza Hut, darling! She was a mess, but came over. Two glasses of wine and a few choice words later, she was like a different woman. It helps, trust me.'

'Fine, I'll give it a go,' I said as we reached the kitchen, and I sat down at the island.

'That's my girl!' said Mum, passing me a chilled glass of French Chardonnay. 'Cheers!'

'Cheers,' I said, knocking my glass gently against hers.

'Right, so how did the big marriage summit go?'

'Honestly? Pretty shit. It felt like he didn't care enough, Mum. The old happy-go-lucky, passionate Joe, the man I married, would have done more. He would have fought for us, gone to couples' counselling at least, but he just accepted everything and agreed to move into the spare room with barely a whimper. It's like all the failures with his writing, all the rejections, the bad reviews, each one has stripped away layers of him, and now he's just fragments of the man I fell in love with.'

'People change,' replied Mum. 'I would never have imagined that your father would have become the man he did when we walked down the aisle. Not that he cheated on me or did anything particularly awful, but he just became boring. He stopped living, stagnated in his shed, while I took care of everything. Although he seems happy now with whatsername in Jersey, so maybe it was just me. People do strange things when they get older and realise they're far closer to death than they'd like. Middle age is a weird time, darling.'

'I know, and I'm to blame, too. I could have done more. Tried harder. Maybe I could have gone to couples' counselling on my own, but I expected more from him. It's like he's wilting, and it's sad to see, but I can't make him care. I can't make him better.'

'It isn't your job, either.'

'It also just feels like over time we simply changed, and the newer versions of us weren't as compatible as the older ones. It's like when you upgrade your iPhone to the newest iOS and realise some of the old apps don't work any more. The old us when Joe was successful, when *The Mornings* was flying high in the BBC ratings, was perfect. Then when *Loosely Translated* flopped, and his career fell off a cliff, we sort of did, too. All the years of financial pain, living mainly off my income and some residual payments from *The Mornings*, all of it took away small chunks of our relationship, dug into it and scooped out bits of our happiness.'

'Oh, darling, I'm sorry, but I'm sure you did all you could.'

'Then why do I feel like a complete and utter failure, Mum?'

That was the crux of the issue for me. Since I was a little girl, I had always been a high achiever. I hated failing at anything: school, sports or keeping plants alive. I was captain of the school netball team, and my desire to win and hatred of losing were my key attributes. My parents always said I was the little girl who never gave up on anything, illustrating this with the family myth about our guinea pig, Nutty. Apparently, when I was eight years old, I found him dead in his cage one morning, and tried to resuscitate him – mouth-to-mouth because I had seen it on *Blue Peter*, although obviously not with a small hairy rodent. Determination was, and had always been, my biggest personality trait. I wasn't the most intelligent pupil in school because that award always went to Nicola Birch, but it didn't stop me from trying to get better GCSE results than her. I ultimately failed but I never gave up and only missed completely straight As by getting that one bloody B in geography – thanks, Mr Morgan! When we had Dolly, and with Joe doing so well in his career, I stopped training to be a solicitor to stay at home and raise Dolly. I hated stopping my training, but it was for the best job in the world of being a mum. However, the minute Joe's career started fading, and Dolly was in school, I returned to the world of law and became a paralegal. Now, with my marriage all but over, and Dolly moving away to university, I was exploring the possibilities of becoming a full-time solicitor once again. I hated failing at anything, but the problem with marriage was that it needed two people to believe in it, and not give up.

'Trust me, darling, the last thing you are is a failure!' said Mum with a sort of Blitz spirit in her voice.

'Thank you,' I said, reaching across the island and placing my hand softly over hers.

'You are welcome, and if you need anything, you know I'm here for you. Me and Martin.'

'Oh, right, yes. How is Marma, I mean, Martin and the haemorrhoids?'

'He's been better, but he'll be fine. He's got a classic car show in Gloucestershire next weekend, so hopefully he can drive to that. His old Austin-Healey has about as much suspension as a cheese grater, so it's a bit of a sore ride at the best of times.'

'Poor old Martin.'

'Poor old me. He wants me to apply the haemorrhoid cream!'

'Oh, Mum,' I said, laughing, and then taking a sip of my wine. Maybe Mum was right and a good natter and a glass of wine were helping. Mum fetched a bowl of olives, some crackers and cheese, which she put out on the island for us to nibble on, before she looked across at me.

'Are you one hundred per cent sure you and Joe are done? Are you completely convinced your marriage is over?'

'I fear our marriage is like one of Martin's old cars.'

'Cars? Sorry, you've lost me.'

'You know how some cars gradually get worse over time, slowly bit by bit they break, you try and fix them, but one day you realise you've done your best, but it's time to trade it in for a newer model? Other cars have a massive crash, and they're immediately a write-off. I think Joe and I just gradually came to a halt, and despite having a good look under the bonnet, we've both realised it's probably just fucked.'

'You're sure there's no chance you'll be able to get it back on the road?'

'I don't think so,' I said glumly because it made me incredibly sad. 'And the worst part is that we're stuck together in that house. We can't afford to sell it at the moment, we can't afford to rent something else, and so we're just stuck together.'

'What about when Dolly is gone?' said Mum, before she popped a large green olive in her mouth.

'I have no idea.'

'You do know I'm more than happy to help. I could give you some money, we have the spare room here, so you can always stay with us, and—'

'Mum, we will figure this out, but thank you.'

'Well, if you change your mind, you know where I am.'

I appreciated Mum's offer, but the truth was I would need a lot of money to get back on my feet, and I didn't want to burden her with that. Plus, I was an adult, I had got myself into this situation, I would somehow get myself out of it. Despite Joe's lack of concern and emotion when it came to us, I was still a fighter with a career in law, and I would find a workable solution because that's what I was good at. I was a problem solver.

'We're going to tell Dolly tonight.'

'How do you think she'll take it?' said Mum, a look of concern on her face because she adored Dolly. She was her only grandchild. Marmalade had been married before but had no children of his own.

'Not sure. She knows things between us aren't great, obviously, she isn't stupid, but separating is something else. I hope she's okay, and it isn't like someone has cheated or that Joe and I hate each other. We've just fallen out of love. Hopefully it makes things easier.'

'Hopefully,' said Mum. 'But then again, when your father and I broke up, under similar circumstances, I remember you were angry at us for years.'

'I don't think it was years, Mum.'

'Trust me. It was years!'

I ended up staying at Mum's for lunch. She had some leftover pizza, which she heated up with a small salad, before I had to head home. I said goodbye to Mum on her doorstep with hugs, but before I left I had one last question for her.

'Whatever happened to your friend, Gloria Parker? The one with the cocker spaniels. Was she okay in the end?'

'Eventually, yes. After "trousers-around-ankles gate", it took her a little while to get herself together, but now she's living in Broadstairs with a woman.'

'Oh, right.'

'So, you see, darling, there's always the chance for a second bite of the apple, or in Gloria's case, a change of fruit completely!'

We said goodbye, and I started walking. The rain had eased off, and I always loved the smell of the air after rain, and the way everything seemed fresh and new. Maybe I would get my second bite of the apple like Gloria, and who knew, perhaps it would be even sweeter than the first. Although, as I put my earbuds in and listened to some music, all of that felt like years away.

I took my time and slowly weaved across Brighton back towards Seven Dials, where our house was. I was listening to a Spotify playlist and 'Chasing Cars' by Snow Patrol came on, and I was instantly transported back in time.

The year was 2006, and the second series of *The Mornings* was on, and doing better than the first. Joe and I were living in our flat in Archway, I was pregnant with Dolly, and Snow Patrol released 'Chasing Cars'. It became the song of that part of our lives, and seemed to always be on no matter where we were. Whenever I heard it now, I was back in our old flat with its crap furniture, and the view of the church out of the bedroom window. Joe and I had been so happy, still in our twenties, and living the London dream. We had only just begun talking about the possibility of moving to Brighton once Dolly was born. As I was walking home, listening to 'Chasing Cars', I couldn't help but cry, the weight of tears behind my eyes desperate to escape, because the song that had been so much of us when we were happy now felt like the death knell of our marriage.

Chapter Four

Joe

Our house was a three-bed terraced property in the Seven Dials area of Brighton. We bought it in 2008 before the house prices in Brighton shot through the roof and doubled in value over the following years. The house had been in the same family for over fifty years before us, so it needed a lot of work, some good old-fashioned TLC, which we were happy to do, and so after just one showing we put in an offer, which was accepted, and our move from London to Brighton was rubber-stamped. After the flat in Archway, it felt enormous and ever so grown-up, but we were excited by the opportunity to renovate a house and make it exactly how we wanted it.

Set over three floors, it boasted a number of original Victorian features, wooden sash windows, ornate corni-cing, cast-iron fireplaces and a large walled garden with mature trees and shrubs. Over the next ten years, we added the downstairs extension, which meant we had the fashionable kitchen diner, plus bifold doors to the back garden. We added a new modern bathroom upstairs, and a utility room off the kitchen. Freya kitted the whole house out with some lovely decor, furniture and soft furnishings from various upscale retailers as well as some upcycled antique gems. It truly was our dream home, but it seemed that once we had made it perfect, every square inch full of everything we had ever wanted, my career tanked, our marriage started to gradually fall apart piece by piece, and now we faced the prospect of having to sell it. It was almost as heartbreaking as the break-up of the marriage itself. It felt like we had spent so many years curating the perfect life to then wake up and realise that, actually, it wasn't as perfect as we had thought all along.

Freya ordered the takeaway from our usual Indian restaurant, which was utterly delicious, and because they knew us so well, they always popped in a few extra bits and pieces. Freya laid everything out on the kitchen island, and we were helping ourselves to the little containers which were full of rice, curries, and then the poppadoms with various dips, which were Dolly's favourite. Dolly was still in her pyjamas, as she hadn't been outside all day. She said she had been studying in her room, which I believed because, unlike me, she was a diligent student, who had ambitions of getting straight As in her A levels and going to Durham University to read English. At her age, I was more concerned with drinking, comedy and girls, and not necessarily in that order. I performed well enough at sixth form, and went to a decent enough university, where I got a perfectly reasonable 2:2 – a drinker's degree – but I was always just doing enough to get by, while my real passions were outside of education. So many evenings when I should have been studying or writing essays, I was at comedy clubs or watching sitcoms, studying for the career I knew I wanted.

Dolly was somehow a perfect mixture of Freya and me. She had my dark hair, dark eyes, and Freya's pale skin. She was reasonably tall, slim, and had her mother's dogged determination and drive, but somehow my creativity and love of the English language. Today she was in baggy checked pyjama bottoms, a grey hoodie, and her scraggly hair was loosely tied back in a ponytail with one of the many scrunchies I would often find lying around the house. The family bathroom often felt like a graveyard for used scrunchies. She had on the same glasses she'd had since secondary school, that were slightly broken, probably with the wrong prescription, but which she refused to replace – they were good luck, apparently. She was filling her plate full of chicken korma, pilau rice, garlic naan, saag paneer, onion raita, mango chutney, mint yogurt and a whole extra plate of poppadoms. She grabbed a can of full-fat Coke from the fridge and sat at the table.

'Thanks. This is the first proper meal I've had today,' said Dolly eagerly.

'I know you want to do well at college, love, but you need to keep your strength up,' replied Freya, with a sort of 1980s advice vibe because Dolly had always been successful, whether her strength was kept up or not. During her GCSEs, we often had to bring food to her room, or she would forget to eat altogether. I feared that when she finally got to university, she would live off cereal, snacks and endless cups of coffee, which would actually be better than my diet at university, which had been largely alcohol-based. At least Dolly had the occasional smoothie with fruit and sometimes vegetables and she drank water, while my choice of a quick snack back in the day was more likely a Pot Noodle, and water was only ever consumed as tea or coffee.

'I'm fine. I had two coffees this morning, a Snickers for lunch, and they're always claiming they give you lots of energy. Plus an apple, so one of my five a day!'

'Still, love, you need to do better. We can't have you fainting mid-exam,' said Freya.

'It would reflect very badly on us,' I said.

'That's not what I meant,' said Freya pointedly.

'I'll try and do better,' said Dolly. 'I wouldn't want to bring shame upon the family name.'

'Good family name,' I added with a smile.

'Sorry, good family name,' said Dolly, and she looked at me and smiled back.

Dolly and I had always been close, and we shared the same sense of humour, which I think frustrated Freya somewhat. They were close but in a different way. They were mother-and-daughter close, while we shared something slightly more cerebral. We connected on a deeper level that often didn't need words and included lots of silly in-jokes and repeated banter. Dolly and I had always laughed a lot, and she had made comments about wanting to write comedy, or maybe even perform, which made me incredibly proud.

Freya and I filled our plates up, too, while Freya poured herself a glass of white wine and I got myself a can of Camden Hells lager from the fridge before joining Dolly at the table.

I looked across at Freya, she looked back at me, and I knew that neither of us were excited at the prospect of breaking Dolly's heart. I hated the thought that we were letting her down because, whichever way you sliced it, we had failed and, in doing so, we had also failed her. Freya and I loved her so much, and yet it wasn't quite enough to keep us together. At least we were waiting for her to move out before the actual separation, which was something. But then she would have the difficult decision of whose house she would go to during breaks from university. With the family house gone, it would undoubtedly become something of a game-show-style backwards and forwards between Freya and me with elation for the winner and commiserations and possible bitterness for the loser. Whatever way you looked at it, we had let her down, and the future wasn't the Disney version of a family we had spent years doing our best to make a reality.

'So,' said Freya when we were about halfway through our meal. 'There's something we need to talk to you about, love.'

Dolly stopped eating and looked across at Freya. I was beginning to sweat, but I didn't know if it was because I was nervous or whether it was the heat from the madras curry I had ordered. It felt like we were drawing the curtains on her childhood and, after this, everything would be different. Freya looked across at me for support. She obviously wanted me to help break the news. Perhaps my 'special relationship' with Dolly might somehow help soften the blow, and maybe I could sneak a joke in there and make everything better.

'Dolly,' I said, and she looked across at me. 'You know that your mother and I have been having some issues for a while now. We haven't been happily married for quite some time.'

'Okaay,' said Dolly. Another crunch as she popped a poppadom in her mouth.

'Well,' I replied, looking across at Freya, who gave me an encouraging nod. 'We've decided that what's best for us, for our future, is to separate.'

I said the word and we both looked across at Dolly, trying to gauge her reaction. Would she burst into tears? Would she dash out of the room in horror? Laugh?

Be angry? Disappointed? Sad? Neither of us knew how she would respond, but I don't think either of us were prepared for her actual response, which came swiftly, and with barely a flicker of emotion.

'Right, okay,' she said brightly, as if we had just told her we were changing our brand of toilet paper. She didn't seem bothered at all, which was a very strange reaction indeed. To confirm her feelings upon the matter, she dipped another piece of poppadom in yoghurt, and then popped it in her mouth with a loud crunch.

'Did you hear what your father said?' said Freya, sounding concerned.

'Uh-huh,' said Dolly, her face giving nothing away.

'You aren't a bit sad about it?' ventured Freya. 'Or angry? Disappointed? It's okay, whatever you're feeling, love, you can tell us.'

Freya and I looked across at each other, both worried by our daughter's apparent lack of emotion about our separation. Dolly wasn't an unemotional person by any stretch of the imagination. As a young girl, she was always full of love, empathy, and she was never shy about expressing her feelings. Even as a teenager, she was never one of those grumpy, short-tempered teenagers, who retired into themselves, and barely said a word to their parents other than the occasional mumbled request for a new app on their phone or money for clothes. I had always felt like Dolly was an open-ish book, but now she was reacting to our news with barely a flicker of emotion.

'I'm sad, obviously,' said Dolly finally.

'Sorry, but you don't seem very sad,' said Freya. 'You seem almost, I don't know, ambivalent.'

'Well, I'm not,' said Dolly with the same level of control. 'I think it's sad.'

'But?' I asked.

'But nothing,' replied Dolly.

'Nothing is going to change until after you leave for university,' said Freya, trying to reassure her. 'Your dad will move into the spare room, but otherwise it's business as usual.'

'Business as usual!' I reiterated for some added assurance, although I couldn't help but feel like I was jumping on board with a position we all knew was essentially bollocks. We both looked at Dolly, hoping for something slightly more emotional or something that said she cared.

Instead, she stood up, and said, 'I'm going to my room to study.'

'You didn't finish your food,' I replied.

'I'll get it later,' said Dolly, disappearing out of the room, and then we heard her feet on the stairs, and then her bedroom door closed with a thud. I looked across at Freya.

'That was strange.'

'It was,' said Freya. 'Do you think she properly understood?'

'I mean, we were quite clear and she's a smart girl.'

'Right, agreed. It's just… I don't know. Should one of us go and talk to her? She's clearly not handling this very well. You know how much she enjoys an Indian.'

'Maybe leave it for now. Give her some space, and I'm sure she'll get some food later.'

'Right, okay.'

'She'll talk when she's ready,' I said, and Freya looked across at me and I knew exactly what she was thinking: *Like you, you mean?*

Freya and I ate the rest of our food in a strange, uncomfortable silence before tidying everything away in the same strange, uncomfortable silence. Tonight hadn't gone how either of us had imagined, and I think we were both feeling a little unsure about what was going to happen next. It felt like the last six months had all been leading up to today: when we would separate, tell Dolly and then put the wheels in motion. The nights we had spent in deep conversation talking about our marriage. What had happened. Could we fix it? Should we get couples' counselling? We had spent so many hours talking, trying to work out a solution, our marriage like a giant jigsaw puzzle we just couldn't complete, no matter how we looked at it, and we had looked at it from every possible angle, but now that we had decided to put the puzzle pieces back in the box, everything felt underwhelming. Despite us agreeing it was a positive decision to separate, as we got ready to head upstairs to bed, it felt like anything but.

The spare room was at the front of the house, and it contained a bed, a wardrobe and my desk. I had chosen that room for my office because the window looked directly out to the street, so I could hear the mutterings of conversations, the whir of traffic and life, which inspired me when I wrote. Plus, it got the morning sunshine, which was when I worked the best. The room was large, airy and had a wonderful light to it, but now it was also my bedroom I felt a slightly different vibe. More student accommodation than modern workspace.

'Everything all right?' said Freya, poking her head around the door.

'Thanks for putting sheets on the bed. You really didn't have to.'

'It's fine,' said Freya, and then we had another painfully long silence.

'What did your mum say about it?' I asked finally.

'Just that it would be okay in time. She got over Dad, and her friend Gloria is now a lesbian, so you know, second lives.'

'Right, okay, sounds… encouraging?'

'Yes. I suppose.'

Another pause.

'Marmalade has haemorrhoids,' said Freya finally.

'Oh, blimey. Poor Marmalade.'

'Poor Mum, actually. She has to apply cream to the affected area.'

'What a pain in the bum!' I said, and we both laughed, more out of nerves, it seemed, than with genuine laughter, but it helped. 'This is fucking weird, isn't it?'

'It is, but it's day one, Joe.'

'Right, day one. I hope Dolly is okay.'

'She'll probably be angry at us for a few years.'

'A few years?' I said incredulously. 'I hope it isn't that long.'

Freya stood by the door and looked at me, and I don't think either of us knew what to say next. Day one of separation and it all felt strange and surreal. This was the woman I had spent so long married to, seen naked from just about every possible angle imaginable, and now we were acting like awkward, hormonal teenagers.

'Night, Joe.'

'Night,' I replied, and then she left me alone in my new bedroom.

I hadn't moved all my stuff into the room yet, but I had enough to begin sleeping in there for the night. I lay in bed listening to the gentle hum of traffic outside. I heard Dolly moving around the house as it got late, and she went back downstairs to get some more food. I thought of Freya in our old bedroom, and despite being in the same house I had been in for the past fifteen years with the same people, it was the first time I had felt alone in it.

Chapter Five

Freya

Three years before Joe and I sat in a coffee shop and made the arrangements for our separation, we were in bed one night, side by side; he was on his phone, and I was on mine. I was doomscrolling through my Facebook feed when I noticed something odd, and on further inspection, it seemed my initial suspicion was proved correct.

'I think Emily and Nick have broken up!' I said.

'What? Emily, your old university mate Emily, and tall Nick?' replied Joe, resting his phone on the bed for a moment.

'I was just looking through some photos she put up on Facebook, and Nick's not in any of them. It's just her and the kids.'

'That doesn't mean they've broken up, though, right?'

'It doesn't, but then I went back through her old photos, and noticed a pattern. Nick's not been in any photos for a good six months. He was in photos, and then he wasn't. I cross-checked that with her Instagram account and it's the same. She even deleted all the photos of them together. Nick's been cancelled!'

'Nice work, Sherlock.'

'I can't believe it. Nick and Emily were amazing together. They were the "it" couple at university. Remember their wedding?'

'Yeah, it was grand.'

'Why are you saying grand? You aren't Irish.'

'Sorry, I've been writing an Irish character for a thing, and he says "grand" a lot. Maybe too much. I should probably learn some other Irish words other than "grand" and "feckin' eejit".'

'Probably,' I said, looking across at him. 'Joe, promise me we'll never break up.'

'Never going to happen.'

'Why? It happened to Emily and Nick, and I thought they were nailed on for life. They were the couple most likely to die in each other's arms at ninety, and now they're probably haggling over child support.'

'So many reasons, Freya, but really the main thing is that the thought of having to go through all my social media accounts and delete all the photos of you seems like a lot of work.'

'You knob,' I said, punching him gently on the arm.

'But seriously, we're okay.'

'Just okay?'

'Better than okay. There's nothing in the world that could break us up. Just because Emily and Nick couldn't make it, it doesn't mean we won't. I'm afraid you're stuck with me.'

I put my phone down, slid across the bed towards Joe, cuddling into him. He was right, we would be fine. Maybe Nick cheated, or Emily had an affair. Perhaps there was something else going on I didn't know about. Maybe they had just fallen out of love. I would text her in the morning and find out, but at that moment, I was with Joe, and we were going to be fine. Better than fine, we were going to be feckin' grand!

–

My office was in one of the gorgeous white Georgian townhouses on the border between Brighton and Hove. The building had five floors in total and our solicitors' took up three of them. Becket, Godwin & Anderson had been in the same building for as long as I had worked there, and I loved walking into work each morning. The office space, despite being in a charming old building with bags of original character, was modern and fresh. It was minimal in design with lots of Scandinavian-inspired furniture and plenty of green plants that helped bring the outdoors in. The partners, Sam Becket, Brian Godwin and Claire Anderson, were all lovely and had made me feel like a part of the family from day one. I had been there for nearly ten years now, and I was already in discussions with them about continuing my studies and becoming a fully fledged solicitor, and they were completely on board and said they would do whatever they could to help.

Becket, Godwin & Anderson were like a second family, and my best friend in the family was Lucy Bailey. Actually, she was more like a sister, and she worked on reception and so was the first person I saw each morning when I walked in.

'Morning,' I said, walking up to her small reception area where she lived for most of the day. 'Receptionist' was something of a misnomer to what she actually did. She was everyone's personal secretary, office manager and the person in charge of making sure that everything ran smoothly. We never ran out of coffee, biscuits or toilet paper because Lucy made sure we didn't. When it was someone's birthday, she bought the cake, and the card for everyone to sign. If Becket, Godwin & Anderson were a family, she was the matriarch. Today she was sitting behind reception, sipping on a coffee and opening the morning mail.

'Morning,' said Lucy.

Today Lucy had her brown hair tied back neatly in a ponytail, two silver earrings hanging from her ears and above her slender neck.

'Good weekend?' I asked, desperate to tell her about mine but at the same time desperate not to. She knew Joe and I were having problems; we had discussed the less-than-finer points of my marriage many times over lunchtime sandwiches, but she didn't know the full extent of them.

'Not bad. The usual. George and Henry both had cricket in Lewes all day Saturday, so that was it really. Stuart worked most of Sunday, but after Cold Water Club, so I had that time just for me, which was lovely.'

'Ah yes, Cold Water Club. How's it going?'

'Freya, it's brilliant. You should come along. There's no better start to the day than a brisk dip in the sea, followed by a flask of hot tea, and a good natter with mates.'

'Brisk? I think it's probably a bit chillier than brisk. Doesn't it freeze your nipples off?'

'You get used to it, and it makes you feel so alive. You should come once, and if you totally hate it, I won't bug you again. Promise.'

'I'll think about it,' I said, as Sam Becket came walking in behind me, carrying his folded-up Brompton bicycle.

'Morning, ladies,' he said in his deep, warm voice.

'Morning, Sam,' we replied in unison.

Sam Becket was tall, handsome, recently turned fifty, and divorced from his wife, Helena. He had two grown-up children and cycled to work on his foldable Brompton bicycle. Every day, you would see him outside folding it or unfolding it, and he stored it in his office. He had already taken his helmet off, his now slightly greying hair beneath, cut short and neatly groomed, and he was wearing a navy suit with smart brown leather shoes. He always smelled incredible, too, and was one of those men that had a signature scent. I wasn't sure what fragrance he used, but it had hints of citrus, maybe bergamot, something spicy and warm, and with deeply woody undertones. He definitely had the handsome, middle-aged solicitor thing down to a tee, and there had been talk since his divorce about whether he was dating again. Sam walked past us, and then up the stairs to the second floor and his office, his bicycle in one hand, and his leather briefcase in the other.

'Do you want to get lunch today?' I asked Lucy. 'I need a chat.'

'Sounds ominous.'

'It's not, it's just something.'

'Then I'm in. I didn't have much for breakfast, and I quite fancy a nice sandwich or something. About twelve thirty?'

'Perfect. See you then,' I said, and then I walked up the stairs towards the space where my desk was, in an office I shared with two other more junior paralegals. I settled in, got myself a coffee from the kitchen, and then got to work, grateful to be busy to take my mind off Joe and Dolly's reaction to our news. I had barely seen her since we told her. She had been in her room all of that night, and then she went to Maya's house all of the next day. I had texted her, and asked if she was all right and wanted to talk, but she said she was fine, just busy with college work, and so I left it, but I couldn't stop worrying about what it might mean. Sometimes Dolly felt like a code I couldn't quite crack. I wanted to be closer to her, wished we had that classic television mother–daughter relationship, that I was the one she went to for advice, but we had never quite had that. If anything, she was closer to Joe, which was something I'd always had a hard time with. I wasn't jealous of their relationship, and I was glad she had someone she could talk to, but I also quite wanted that person to be me.

It was bright out, and Lucy and I walked from the office to an artisanal cafe nearby. I didn't often have lunch with Lucy because we were generally both too busy, but I needed to talk to her. Lucy's husband, Stuart, was good friends with Joe, and I didn't want Lucy finding out about our separation from him. I had no idea whether Joe was going to tell Stuart, but I couldn't risk it, and it would be good to get her perspective.

'What's going on?' Lucy asked, tucking into her sandwich.

I was nervous about saying the words out loud. I had talked to Mum, and Joe and I had told Dolly, but this felt, if anything, slightly scarier. Lucy was a friend and once it was out in the real world and people other than close family knew, it would make it seem more real. It would be news. I took a small breath and then I said the words I had been rehearsing all morning.

'It's me and Joe. We've decided to separate.'

'Oh, shit, Freya, that's…' She paused for a moment, probably trying to choose the right words. She placed her sandwich back on the plate. 'Really shit. Are you okay?' She reached a hand across the small table and placed it momentarily on my arm for support.

'I'm fine, I suppose, given the situation. It's been coming for a while, so.'

'Really? I knew you were having some problems, but I suppose I just thought you'd figure them out. I mean, we all have our ups and downs, don't we?'

'We do, but the last year or so has all been down for us, I'm afraid.'

'I'm so sorry. You know if you need anything, I'm here for you. Stuart, too.'

'Won't he be on Joe's side?' I said without realising what I had actually said.

'We don't have to take sides, do we?' said Lucy, an expression of concern flashing across her face like a heavy cloud suddenly moving in front of the sun.

'No, sorry, shit, I didn't mean it like that,' I replied quickly. 'I just meant, you know, because they're mates and men, that's all.'

'Right, good,' said Lucy, and I took a bite of my cheese toastie, and then a sip of my coffee.

'To be honest, it feels strange. Like, it's not really happening,' I said, after a moment.

'What do you mean?'

'I don't know, but you imagine the end of a marriage, and you think of countless fights, long emotional talks late into the night, and just something big and gargantuan coming between you like an affair or a midlife crisis. You think that after almost nineteen years, it would feel like someone had ripped my heart out, like I did when Adam Turner dumped me at eighteen, and I cried for a week and refused to eat. But this, it just feels too… civilised.'

'I mean, this is Joe we're talking about.'

'And?'

'He's just not very emotional, is he? Have you two ever had a huge fight? You know the sort when you're screaming in each other's faces, and you want to kill them?'

'Well, no, but I always thought that was sort of a good thing. Have you and Stuart?'

'Oh, yes. Usually before the best sex ever! Stuart's passionate, I'm passionate, and sometimes it bubbles over, but I think it's good. We get everything out in the open. It's like how sometimes you need a really big thunderstorm to clear the air. Joe always seemed like the sort of bloke who was just a bit, I don't know, apathetic. Sorry, I'm not trying to be callous.'

'No, no, it's fine. Maybe you're right. He hated arguing, and so we didn't. So many things were never said, or discussed because he couldn't handle it. I don't think it's that he doesn't care enough, but that, well, if you met his dad you'd understand. They're exactly the same. If anyone so much as mentioned a feeling, or heaven forbid shared something too personal, it was like you'd taken a shit in the middle of the room. Even when Joe's mum died, it was just, I don't know, weirdly unemotional. They're like a working-class version of the royal family.'

'Which is why maybe now it feels like it's limping to a rather sad finish.'

'I hadn't thought about it like that before,' I replied, and the more I thought about it, the more I realised that Lucy was right. Joe hated fighting. He never raised his voice, or engaged with me, and instead we both let the little things fester. Maybe over time all those little things became bigger things and because we didn't deal with them they slowly destroyed us. When I had suggested marriage counselling, Joe had declined and repeated the same mantra over and over whenever the topic came up: *If we can't deal with this ourselves, Freya, then our marriage is already over.* What he hadn't considered, and what I hadn't either, was that maybe what we really needed was just to scream at each other a bit.

'I think what you need is Cold Water Club. It will literally change your life!'

'Change my life?' I asked, because I didn't understand how standing in the freezing cold sea at seven o'clock in the morning would change my life.

'Guaranteed,' said Lucy with a smile.

'Fine. I'll come.'

'Yes!'

'But just once, and if I hate it or get life-threatening hypothermia, you'll leave me alone?'

'On Stuart's life,' said Lucy before we got back to our sandwiches, my mind suddenly feeling somewhat lighter because maybe Cold Water Club was at least something new, and maybe Lucy was right about shouting at Joe – was it the solution we had been searching for all along? Whether either of those things would ultimately change anything I didn't know, but it was surely a move in the right direction. Actually, it was just a move, and moving felt good because for so long my life had felt stuck and unmoveable, and perhaps just doing something different was all I needed to feel alive again.

Chapter Six

Joe

Dinner time had always been the one time when we would get together as a family and share the details of our day, and despite whatever else was going on, we had that. Also, I think that, because I worked from home alone all day with just my thoughts, it was something I particularly looked forward to. I was the house chef, and I loved trying out new recipes on Freya and Dolly, and so for me dinner was always one of my favourite parts of the day. It was important, or it had been, before. Now, with Freya and I separated, and Dolly being weirdly ambivalent about it, the tension in the house was palpable and so dinner was different. Today, I was in the middle of cooking my famous spaghetti bolognese – only famous in our house and for wildly unspectacular reasons – when the front door opened, closed, and then Freya came walking into the kitchen.

'Oh, you're cooking,' she said, standing next to me suddenly.

'I am. We hadn't discussed dinner time, and so I just thought—'

'No, no, it's, umm, fine, I just didn't—'

'What?' I said, turning away from the hob and facing her. I had just put the spaghetti in, and was monitoring it while the sauce was in a separate saucepan, being kept warm on a low heat. I'd made a two-hour bolognese sauce, and I still needed to grate some Parmesan cheese. 'Shouldn't I have cooked?'

'No, Joe, honestly, it's fine, really. I, umm—'

'Something smells good,' said Dolly, suddenly walking in behind Freya. 'Hi, Mum.'

'Dolly, hi,' said Freya.

'I'm literally starving,' said Dolly, walking across to the fridge and grabbing the orange juice, before she walked across to the side, got a glass from the cupboard and poured herself a large glass.

'Do I have time for a quick shower?' Freya said, turning back towards me.

'Umm, yes, sure,' I replied.

Freya awkwardly smiled before she left the room, while Dolly sat at the dining table.

'Do we have garlic bread?' she asked. 'I'm literally craving it.'

'We do not.'

'Disappointing.'

'Sorry,' I said, and when I looked across at her, she smiled at me. 'How was your day?'

'Yeah, you know.'

'No, I don't know, Dolls, that's why I asked.'

'Oh, you want details. Such a boomer move,' said Dolly, and I could tell from the tone of her voice that she was playing with me. We did this. A jovial backwards and forwards, and it was what we were good at. I was close with Dolly, but it had its limits. We were close when it came to things that weren't too personal or difficult.

'That would be great, Dolls, and FYI, I am a part of Gen X,' I said, putting a fork into the boiling water, and giving the spaghetti a spin to make sure it wasn't sticking.

'Let me see,' said Dolly. I heard the shower being turned on in the en suite in my old bedroom. Earlier, I had moved all my toiletries into the main bathroom I was now sharing with Dolly and her million bottles of 'stuff'. 'My day was fine.'

'Fine? That's not details. That's fluff.'

'Are you sure we don't have any garlic bread?' said Dolly, and I just gave her a look before I turned back to the stove and stirred the spaghetti again.

I honestly hadn't considered not cooking dinner, but when Freya came in, I could immediately see that she hadn't expected it. We had discussed finances and our distinct lack of them, housework and other living arrangement things, but we had neglected dinner. We had said something generic about being flexible with dinner time, but what did that mean? Was I supposed to check each and every day who was home for dinner? Perhaps foolishly, I had thought we would carry on as usual. Without dinner, we wouldn't have a time to catch up, a moment to still be a family, and the idea of not doing it hadn't entered my head. Business as usual, right?

I finished cooking, and started serving as Freya came walking back into the room. She was in her pyjamas, her damp hair tied back in a loose ponytail to keep it out of her eyes. She looked just like she had a thousand times before, post-work shower and walking into the kitchen for dinner. The only noticeable difference was that she was definitely wearing a bra. In years gone by, she had often returned home from work, and immediately taken her bra off with a smile and a sigh, saying how good it felt – I would often joke or say something about 'letting those babies breathe' or something else along those lines. She wouldn't usually put a bra on post-shower unless we had guests, but once again, that was very much then and this was very much now. Two very different time periods.

'Thanks for dinner, it smells great,' said Freya, sitting down at the table.

'You're welcome,' I said, walking across with a plate of spaghetti bolognese for Dolly and placing it in front of her. 'Cheese?'

'Please,' Dolly replied.

I brought across the block of hard Parmesan and the grater.

'Say when,' I said, and started grating cheese over the top of her meal like I had done hundreds of times before.

'When,' said Dolly when she had a small mountain of Parmesan over the red sauce so it looked like snow. I walked back to the side and brought Freya's plate of food over.

'Cheese?' I asked Freya.

'It's okay, I can do it,' she said with a forced smile.

'Yes, right, okay,' I said, handing her the grater and the plate with the block of cheese on.

All of this felt so unnecessary. Grating her own cheese, making her own dinner, doing her own washing, and I got it, we were separated, but did that mean I couldn't do anything for her any more? If I was popping the kettle on for a cup of tea, was I banned from asking if she fancied a cup, too? Was I still allowed to text her from Tesco and ask if she needed anything? What was next and where would it end?

I got myself a glass of red wine, and then offered Freya a glass but she declined, fetching herself white wine from the fridge. Dolly was vigorously stirring her cheese through her spaghetti, and then Freya sat down with her wine, and then I grated some cheese over the top of my bolognese, and it was time to eat. Everything was basically the same as it always had been, except for the fact that every slight thing we did felt ridiculously self-conscious and completely different. Every word and movement was under the microscope. I glanced at Freya, she returned my look, and I think both of us knew what we had to do. We had Dolly, and she was the main/only reason why we were even doing this. Without her, this would have been even more excruciatingly awkward. She was the glue that was holding this shitshow together.

'How was your day, love?' said Freya, looking across at Dolly with a hopeful smile.

'Fine,' replied Dolly.

'Still just fine?' I asked.

'What's that?' said Freya.

'I asked her before about her day, and all I got was "fine" despite requesting details.'

'Fine isn't details, love,' said Freya.

'That's what I said,' I said, and we both looked across at Dolly, who was expertly twisting spaghetti on to her fork.

'I don't know what you want me to say,' said Dolly. 'My day was fine. How was your day, Mum?'

Dolly and I both looked across at Freya, who looked uncomfortable being put on the spot like that. It was as if we had suddenly shoved a camera in front of her face and asked her a problematic question live on TV. Obviously she couldn't just say fine. There was a pause, an awkward silence that stretched across the table. This was the new reality of us. Whatever she shared with Dolly she would need to share with me, and perhaps she wasn't comfortable with that. We were in a war situation and information was king. Secrets needed to be kept and loose talk could potentially cost, well, not lives exactly, but something else. This was all new to me and, honestly, I didn't know the rules yet. It was like playing a game of cards I hadn't played before; it would take time, and while I was still going through the rules, I would definitely lose quite a few hands out of sheer stupidity.

'My day was good. I had lunch with Lucy, which was nice, and I was given a new case to work on, and—'

'It's okay, you don't need to drag it out because of me,' said Dolly.

'I wasn't, I—'

'How's Lucy?' I asked, before I shovelled a forkful of spaghetti into my mouth.

'Yes, all good,' said Freya.

A silence. Dolly looked across at me. I looked back at her.

'Great,' I replied to Freya.

Another pause.

'Maya is pissed off with me,' said Dolly suddenly.

Freya and I looked across at her with relief. Something meaty to get our conversational knives and forks into.

'What, why?' said Freya.

'Don't know. You know Maya, she's… temperamental.'

'Right, yes, totally,' I replied, but I didn't know because I had only met her a handful of times, and I had no idea if she was temperamental or not. Apparently, she was.

'I had a friend around your age,' said Freya. 'Shelly Barnes. I thought she was a good friend, we had known each other since primary school, but she would change gears faster than a Formula One car. One minute we were as thick as thieves, sleepovers, and talking about boys until the early hours, then the next day, it was like you'd physically assaulted her family.'

'What happened with you and Shelly? Did you stay friends?' asked Dolly.

I looked across at Freya because I had never heard this story before.

'It was just before my seventeenth birthday. I was having a house party and I had invited everyone we knew from college, and Shelly and I had a huge fight. She claimed I was only having the party because she had mentioned that she was having one, and apparently I stole her thunder. Long story short, she turned up drunk, tried to set fire to the sofa, and attacked Simon Thompson with a frozen cheesecake because she thought I was trying to get off with him.'

'Oh my God!' said Dolly. 'That's crazy.'

'How have I not heard this story before?' I asked incredulously.

'I don't know but it was insane,' said Freya.

'What happened to her?' said Dolly.

'I never saw her again after that night, and her family moved to Swindon soon after.'

'So, the moral of the story is?' I asked.

'Don't make friends with psychos?' conjectured Dolly.

'I don't know. I'm sure Maya isn't like that, but I suppose the moral is, sometimes friendships don't work out and that's okay. There was a time when I thought Shelly and I would be friends forever, but then she tried to burn my house down,' said Freya, and we all giggled, and it felt good to just laugh together at the table. For a wonderful moment, all the awkwardness evaporated and we were just us again, eating, talking and acting like a proper family.

Unfortunately, once the laughter died down, the rest of dinner played out more like the first half had, like a challenging play you had been ushered along to see with a friend because they had a spare ticket, but you spent the whole time trying to work out what the hell was going on. There were long, difficult stretches that were hard to watch, and broken, stilted conversations that seemed to be heading nowhere, until finally it was time for the last scene, where hopefully some of it made sense and you had a clearer idea of what had just happened. Dolly eventually left and headed back upstairs to study, and Freya and I were cleaning up. I felt like I had to say something.

'I'm sorry about dinner,' I said, rinsing a plate under the tap before placing it into the dishwasher.

'No, it's fine, Joe. We didn't discuss it, so it's just… it's fine.'

'Details please,' I said, looking across at Freya.

'I don't know what the answer is, Joe. Being separated, and yet still having dinner together every day feels a little strange, but also not eating together feels like…'

She stopped, I stopped, and we both stood in the kitchen and looked at each other.

'Strange, too?' I ventured.

'Something like that. Can we just play it by ear?'

'Of course,' I replied. 'I still can't believe the Shelly Barnes story.'

'I know. I hope Maya isn't another Shelly Barnes.'

'I doubt it. It sounds like Shelly Barnes had real mental health issues. Have you ever tried finding her on Facebook?'

'Once, but she has no online presence.'

'Maybe she's in prison for arson or grievous bodily harm with a Cornetto,' I said before we got back to cleaning up, and Dolly was upstairs in her room, and it sort of felt like everything was the same but at the same time I knew it wasn't. Changes were happening, albeit slowly, but I knew that bigger changes were coming and soon, and we needed to prepare ourselves for them.

Chapter Seven

Joe

The first time I saw Karen was six months ago. I knew I needed help, but I didn't want to tell anyone or go to Freya because I didn't want her to worry, and so I kept it to myself. I still do. Karen O'Neill, my therapist, my secret, and the one person in the world who knows everything about the annoying fucking demons in my head. She was the only person I told about my panic attacks. It was when I knew I needed help because this thing in my head had become bigger than me, and I had no idea how to deal with it. At first I thought it was just me being stupid, weak, and that I needed to stop thinking about it, get my head down, work harder, and it would go away by itself. I needed to stuff it down, pretend everything was fine, but it didn't work like that, and the panic attacks got worse. But with Karen's help, I have managed to calm the voices in my head and understand myself better in the process, and yes, I know, I'm a massive fucking fraud and a piece of hypocritical shit because I refused to see a marriage counsellor with Freya, but this was different. I could just about deal with my own pain, my fears and deep-rooted anxieties, I didn't have the emotional bandwidth to deal with Freya's, too. I rationalised everything with the premise that if I could fix myself, then maybe I might be able to somehow fix my marriage, too.

Karen's office was in a semi-detached house next to Wish Park in Hove that had a large children's playground and a small cafe that served surprisingly good coffee. The house had been taken over with mental health professionals, and Karen's office was in one of the old upstairs bedrooms. It was a simple room with just her desk and chair, and then two comfortable chairs in front of her desk. When I first saw her, I was disappointed she didn't have a sofa like they always have on American television shows, and she said that wasn't really her thing, but that if I was more comfortable lying down, she was happy for me to lie on the floor. I could even bring along a yoga mat if that was something I wanted to pursue. I said I would sit. She had prints of pretty landscape paintings on the wall, a tall, leafy plant in the corner, and it always smelled lovely. It was a beautiful, clean space with a comforting, peaceful vibe. I supposed that's what she was going for.

'So, Joe, how are you, today?' said Karen with a relaxed, open smile, and I knew I would need to tell her that Freya and I had decided to separate. Karen was from Ireland, and somehow her accent always helped me open up. It was soft, smooth and mellifluous.

'Fine, I suppose,' I said before I paused. 'Freya and I have decided to separate.'

'Okay, Joe, that's big news,' said Karen, sitting up slightly taller, and jotting something down in the notepad she had in front of her. She always took notes during our sessions, which was slightly jarring at first, but I'd become used to it, and now I barely registered it. 'We should definitely discuss that. How do you feel about it?'

'Sad, obviously. We've been married for nearly nineteen years, and the fact it's come to this feels a bit like a failure.'

'What do you mean by failure, exactly?'

'Exactly that, I suppose. We failed. We set out to be together for the rest of our lives, and now we're not. It feels like we failed.'

'But do you think of your marriage as a whole as a failure?'

'No, of course not. We were really happy for most of it. We had Dolly, moved to Brighton, and created a wonderful life together.'

'So if you're saying that for the most part, your marriage was a success, why now do you deem it a failure? For most things in life, I think we can agree, that if it was a success for the majority of the time then we would call it a success, right? So, why in a marriage do we judge it differently? Why use the word failure?'

I looked out of the window for a moment. A warm ray of sunshine lent a soft glow across the room. Outside I could see a tree with a wonderfully eclectic array of branches, and then other suburban houses in the middle distance. I looked at one of the prints on the wall, a gorgeous English countryside scene, and I longed to be outside, perhaps walking on the South Downs. Despite living so close, I hadn't been walking for quite some time. I think I had just forgotten about it. I could drive for twenty minutes out of Brighton, and then walk for days through the most idyllic countryside on earth, and yet I didn't, and I had no idea why when it was all I craved at that moment.

'I don't know,' I replied, looking rather uncertainly at Karen. 'Maybe because marriage feels different. More personal. Freya and I were happy, and now we're not. I wish we could be happy again, like we used to be, but I don't know how we do that. Going backwards feels impossible and moving forwards even more so. Falling in love with her felt so easy, but maybe staying in love was the hard bit we just didn't see coming.'

Karen looked at me across the table. I never quite knew what she was going to say or suggest. The truth was, I hated therapy. I despised the idea of sharing my deepest, darkest fears with a complete stranger. I only came to her because I felt like I had no choice. When it came down to it, I was more scared about what might happen if I didn't get help than the help itself.

After years of professional failure, I was terrified I was done, that my career as a writer was over, and then what would I do? If I couldn't provide an income for my family as a writer, what was I? Perhaps it was just a classic midlife crisis. A crisis of identity. Being a writer was all I had ever wanted to be, and if I wasn't that, what was I? My heroes growing up weren't athletes or world leaders, but comedy writers. I grew up inspired by the great sitcoms of the Seventies, Eighties and Nineties like *Fawlty Towers*, *Only Fools and Horses* and *Blackadder*, and it was all I aspired to be, and then it happened. My own sitcom on the BBC was the holy grail. My dream had come true, and it felt like winning the lottery, but when it was gone, it felt like my heart had been ripped out. Some days I sat at my desk, and wrote nothing, because the pressure seemed too great, and others I would bash away for months at something, which would end up in the bin. I was anxious, couldn't see the light at the end of the tunnel, and then, of course, the panic attacks started, paralysing moments of intense self-loathing, and that's when I came to see Karen.

'I have a question for you,' said Karen, putting her pen down on her desk, and then looking back across at me. 'If I could give you one wish, what would it be?'

She had pulled that one out of the bag, and I had no idea what my answer might be. Actually that was a lie. I had two answers, and I was weighing up which one she wanted me to say. Sometimes therapy was just about playing the game.

'Just one wish?'

'Yes, Joe. If I could grant you one wish in the entire world, and before you answer, it can't be for more wishes. You have one wish, what would it be?'

There were obviously two clear front runners for this question. One wish would be for Freya and me to be in love and as happy as we once were. The second wish would be to have a successful sitcom on television again. She knew this was my biggest hope for my life, and she was using it against me.

'I have an answer, but it has a caveat.'

'Go on.'

'If I had one wish, it would be to have a successful television series again, but the caveat is that I genuinely think if my career hadn't gone to shit then Freya and I wouldn't have reached the point we have now. I think if I could be successful again, then maybe there would be a chance for my marriage, too.'

I looked at Karen with a smile, hoping I had given her the right answer or at least an answer she would agree with, but when she looked at me, it was clear I was wrong – although I'm sure she had once said to me that there weren't any wrong answers in therapy.

'Joe, why do you always associate your professional success with your personal happiness?'

'Because that's how I see it. I need to be happy and successful with my work to be happy and successful in life. Isn't that how everyone thinks?'

'So you believe that if you reached your professional goals then everything else in your life would just fall magically into place?'

Karen always had a way of looking at things that was different than mine. She liked to twist whatever I said into something else. It was quite a gift, which was why she was obviously a good therapist. I didn't see the world in the same way with the same complicated narratives. Why couldn't it be as simple as when I was happy at work I was happier with myself, and therefore a better husband and father? What was so wrong with that narrative?

'I think for me, personally, being a success, being able to provide for my family while being creative is integral to being happy. I need that something to aim towards, that goal, however achievable or not, because it gives me meaning.'

'But what happens when you reach your goal? Because you've reached it once before—'

'Twice, actually, if you include my doomed second sitcom.'

'Okay, twice, and yet here we are. Surely, it demonstrates that actually, what really counts in life isn't always money or success, but enjoying the process. Life is happening now, not in some faraway place in the past or the future, and you need to embrace and enjoy life today. Learning to accept our current reality, however far removed from the dream, is integral to being content, Joe, and that is something I think we need to work on.'

She leaned down, took her pen, and wrote something on her paper. I wasn't ever allowed to see what she had written down, but I had my suspicions. I generally thought she wrote something when she thought it sounded good, and maybe she could use it again because that was exactly how I worked, too. I saw her point, but it didn't detract from my overall feeling that at the end of the day, I really needed to get a show on television again. It genuinely felt like the cheat code to my life.

'Your homework this week, should you choose to accept it—' said Karen.

'*Mission Impossible*, love it.'

'I thought you'd appreciate it. Your homework this week, should you choose to accept it, Joe, is to really think about your marriage. What happened, and if you could go back and change something, what that might be?'

'Okay,' I replied, before she told me our session was over. I thanked her and then I was outside on the pavement, deciding what to do next.

It was a beautiful day, and I thought for a moment about going for that walk on the South Downs, but I would need to go home first, get changed, and then drive out of Brighton, and I needed to have something for lunch, and it was already two o'clock, and so I decided to go for a walk on the beach instead. I would walk home to Brighton along the front, and perhaps I would do the homework Karen had assigned me. Why had my marriage failed? Was it all to do with my work? With me? How had we gone from being so happy together, to separation, and whose fault was it? Was it anyone's fault or just one of those things? People got divorced all the time, and surely not all of the reasons were that complex. Sometimes, wasn't it just a case of people falling in and then out of love?

I had a lot to think about, and I had a meeting with my agent, Carl, in London soon, and I still didn't have an idea for my next project. My mind was full of so many problems, each like a ball, flying around my mind, crashing against all the other balls, and I was trying to stop them from moving so I could reach in there and grab one of them. I needed something solid to hold on to, to feel like I was getting somewhere, but the harder I tried, the more it felt like more and more balls were being added, and they were moving faster and faster, and it was impossible to get one and hold on to it for any length of time.

Chapter Eight

Freya

It was ridiculously early for a Saturday morning, freezing, and Cold Water Club were meeting in the car park by the beach. It was my first experience of cold water swimming, and I was sensibly nervous about the temperature, but also because underneath my warmest winter puffa coat, woolly hat and gloves, I had on a one-piece swimsuit I hadn't worn since last summer, and I had definitely gained a little winter weight – which might actually protect me from the harshness of the icy water, so was not all that bad in reality. This seemed like a terrible idea at seven o'clock on a weekend morning when I could be lying in bed. Instead, I was in the car waiting for all the other ladies to turn up. I was listening to Radio 2, and trying to wake up and warm up, when there was a sudden and very loud rapping on my car window that scared the hell out of me. I jumped, and then looked out of the window and saw Lucy's face staring back at me with a smile. I pressed the button to lower the window.

'Jesus Christ, Luce, you scared the living daylights out of me!'

'A very underrated Bond film. Ready for a dip?'

'What if I say no, and yes, a great song by A-ha, but Timothy Dalton?'

'Come on, it will be fun,' said Lucy with a warm smile. 'And never knock Dalton!'

I got out of my car, and gave Lucy a quick hug, and I could see the other members of Cold Water Club congregating near another car, all trying to keep warm. Apart from us, there were a couple of early morning joggers, and a few dog walkers, but otherwise it was empty. Lucy offered to introduce me, and so I walked over and met them one by one. First up was Debbie, or Debs as she introduced herself. Caroline was originally from Edinburgh, and I instantly loved her Scottish brogue, and her bright, bubbly personality. Then lastly, I met Helen and Amy. Four lovely women, along with Lucy, who met at the beach at least four days a week to slowly wade into intensely chilly water for fun. I was already questioning my life choices.

'You're going to love it,' said Scottish Caroline as we walked slowly towards the beach. 'Can't beat an early morning dook to start the day.'

'I'm not so sure,' I replied, already feeling quite cold, despite my woolly hat and gloves. I could only imagine how chilly I was going to feel after being in the choppy water. 'Sorry, what exactly is a dook?'

Caroline laughed. 'It's Scottish for, you know, a duck, or plunging. Dook.'

'Oh, right. I love it.'

'Aye, me, too. The cold water really connects your mind and body and afterwards you'll feel a natural high, and also an incredible inner peace. You'll feel like you can do anything, conquer any mountain that comes your way. Trust me, it's changed my life.'

'That's what Lucy said, too.'

'Then maybe there's something to it,' said Caroline with a bright, warm smile.

'Or it's one of those cult situations and I'll end up on the *News at Ten*,' I replied, as we walked down to the pebbly beach from the car park.

I had brought warm clothes to change into afterwards, a towel, and a flask of hot tea that I left on the beach. Suddenly, as we started towards the sea, I could see why Lucy loved it so much. There was something about being up and about so early in the morning with a group of women and doing something together that felt liberating.

It was one of the things I had been thinking about since Joe and I decided to separate. I had a small group of good friends, but being a wife, a mother and working full-time meant I didn't actually get to spend much time on myself. My life had been my family for so long, but now with Dolly on the verge of leaving home for university, and with my marriage all but over, I was beginning to look to the next chapter and it was a little terrifying. I wanted a good group of female friends, to pick up new hobbies, explore things I hadn't had the chance to before, and perhaps, if I survived today's rather frosty beginnings, Cold Water Club might be a part of my future. These women with their own lives, problems and stories might potentially be a group that could help me move on. Well, either that, or, as I suspected, being fucking freezing might put me off ever going into the sea again.

We congregated in front of the iron-grey sea, the small waves lapping against the pebbles on the beach. The sky was stretched out before us, a blanket of deep blue flecked with eggshell clouds, and a gentle gust that pulled our hair out behind us. It felt for a moment as if we were stepping into the unknown, the great beyond, with nothing behind us. To our left was what remained of the West Pier, jutting out from the sea like a postmodern art installation, and then beyond that the new pier, and the beach with its restaurants, shops and attractions I knew so well from the days when Dolly had been little and we had strolled together, eating ice cream, and Dolly had played on the beach, dipping her toes in the water with giggles. Memories unfolded inside me. I looked out at the sea, and it truly felt like I was looking to the future.

'Ready?' said Lucy, turning to look at me.

'Not really, but let's do it before I change my mind,' I replied, and we stepped forward together. Six women on the empty beach, and we walked into the water.

It was fucking Baltic! There was no getting away from it. I had kept my woolly hat and gloves on – advice from Lucy – which I hoped would help me avoid hypothermia, but the ice-cold water on my skin felt like it was burning me. We walked slowly into the water, the group chatting and talking, as if they were just getting coffee. Perhaps it was the way to distract their minds from the immense pain of the bone-chilling sea.

'How's Fran?' Lucy asked Debs.

'Yeah, she's well, I think. She's fifteen, and sometimes it feels like cracking the Enigma code just to find out how she's doing at school.'

'Aye, I know what you mean,' laughed Caroline. 'Mine are twelve and ten, and already it feels like they have a whole world of secrets they're keeping from me.'

'Just you wait!' said Helen. 'It only gets worse, but then one day it gets better. Evelyn and I are closer now than we've ever been.'

'How old is she?' I asked, trying to keep my mind off the cold as we walked slowly forwards, one careful foot in front of the other, feeling the jagged pebbles beneath. I noticed the other women had on black boots, which protected their feet from the pebbles and the cold.

'Twenty-four,' replied Helen. 'Which is crazy. It barely feels like a year since she was at school, and not that long ago since she was playing on this very beach. Now she's working and living in London. She has a boyfriend, who does something in the city, and Evelyn's a teacher.'

'How are you doing?' Lucy asked me.

Was I the only one shivering uncontrollably?

'Okay, just,' I said, as we got deeper and deeper. 'I can't feel anything below my waist.'

'It gets better,' said Lucy.

'Aye, the first time I took a dook, I promised myself never again. I was back within the week,' said Caroline with an encouraging smile.

When we got waist deep, Lucy told me that they were going to dip down to cover their shoulders and start moving around and swimming, but it was up to me if I wanted to do it, too. Because it was my first time, they said I needed to be careful and not stay in too long. I had to slowly build myself up to it. I said I wanted to experience it with them, and so after a short countdown, we all ducked down into the water until it was up to our necks. OH MY FUCKING GOD! I didn't know the actual temperature of the water, but I hadn't been that cold in a very long time or perhaps ever. It was a real shock. Adrenalin was definitely pumping through my system, and I'm sure my brain was trying to understand what was happening and applying the appropriate measures: *Brain to Freya, what the actual fuck are you doing because everything appears to be shutting down, over?*

The other ladies all started moving around to varying degrees. Caroline was full-on swimming, and even got her head wet, while Lucy sort of doggy-paddled in slow circles. Debs and Helen both walked around a bit to help keep warm, while Amy did a few breaststrokes before standing up again.

'You can get out whenever you want,' said Lucy, while she slowly swam around me. 'It's your first time, and you don't want to overdo it. A few minutes is long enough for a newbie.'

'She's right,' said Debs. 'My first time, I only lasted two minutes, and then I was up and out before you could say freezing nips!'

'Okay, I think I'm done,' I said, my teeth chattering.

'We'll be in soon. Get warm quickly,' said Lucy. 'And drink your tea. It helps!'

'Righto,' I said, wading as quickly as I could through the sea and back to the shore.

Once back, I grabbed my towel and quickly dried myself off, before I slipped on the fleece tracksuit bottoms and the top I had brought along, zipped up my long puffa coat and, despite my hands shaking almost uncontrollably, I put on my gloves, and opened my flask of tea. The tea felt so good as it slid down my throat. It was so warm, and it tasted incredible. I sat on the pebbly beach and watched the rest of the women in the water, swimming around without a care in the world, and I wondered if I would ever get to be that okay with sitting in freezing cold water. I watched them, drinking my tea; my body gradually warmed up, and I felt amazing. Caroline had been right: it was like a natural high. I felt giddy with endorphins, and I genuinely couldn't believe how right Lucy had been all along. This might have just changed my life. The future felt terrifying without Dolly and Joe, but perhaps this was the start of something that might become one of the tent poles of my new existence. Without me even realising it, tears suddenly appeared in my eyes, but for the first time in a long time, they were tears of joy.

After about ten minutes, the rest of Cold Water Club emerged from the sea, all looking a bit cold, but none as visibly shocked as me. They walked up to where our stuff was, and started casually drying off, and getting their clothes on, as if they had all the time in the world. I longed to be just like them. I wanted to be further down the tracks – in more ways than one.

'Well?' said Lucy to me, once she had her coat on. 'How was it?'

I looked at her and smiled. 'Fine, you were right. It was incredible. I feel so overwhelmed with energy, like I could do anything.'

'So, we'll see you again soon?'

'Definitely,' I replied, as everyone sat down, and we all drank our tea and chatted about what we had planned for the rest of the day.

On the drive home, I felt such a renewed sense of energy and enthusiasm for the day ahead. Most Saturday mornings at eight o'clock, I would still be in bed, and then I would slowly get up, have coffee, breakfast, and perhaps by ten or eleven we would find something to do, but now I wanted to be productive. I was starving and wanted to eat breakfast, but then I felt the need to make the most of the day.

I parked on the street outside of our house, and then opened the front door and walked in. I didn't know what I was going to find, but I was excited and wanted to tell them about the experience I'd had that morning. I walked along the hallway and into the kitchen, but it was empty. I looked in the living room, and that was the same. Undeterred, I marched up the stairs, but Dolly's door was still closed, which meant she was probably still asleep. I opened it as slowly and as quietly as I could, and I poked my head around the door, and she was still underneath her duvet, one leg hanging out of the bottom wearing a sock. I closed the door, and then walked past Joe's room. The door was closed, and I couldn't exactly open that and check on him, too. I wanted to, but it felt odd, and so instead, I walked to my bedroom, closed the door, and sat on the bed in silence.

I'd had the most incredible experience that morning, and yet I had no one to share it with. I had chatted with Lucy about it back at the car park, but she needed to get home because her boys had cricket, and Stuart was working all day. In years gone by, I would have talked to Joe and Dolly because they were my people, and the thought that they would soon both be gone terrified the life out of me.

I had too much energy at that moment, and I was still on a high, so, without anyone to share it with, I decided to have a shower on my own, and do the one thing I needed at that moment. It was something else I was becoming accustomed to since Joe and I no longer had sex. I still had needs, desires, and without the luxury of a man in my life, I had to take care of that myself. So I got undressed, grabbed my rabbit vibrator from my nightstand, and headed into my en-suite shower for some much needed 'me time'. A phrase that had once been a luxury and used to consist of a nice bubble bath, or time alone to read a book, was now something else entirely.

Chapter Nine

Joe

I got the train from Brighton into London Waterloo, arriving at just after ten o'clock in the morning. I had a meeting with my agent, Carl Newman, and we were having lunch at Quo Vadis in Soho at twelve, but I wanted to arrive early and have a wander around first. I strolled through the always chaotic Borough Market, browsing stalls, and then I got my favourite cup of coffee from Monmouth Coffee Company, and walked through the rest of the market before heading down towards the Thames. It was one of those perfect spring mornings when the weather was cool enough to wear a light jacket, but there was a warmth to the sunshine that lay across everything. I loved living in Brighton, but whenever I was back in London, I missed it. The vibrancy of it, the creative energy it gave me, and I wondered whether leaving London had been my biggest mistake. Perhaps if I had stayed, I would have been a better writer, more relevant, dragged along by the zeitgeist, and perhaps my career wouldn't have stalled in the way it had. Was Brighton nothing more than a retirement home for my career? My marriage?

I strolled along the Thames, sipping my coffee, and then across Hungerford Bridge, taking in the views of the London Eye and the Houses of Parliament, before I wandered up towards Trafalgar Square. I had always found a certain joy in walking in London, and especially on days like this. On the train journey from Brighton into Waterloo station, watching the neat patchwork of countryside fly past my window, I had thought about maybe moving back once Dolly was off to university. Brighton had always been Freya's dream more than mine, and her idea of the perfect place to raise a family. She'd wanted to get away from the hustle and bustle of London, nearer the sea, and Brighton had been perfect for that. But once Freya and I were officially separated, and the house was sold, would I stay in Brighton or move back to London? Could I even afford London again? The sad answer to that was a definite no, unless I somehow got something commissioned and on television again. At the moment, my income was basically nothing, and so as much as I loved the idea of London, it would be impossible even with the sale of the house. Also, most of the people I had known 'back in the day' had moved away to commuter towns, or into the vast London suburbs with partners and children, and so I would have to make a whole new network of friends, which was daunting at my stage of life. Making friends was hard enough in your twenties, but at least then there was a shared experience, a sort of 'we're all in this together' spirit, and we were desperate to make something of our lives and it felt like we needed people to make that happen. But approaching fifty, making new friends, new connections, felt about as painful as running a marathon when you suffered from a dodgy knee, debilitating shin splints, and had zero desire to even run for the bus let alone the full 26.2 miles.

Carl was already sitting down when I arrived at Quo Vadis. He stood up as I walked across to his table.

'Joe, how's it going, mate?' he greeted me, enthusiastically.

'Good, thanks. You?'

'Ah, yes, can't complain.' We shook hands before we sat down.

I first met Carl Newman in 2004, just before *The Burds*, my first comedy, went out on BBC Radio 4. I had been looking for an agent for a while, and then one day I got a phone call from a lady who worked at one of the big agencies in London, who said that Carl Newman wanted to meet me. I was excited because I was twenty-five, had done a few shows, the Edinburgh Fringe, and now I had written a comedy play for Radio 4 that was going to star Jonny Bailey, one of the up-and-coming stars of the stage and screen. I was told to meet Carl in Quo Vadis restaurant which felt to me – a poor, struggling writer, who lived off beans on toast and Pot Noodles – like I had somehow made it before I had actually made it. Carl and I had met there at least once a year ever since.

Carl had gained a little weight over the years, but still retained a certain handsomeness. He still had a sparkle in his eyes, and the very definite whiff of old-school money. Carl came from a long line of entertainment royalty and knew how to wine and dine with the very best. His mother was a well-known actress, who had starred in a number of television shows and films in the Sixties and Seventies, his father was a director and his brother did something in Hollywood. Today Carl was in a sharp navy suit, his now greying hair cut in the same style he always had, and he smelled of the same aftershave he had worn when I first met him. Everything about Carl Newman was signature, from his Savile Row suits to his Creed Irish Tweed Eau de Parfum.

'So, Joe, what's new?' said Carl once we had settled.

'Umm, well, Freya and I have decided to separate,' I replied, and I looked across the table at Carl, who I had heard describe himself as a 'survivor' of three marriages. He was currently dating a woman ten years his junior, and had four children with two different partners. His dating history was, at best, chequered. I had considered beforehand whether to confide in Carl or not, but after some careful consideration decided it was best to be honest about it. Carl had never been one to hide his own relationship shortcomings, and so it felt a little petty not to be truthful about mine.

'Oh no, really? I thought your marriage was one of the lucky ones. What happened?'

'Nothing happened, really,' I said, as a waitress walked across and offered us drinks. Carl ordered his usual bottle of white wine for the table, and we both got water, too. The waitress took our order and walked off. The restaurant was slowly filling up. 'We just gradually fell out of love, I suppose.'

'No one cheated?' said Carl, raising an eyebrow, and I knew exactly why he was asking. He always had to cover his back. If I did get back on television, had slightly more fame and notoriety than I did now, he had to make sure there weren't any skeletons in the old family cupboard.

'No, Carl, no one cheated.'

'Good boy.'

'I just think that, very slowly, we just sort of stopped making an effort, stopped doing the things that had made us happy in the first place, and then one day you wake up and realise, fuck, this isn't really a marriage any more.'

'Sorry, old boy, really. I know I've had my relationship indiscretions over the years, but I always believed in you and Freya. I thought you would make it to the bitter end.'

'Me, too.'

'Well,' said Carl, pouring us both a healthy measure of wine, and then holding his glass out over the table. 'To new beginnings.'

'To new beginnings,' I repeated, chinking my glass gently against his, and then taking a sip.

After a few minutes, the waitress returned and took our food orders. When Carl and I met for lunch, I always knew we wouldn't be rushed for time. It was one of the best things about working with him. He had patience. Some agents might have already given up on me, and to be fair, I wouldn't have blamed them if they had. The last ten years had been unproductive, and unsuccessful in terms of actually getting something commissioned, but Carl had stood by me and supported me throughout. He believed I had the talent and would eventually come good. I was the racehorse you kept backing because I had good form, or the footballer that was going through a bad patch. What was the saying? *Form is temporary but class is permanent.* Carl genuinely believed that, which was why he still wore the same fragrance and was dressed by the same tailors. Everything with Carl was long-term, except, of course, his romantic relationships.

'So, Joe, let's get into it,' said Carl when we were halfway through our main course. 'What are you working on?'

Unfortunately, this was the part of the lunch I wasn't looking forward to. After catching up, chatting about the state of the business, and what he had been working on, the inevitable question about me and my career had followed.

'I was working on the sitcom we discussed last time.'

'Oh, right, yes. The one set in the fictional media agency. Loved it. How's it going?'

'It's not. There was just something not working with it. The characters, or the setting, I don't know, but I've binned it anyway.'

'Riiight,' said Carl, his tone telling me exactly what his next question would be. 'So, what's next?'

What's next? The question that every writer in the world despised. What was next? It symbolised exactly what I hated about being a writer because it almost never mattered what you were working on, whatever success you had in the past, the most important thing was always, what's next? The past was ancient history, the now was very much old news, and the only thing that really mattered was, what was next? I lived in a world of the future.

'Honestly, Carl, I'm not sure. With the separation, and Dolly off to university in September.'

'Young Dolly, off to university already? Fuck me. The last time I saw her, she was just off to secondary school. Does she know where she's going yet?'

'She wants to read English at Durham.'

'Oh, right, wonderful university. My brother, Freddie, went to Durham. She'll love it.'

'So with her leaving in September, Freya and I are living together until then. I have moved into the spare room, but it's a bit tense.'

'I can only imagine. So, you're doing one of those modern parenting things everyone is doing these days. You separate but keep living together out of necessity.

Magpie parenting or something, isn't it? I read an article about it in the *Guardian* a few weeks ago.'

'Something like that. It's just for the time being until Dolly has moved out. Although, if I don't get something commissioned soon and start earning some money, I fear for the future.'

'You have what, five months until D-Day?'

'About that.'

We both paused to take mouthfuls of food, and then Carl looked out of the window for a moment, and as I watched him, I noticed something change in his expression. A flicker of something flashed across his face, and his eyes lit up, and then he turned back towards me. Something was coming.

'Maybe that's your idea!' he said.

'Sorry? What's my idea?'

'For a sitcom. Yes, what could be better? It has everything you'd ever want or need for the perfect series. A couple trapped in a loveless marriage, but under the same roof. A daughter desperate to leave, but having to wait until university. It has everything, Joe. Time, pressure, love, parenting, and all under one roof so a piece of piss to shoot.'

'You're saying I should write a sitcom about my current situation?'

'Why not? I'm sure it's tough, but there must be some comedy in there, too, and everyone loves that these days. Nobody wants a straight sitcom any more, Joe. I'm afraid the era of comedies like *The Mornings* is over. Now it's all about comedy drama, the humour of life, of reality, and what's more dramatic or potentially funnier than two people stuck under the same roof, in a marriage that used to work but doesn't any more? Yes, by Jove, I think it's a genius idea. I mean, really, well done!'

'I mean, it's not my idea.'

'But it will be. What do you think?'

I took a moment to think about it, and perhaps he was right, but how could I write it as I was going through it? Surely I was too close to it. Too involved to make it funny because, trust me, I hadn't found much humour in the break-up of my marriage so far. It had just been fucking difficult, heartbreaking, and also I was sure Freya wouldn't want me writing about the intricate details of our crumbling relationship. In fact, I knew without a shadow of a doubt that she would absolutely hate it. My career, my work, had definitely been one of the defining factors in the breakdown of our marriage, and so using it as my way of moving on would go down about as well as a warm seafood salad for breakfast.

'I think the idea has potential, but I don't know, Carl. I'm literally still going through it. I'm not sure I have the space from it to make it funny. Maybe in a year or two once the dust—'

'In a year or two, Joe, someone else will have written it. Think about it. So many comedies on television are about people getting together, or being married, but there isn't one about a couple that have already decided to split but are forced to cohabit. It's like *The Office*, you know. The joy of *The Office* was watching people that were forced to spend eight hours a day treading the same carpet. They didn't love each other, or often even *like* each other, but they had to be together. Now you focus that down on to two people and a child. They all want to leave but they can't. There's your humour. There's your show. It could be called, oh, I don't know—'

'*House Shared?*' I said instinctively, and Carl's face broadened into a smile.

'Yes!' he said enthusiastically. '*House Shared*. It's perfect!'

Carl and I had lunch for almost two hours where we discussed the finer points of *House Shared*, until eventually he had another meeting and I had to get back. I stayed in London for another hour or so, doing a bit of shopping, until it was time for the train back to Brighton. I wanted to miss rush hour and so I left before it all got a bit much, although as I boarded the train, I quickly realised it was still going to be packed.

Luckily, I managed to find a seat with a table, squeezed against the window next to a mother with a fussy baby and opposite a young man who, despite wearing headphones, was still playing his music so ridiculously loudly I could hear every word of every song – and no, it wasn't something I enjoyed. In years gone by, when money was far less of an issue, I would travel first class, so I could work. There was just something about being on a train that I had always found so creative and sometimes the hour between Brighton and London would seem like five minutes if I was in the zone. It was the gentle rattle of the train, the countryside and towns flying by the window, the casual mutterings of nearby conversations and people talking on phones. Stopping at stations, people getting off, struggling with luggage, and then new passengers getting on, and getting settled.

Today I had my laptop, and I opened it up, and typed the beginning of a new idea. *House Shared*. Maybe there was something in it. I knew Carl was right that it had all the ingredients for a perfect modern sitcom. Comedy and pathos, and something that most people would be able to identify with. It could be about love, marriage, parenting, and that moment in life when you have to let go, whether you want to or not. It could feature flashbacks of when the daughter was small and the couple were happy, and mostly be set in one house, and around Brighton. As I started thinking more and more about it, I began writing things down, just ideas for scenes, character notes, and by the time the train pulled slowly into Brighton station, I had written well over 2,000 words.

As I walked out of the station, and towards home, I got a text from Carl.

> Just mentioned House Shared to my assistant Sara and she loved it! Get writing!

I put my phone back in my pocket and started off through the Brighton streets towards the house where my wife and daughter lived, and where the idea of *House Shared* would be set. I felt that buzz I only got when I knew I had an idea that might actually go somewhere. It only happened from time to time, that spark of creativity, that surge of adrenalin when I felt I was at the beginning of potentially something magical. Ideas like electrical shocks were already popping into my head, connecting to other ideas, as a whole new world began to form in my head, and I felt myself walking a little taller.

I got home and walked into the kitchen, where I saw Freya standing up and looking pensive. Seated at the dining table was my father.

'Dad,' I said, putting my bag on the floor. 'What are you doing here?'

'Hello, Joe,' said Dad, standing up, his large frame filling the space between us. 'I was just passing by and thought I'd stop in.'

I looked at Freya and she looked at me, and I knew exactly what she was thinking.

Chapter Ten

Joe

'You haven't told him about us yet, have you?' said Freya.

We had left Dad in the kitchen, and stepped into the hallway for a private chat because obviously I hadn't told him about us separating and I had no idea why he had popped by. For a start, Dad lived in Colchester, which was nowhere near Brighton, and he never just stopped in for a casual chat because he was Dad. In all the years we had lived in Brighton, this was the first time he had ever showed up unannounced. It felt more likely that Ed Sheeran would pop in for a cup of tea than Dad, and so I hadn't told him about the separation. I hadn't informed Ed Sheeran either for basically the same reason.

'No, of course not. It's Dad. We never speak about anything important.'

'I know. So why is he here?'

'No idea.'

'Are you going to tell him?'

'Well, I…' I said, not sure what the plan was. Freya and I had only been separated for such a short time, and I would sometimes go for months without speaking to Dad, so the idea of telling him hadn't even entered my head. 'No?'

'So he's going to be here, perhaps stay the night, and you want to play happy families rather than tell him the truth?'

I could see her point. It seemed ludicrous not to tell him because he would have to find out at some point, but the thought of actually doing it made me feel queasy. It was Dad. We literally never discussed anything vaguely important or, heaven forbid, emotional. Even when Mum died, we barely talked about it, and her fight against cancer had been subjected to the usual family 'best not to mention it' treatment. Dad was old-fashioned, stiff, unapproachable, and we just didn't have that sort of relationship. Freya and I could be separated for years, divorced, and I could have a new partner, and if Dad knew nothing about it, I don't think either of us would be particularly concerned. I was about to say as much when Dad appeared in the hallway.

'I'm putting the kettle on. Tea?' said Dad.

'Oh, go on then,' said Freya with a bright smile.

'Please,' I said.

'When will Dolly be home?' said Dad. 'I'd love to see her.'

'She's actually staying at her friend Maya's house tonight,' replied Freya. 'Sorry.'

'That's a shame. I probably should have warned you I was coming, eh?' said Dad, before he ducked back into the kitchen, leaving Freya and me alone. She looked at me, and obviously knew what I was going to say, and so she beat me to it.

'Fine. I know what you and your dad are like. I won't say anything about us,' said Freya, and at that moment I wanted to hug her.

'Thank you. I'll try and get him out of here as soon as I can. Promise.'

'You'd better,' said Freya as I heard the kettle come to a boil.

Dad and I had never been close, but we had always had Mum. If our family were a sandwich, Dad and I would have been the bread and Mum would have been the filling. She would have been the butter or mayonnaise, the cheese, meat and all the salad. She made us a proper sandwich, but without her we were just two pieces of slightly rubbish bread that had nothing to keep them together. When she died, Dad and I didn't have her to make our relationship bearable so we just didn't see much of each other. It was easier keeping our distance and, the longer we did it, the more our relationship seemed to have become set in stone. Which was why him turning up suddenly out of the blue was suspicious. The last time I had spoken to him was on his birthday, and that was short and cordial like all of our interactions. Now he was sitting in my kitchen, drinking tea, and I had to know why he was here.

'So, Dad—'

'Yes, Joe,' said Dad, slurping on his tea.

I sat opposite him, and took a sip of mine. 'Why exactly are you here?'

'Like I said, I was passing.'

'Passing? You live in Colchester, Dad, which is roughly a two-and-a-half-hour drive away. The last time you were south of London, the brightest minds were still debating whether the Earth was flat. Honestly, Dad, what are you really doing here?'

I looked across the table at my father, and it was hard not to see myself in him. We had the same eyes, similar hair, and sometimes I would catch myself standing a certain way or making a gesture, and I knew it was just like him. Growing up, I had been determined to be nothing like my old man, and I thought I had achieved it by going into comedy when he had worked in factories his whole life. I was different than him, lighter, more open, and hopefully a better dad and husband, but over the last few years I had seen the parts of him I had always found difficult infiltrating parts of myself. Dad had always been more comfortable mending objects than people. His love language was DIY or perhaps, even better, just keeping out of the way. After another sip of his tea and a moment of silence, Dad put his cup down and then looked across the table at me.

'Joe, there's something I have to tell you,' he said, a serious expression settled on his face. Memories of the day Mum told me she had cancer jumped into my head, swirling around like nightmares that were so unfortunately true. The awful tears, and the unbearable weight of her words that sucked every last breath from my body until I could barely breathe. *I'm dying, Joe.* I couldn't stand the thought of lightning striking twice. 'I'm moving.'

'What?' I heard myself saying with a large dose of incredulity.

'I'm moving.'

'Okay, right,' I said, a relief washing through me that at least he wasn't dying. We weren't close but he was still my father.

Dad had lived in Colchester all his life, born and bred, and the idea of him not being there felt sort of ridiculous, like taking an animal that was native to hot African savannas and popping them down in Iceland – the country, not the budget supermarket. I had always imagined that Dad would live and die in Colchester. He was probably just moving to a nearby village or something. His face that had been so serious, so heavy, suddenly smiled and became lighter. He looked, for the want of a better word, happy. It was very unsettling.

'Moving where, exactly?' I asked.

'France,' said Dad, and I looked at him, and I laughed.

'France? The country? You? You're joking, right?'

Freya walked into the room and sat next to me. She picked up her tea and took a sip. 'What's happening?' she asked, probably sensing the crazy energy in the room.

'Dad said he's moving to France,' I said.

'The country?' said Freya incredulously.

'I met a woman. Her name's Juliette, she's French, and we're moving to France together. Provence, to be precise.'

'Oh, right. Wow!' said Freya. 'That's—'

'You're moving to actual France?' I said, suddenly feeling something else other than shock and confusion. Dad was supposed to live out his life in Colchester. I was supposed to be a comedy writer in Brighton with Freya and Dolly. Mum wasn't supposed to have died from cancer. Why was nothing what it was supposed to fucking be?

'I am,' said Dad with a brightness as if the light bulb that had been inside of him that had been dead for years had suddenly been replaced and turned on. It was blinding.

Dad went on to explain that he had met Juliette about six months ago, and they had just clicked. She was in Colchester visiting family, and after dating long-distance for a few months, they had decided to take the leap.

'I just… I can't believe it,' I said. 'What's she like?'

'Juliette?'

'No, Dad, Claudia Winkleman. Of course Juliette.'

'She's a bit younger than me. Sixty-two, to be precise. Divorced with four children—'

'Why didn't you tell me about her sooner?' I said suddenly, and Dad looked momentarily uncomfortable. He paused before he answered.

'To be honest, Joe, I couldn't quite believe my luck that I could fall in love again at my age and that someone would fall in love with me. I suppose I was just waiting for something to go wrong.'

It was perhaps the most honest, emotionally vulnerable thing my father had ever said to me. I didn't know what to say. This was Dad. This was me. I felt a lump slide down my throat. I wasn't going to fucking cry, was I?

'Well, I think it's fantastic!' said Freya. 'Being brave enough to do something like that later in life is to be commended.'

'Thanks, love,' said Dad, before slurping more of his tea.

With Dad's news rather killing my optimism about my new sitcom idea – because how could I possibly even think about that while Dad was telling us all about his new French girlfriend? – Freya arranged for dinner, while Dad told us more about Juliette. He even, incredibly, started speaking French, which was bizarre, and it seemed he had a new lease of life. Freya ordered pizza, and Dad regaled us with stories about the old farmhouse they were in the process of buying in France and how they were going to renovate it, and turn it into a luxury bed and breakfast. He even had a brand-new iPhone, which was quite the upgrade from his old flip phone, and he showed us some photos of their new place and it looked idyllic. Dad was like a new man. I couldn't believe that all of this had happened in the last six months and it terrified me. If my father could completely change his life, what was stopping Freya from doing the same, and Dolly, too? What if everyone else around me changed and became better, happier, and I stayed the same or became worse? I was stuck being a comedy writer but if it failed, if I failed, what would become of me?

As it turned out, we spent so long eating and talking about France that Dad decided to spend the night. While Dad and I cleaned away dinner, Freya raced upstairs and put some new sheets on my bed for Dad, and moved all my things back into the marital bedroom, so he wouldn't suspect anything. Eventually, it was time for bed after what had been perhaps the most surreal night of my life.

'Night then,' said Dad on the landing.

'Night, Dad, and…'

'And?'

'I'm really happy for you. Glad you've found someone.'

'Thanks, Joe.'

'Guess I'll be seeing even less of you once you move.'

'You'll always be welcome in France. Once we get everything sorted.'

'A cheap holiday at the family B & B. Now there's a phrase I never thought I'd be saying,' I said, and we both chuckled, even though the whole thing still felt completely barmy. 'I can't wait to meet Juliette.'

'Yeah, she's coming over in June.'

'Okay, all right. I still can't believe all of this, Dad.'

'You know the funny thing, Joe? Neither can I.'

'Really?'

'I always thought that after your mum I'd see out my days in Colchester. I had no reason to think I'd meet someone else, and certainly not from France. Life can surprise you sometimes.'

'It certainly can,' I said, and for a moment I thought about telling him about me and Freya, but before I could he opened his mouth and said, 'Well, good night then, Joe. See you in the morning.'

'Right, night, Dad.'

I smiled at him, he smiled at me, and for a moment I thought he was going to hug me, but instead he gave me a quick clap on the shoulder before he wandered off to brush his teeth, and I walked into Freya's bedroom still completely and utterly gobsmacked. My father was like a new man, and if we weren't careful, we might start discussing things like love and relationships instead of always reverting to silence or football.

Freya was sitting on the bed and I gingerly walked across and sat next to her. It was uncomfortable. I could wait until Dad was asleep, and then sneak into Dolly's bedroom and sleep in there, but what if Dad got up in the night and for some reason looked in Dolly's bedroom or woke up before me and saw me coming out? I knew it was silly, but I couldn't tell him so the best solution was to share Freya's bed. It was only one night. How awkward could it be?

'I'm sorry,' I said, turning to face Freya. 'I can sleep on the floor if you like.'

'Just stay on your side,' said Freya, somewhat coolly. 'And we'll be fine.'

'Got it,' I replied, as Freya stood up and got ready for bed.

We both moved around the room and into the en suite brushing our teeth, and Freya made a big deal about going into the toilet/shower room to get changed before emerging in full pyjamas and a bra – as if just seeing a flash of side boob would mean I'd be unable to control myself. It was like all the years we had been married meant nothing. She turned off the light before I clambered into bed next to her. Luckily our bed was quite large and there was plenty of space for both of us, and with a sort of no-man's land between us. I'm sure if Freya had her way, she would have erected some sort of temporary barbed-wire fence, just to be on the safe side.

'Good night,' I said.

'Night, Joe,' Freya replied, and we lay in the dark, so close to each other, and my father was in my bedroom, and the house had never felt stranger. Before I fell asleep, I thought more and more about my new sitcom, *House Shared*. Perhaps it was my last chance to get something commissioned and really make something of myself because, if this didn't get anywhere, Dolly would be off to university, Dad to France, Freya to goodness knows where, and what would I have left? I had to make it work, and so despite the obvious moral implications of not telling Freya and using our marital pain for some sort of professional gain, I knew I had no choice. I rolled over and in the faint light I could just make out the shape of Freya's shoulder next to me. She sighed, moved and then rolled over so she was facing me.

'Stop looking at me,' she whispered.

'I'm not. I was just thinking.'

'About what?'

'The future.'

'Sounds terrifying.'

'It might be.'

'Or maybe it will be brilliant.'

'Maybe.'

A pause.

'I can't believe your dad is moving to France.'

'It makes me wonder.'

'What?'

'If there is a version of this world where my dad lives in France and runs a bed and breakfast with a French lady called Juliette, perhaps there is a version of life where you and I are happy again.'

I could just about make out the shape of Freya in the dark, but I couldn't see the details of her face. She didn't say anything and then, after a minute, she rolled away from me again, so she was on her back looking up at the ceiling.

'Night, Joe,' she said quietly.

'Night,' I replied, and then we both tried to get some sleep.

Chapter Eleven

Freya

I was waiting for my toast to pop out of the toaster, sipping on coffee, while the morning show on Radio 2 played in the kitchen from the old radio we had bought years before. Dolly was at the table, munching her way through a huge bowl of Crunchy Nut, although nowadays she preferred almond milk to regular milk, and Joe was sipping on a cup of tea, while doomscrolling through his phone. Outside it was a bright morning, and inside our kitchen this was a perfectly regular family morning getting ready for the day ahead. The sort of morning we'd had a thousand times before when it used to be me telling Dolly to hurry up and get her stuff ready for school, while Joe made us breakfast, before I dashed off to work, dropping Dolly at school on the way, both of us saying goodbye to Joe at the front door with hugs and kisses. It was routine and it had felt during those days, in the middle of it all, like they would go on forever. But that was then, and this was now, and things had changed so much they were barely recognisable.

Whereas then the atmosphere had been familiar and comfortable, now it was riddled with excruciating awkwardness, each of us second-guessing what to say, how to say it, and what to do next. Before, we would move around the kitchen with a synchronicity, each of us doing something different, but it worked, and we knew the patterns of our morning routine. Now it was mumbled apologies for bumping into each other or for getting in the way, almost like strangers inhabiting the same space for the first time. It was like the early days of university when you were just getting to know people, but at least then we had alcohol to soften the blow. For so many years, it had felt so natural, but now just making coffee, toast, and trying to have a vague conversation about the day ahead felt like the most complicated thing in the world.

My toast popped, and I put it on my plate, and walked across to the side to add butter and marmalade, as Joe got up to fetch himself a bowl of muesli. Just the simple act of the two of us in close proximity to each other, moving about the same space, caused both of us to tense up like a couple of teenagers on a first date.

'Sorry, I just need to grab a spoon,' said Joe, reaching towards the cutlery drawer.

'No worries,' I replied, stepping aside, and Dolly looked up from the table. I'm sure she could feel the tension that sat heavily in the room the way cigarette smoke used to be in pubs before the indoor smoking ban.

I glanced at Joe, he looked at me, and I thought about the conversation I'd had with Lucy about Joe and me not really arguing. Did I want to scream at him and tell him exactly how I felt? A part of me did, obviously, but it wasn't something that came easily to us. We had been together for so long, and enormous, ugly arguments had never been a part of us. The very fabric of our relationship had been founded on something much more congenial, and much like the US Constitution, it felt like once it had been written it was impossible to change without some serious fucking work. I smiled awkwardly at him, he smiled uneasily at me, Dolly glanced across and slowly shook her head, and then we both continued on, trying to act as normal as possible, as though everything was perfectly fine, when it really wasn't.

'How are you doing, love?' I said to Dolly, sitting opposite her with my toast.

She was on her phone, and she glanced across at me for a moment, a face full of ambivalence. She had never been a morning person.

'Like you care,' said Dolly, her voice sharp and pointed.

'What? Of course I care, love.'

I saw Joe out of the corner of my eye, and he had stopped what he was doing and was looking across at us like someone who had just witnessed a minor car crash. Dolly huffed and stood up, her bowl of cereal unfinished. She slipped her phone quickly in the back pocket of her jeans.

'Whatever,' she said, and then she walked out of the kitchen, along the hallway, and I heard her feet loudly on the stairs. I glanced across at Joe and he shrugged his shoulders and screwed his face in a sort of 'what was that all about?' way before he continued doing what he was doing, while the radio was playing '2 Become 1' by the Spice Girls, and the irony wasn't lost on me. Our household had very quickly turned from one family into three separate people uncomfortably occupying the same space, all wondering where the hell this was going to end. Our party line that it was 'business as usual' was quickly being picked apart as the lie it probably had been from the start.

I was worried about Dolly because one of my big fears was that my separation from Joe would permanently harm our relationship. She was leaving home soon, and I had recently heard a statistic that by the age of eighteen we had already spent ninety per cent of the time we'll ever spend with our kids. That meant that after she moved to university, our relationship would be forever changed. I would only see her fleetingly, and the relationship we had when she left might be set in stone for the rest of our lives. It terrified the life out of me, but at the same time I felt almost helpless to stop it from happening, in the same way I felt helpless about the state of my marriage to Joe. No matter how much I wanted to, I couldn't go back to how things were when Dolly was young and innocent, and Joe and I were happy. It was like that version of us was behind a wall, and I could hear it, almost feel it, but I couldn't get over or around that wall to actually see it or be close to it again.

I closed the front door behind me, stepped outside and took in a deep breath of fresh air, and I almost wanted to cry. It was such a relief being outside because the morning had been awful. Dolly didn't say another word to me before I heard the front door slam shut and she was gone and off to college. Joe and I didn't speak either, tiptoeing around each other, neither of us sure what to say to the other. All our relationships were strained, and I just wanted to fucking scream, but I couldn't. I had to keep it inside, push it down, because I didn't have a choice. I needed to speak with Dolly, but she was an adult, and I couldn't force her. Joe and I were in such a strange place that I didn't even know what to do with him, or what to say, and so I said nothing. Instead, I started the walk to work where at least I could bury myself in my cases, and hopefully for eight hours forget about everything. Work had become the distraction I needed to stay sane in a world I barely recognised any more.

It was the end of the day, and I was heading out of the office, not overly excited to get home, when I walked outside and there was Sam Becket, Brompton bicycle in his hand, readying himself to head home. Trousers clipped at the bottom, he looked in many ways so old-fashioned, or classic, it depended on how you looked at it.

'Freya. How are you?' said Sam brightly.

Today he was in a grey suit, black shoes and a navy tie. He looked, as always, remarkably handsome. He was always so clean-shaven; it was almost impossible to imagine him with any facial hair at all. Joe always had a certain amount of beard, no matter how often he seemed to shave. Although being a stay-at-home writer had given him the little encouragement he needed to grow a beard. He kept it reasonably short, but was never clean-shaven like Sam.

'Good,' I replied, although clearly a lie. 'Heading home on the bicycle?'

'You can't beat it after a day in the office. It's nice to feel like I'm doing something slightly physical. Brush away the cobwebs.'

'Totally understand. I walk, which is something. Well, have a—'

'Do you mind if I walk with you?' said Sam suddenly, and I was momentarily unsure how to reply. Sam and I had a good relationship, friendly, professional, but once outside of the office, it ended. In all the years I had worked at Becket, Godwin & Anderson, we had never walked home together. It felt like something was definitely afoot, or amiss?

'Sure, great,' I said far too excitedly, before I added with a touch more poise, 'Is there something you wanted to discuss?'

Sam looked at me, smiled, and then picked up his bicycle that was still folded up. 'Let's start walking first, eh?'

I smiled back, curious, and we started walking. When I was alone, I would usually walk reasonably quickly, but with Sam and his bike, we strolled. It was a lovely evening, warm for the time of year, and it felt nice being with Sam. It was, despite my insecurities about why we were walking together – and wasn't Sam's house in the opposite direction? – comfortable.

'So, Freya, how are you?' said Sam after a minute's silence – not the sort of silence used to commemorate a death, a tragedy, or remember fallen soldiers – it was just about a minute long.

'Good, yeah. Although slightly concerned I'm about to be fired from my job.'

Sam laughed. 'Gosh, no, it's nothing like that.' Now it was his turn to look mildly uncomfortable. 'Freya, please tell me to shut up if I'm overreaching, but having gone through a somewhat difficult divorce myself, I wanted to offer my support. I heard about the separation.'

'Oh, right,' I said, making a mental note to have a word with Lucy. She must have let it slip.

'And honestly, Freya, if you're uncomfortable discussing it, please tell me to shut up and we can discuss anything else. Football? Are you into football at all?'

'No, Sam, I'm not into football.'

'Oh, good, that's a relief, neither am I.'

'More of a rugby man, I assume?'

'Not really a sports man at all, if I'm honest. I like to exercise, but I'm not into watching sports. The theatre, yes. Even the opera over a game of men kicking a ball around a large patch of grass.'

I laughed. 'Oh, Sam, thank you.'

'For what?'

'I don't think I have laughed all day.'

'You are welcome,' said Sam with a soft smile, as we continued to stroll somewhat aimlessly in the direction of my house. We had already missed one of the roads I would usually walk down, but I didn't say anything, and so we just kept wandering.

'You're right that Joe and I have separated. It's really shit, weird, and we're still trying to figure out exactly what all of it means, but I appreciate your support.'

'If there's anything you need, legal or otherwise, you know I'm here for you. The whole team is here for you. I just wanted to let you know that you aren't alone in this. It was one of the things I felt at the beginning of my divorce. I tried to deal with it on my own, keeping it a secret because I was embarrassed, but it didn't help. Sharing it did. Getting help did, and that's what I wanted to say to you today.'

He was being so nice and supportive, I almost wanted to cry.

'Thank you,' I said, keeping the tears at bay. 'The thing that's hard at the moment is that we still live together. Until Dolly leaves for university, we're stuck in this strange, surreal place.'

'Right, yes, we did the whole bird-nest parenting thing where the kids stay in the home, and the parents switch out. I had the weekends.'

'How did that work out?'

'Okay, I suppose. I think the thing is that none of it is ideal, is it? We see it all the time at work, representing couples in divorce settlements is never easy. You're untangling years, sometimes decades of finances, children, property, and on top of that there are feelings, infidelities, and it's a mess, Freya, but people do it, and we move on. I would say that now my relationship with my children is good, and my relationship with Helena is tentatively getting better. It's amicable. Separation is hard, but if it's the right thing to do, then stick with it, ride out the bumps, and eventually you'll find some smoother ground.'

'So the headlines are that it's shit, messy, but in the long-term, I might survive with my relationships vaguely intact?'

'Something like that,' said Sam with a reassuring smile, and in that moment I felt a sense of calm come over me. Sam had been through this and he had survived and come out the other side, and just knowing I had his support and friendship meant the world.

We kept walking until we were about five minutes from my house and I finally had to say it. 'Sam?'

'Yes?'

'Isn't your house in the opposite direction?'

'Ah,' said Sam. 'Yes, but on the old Brompton it isn't far, and I wanted to have this chat. Make sure you were okay.'

'I appreciate it, but I'm nearly home now. You can head off if you want.'

'Will do,' said Sam, and we both stopped. It took him a moment to unfold his bicycle, and then he put his helmet on.

'Thank you,' I said. 'It's nice to know I have your support.'

'Always, and Freya, if you need anything, just fancy a chat, or maybe a drink, let me know,' said Sam, and he reached across and put his hand on my arm for a moment. 'Okay?'

I couldn't help feeling a rush of excitement at his touch. Was he trying to convey something to me that perhaps in the future, when I was ready, that maybe he was interested in something more than just a friendly, professional relationship? Was that even possible given our current employer–employee status? Was I reading far too much into a simple friendly gesture?

'Okay,' I said, feeling my cheeks redden, as he got on his bicycle.

'See you tomorrow,' said Sam, and I smiled at him before he was off, and I walked the rest of the way home. As I walked, I couldn't help but feel happier because, after such an awful day, Sam reminded me that I had people. I had friends like Lucy and perhaps the rest of Cold Water Club, Mum was close by, and now I had Sam, too. For so long I had been one part of a couple, and tearing myself away from that felt impossible – like a once great double act trying to forge solo careers – but Sam had done it and got the T-shirt, or in his case probably a very expensive and well-fitted shirt, to prove it. I had people and a career that would require lots of my time, and that was something to be thankful for. I smiled to myself because for the first time in a long time, I felt the exhilaration of possibility, and of potentially imagining a future beyond my current existence, and after that morning when I had left the house feeling like utter shit, it definitely felt like a bit of a win.

Chapter Twelve

Joe

I typed the title, *House Shared*, on the opening page, and then I added, *Pilot Episode* by *Joe Wallace.* I pressed enter until I had moved the cursor on to the next page. A blank page and the beginning of a new sitcom. Only this wasn't just a sitcom, this was my life I was attempting to replicate on the page. It felt different to anything I had done before, and also quite duplicitous because I knew Freya wouldn't appreciate me spilling the guts of our marriage on to the page for laughs. The thing was, though, I was desperate. This had to be a success, or I would be returning to education and becoming a teacher or perhaps a lecturer because that was literally the only other job I could see myself doing. I could write a novel, but that had about as much chance of success as writing a sitcom and even less financial gain, from what I had heard. No, I was putting all my eggs in one basket, and this was the basket. I was forty-five, recently separated from my wife, my daughter was soon leaving home for a town at the other end of the country, and I only had one fucking basket! A thoroughly depressing thought, but I had to get my head down and hope this worked because the alternatives didn't bear thinking about.

I wrote for a few hours before I stopped typing and read it back a few times. Was it too close to the knuckle?

Was it basically just repeating the same conversations I had with Freya verbatim but with a few jokes added to the mix? Were the characters too similar to Freya, Dolly and myself? Would she end up suing me for libel? I didn't know, but it was just a first draft, and it would change anyway. The thing was, I liked it. It had a good ebb and flow, and the characters were already so real in my mind. They always say 'write what you know', but surely this was taking the piss. This wasn't creating something based on something that had happened years before, or stories I had patchworked together, this was literally happening as I was writing it. It felt a little more than risky.

I wrote a few more pages before I took a break and made myself a coffee. While I was waiting for the kettle to boil, I had a look on the fridge door and saw the housework schedule Freya had made at work, printed off, laminated and then stuck to the fridge with a magnet. I needed to clean the floors, clean the downstairs loo and the main bathroom. I was a forty-five-year-old comedy writer, and yet I felt like a child being told what to do for pocket money. The irony was, I had done all those things for years without evening thinking about it, but now it was written down on a schedule, something about it just annoyed me. Why couldn't she trust that I would do the jobs that I had already been doing for years without having to check up on me? Why did we need a laminated schedule stuck to the fridge? The kettle boiled and I made myself a coffee, before I headed back upstairs to my office to work. I would do my housework later.

After another couple of hours of writing, I felt the need to get out and see people. Since the separation, I had been largely wallowing, and apart from my visit to see Karen, which was not exactly an exercise in levity, I hadn't done much else. I texted Stuart and Barney to see if they fancied a drink, which fortunately both of them did, and we arranged to meet at a pub in town later that night. Stuart would usually come for a drink if he wasn't working or ferrying his boys around Sussex for cricket matches, which he often was. Barney was my token single friend, and generally up for a pint. I met Barney in London years before, as he worked in media, too, and he had moved to Brighton a few years ago to 'escape the rat race', he claimed, but I think also because he had dated every woman in London and needed a new pool to tempt into a relationship with him. I didn't know what it was about Barney, but he could never seem to hang on to a woman for long. He dated but none of them stuck. He was a bit like Blu-Tack – a safe bet at the beginning, but you knew that eventually things would become unstuck.

We were meeting at the Mash Tun pub in The Lanes because it was a nice evening and we could sit outside and watch the world go by. It was always a busy area of Brighton, and the pub was packed as I walked up and saw Stuart and Barney already outside with a couple of pints.

'Hello, chaps,' I said, walking across.

'Ah, there he is!' said Barney with his usual enthusiasm.

'Hello, mate,' said Stuart.

I gave them both a quick handshake before I ducked inside, got myself a pint and then returned and joined my friends. Stuart was tall, burly and good-looking in a sort of dashing Emily Brontë way. He was originally from Yorkshire, so had a certain directness about him, a natural simplicity in the way he was and looked that I had always envied. He had played cricket to a high level, but now ran an English language school in Brighton, was married to Lucy and they had two boys. Barney was almost the exact opposite of Stuart. Whereas Stuart was tall and still in decent shape because he was a runner, Barney was shorter, squatter and did very little exercise as far as I knew. He had once mentioned a Zumba class, but that didn't bear thinking about. Barney dressed smarter and was still a part of the London media scene, while Stuart was dressed in comfortable dad clothes. Two very dissimilar people but equally good mates.

'How's it going?' said Stuart, an expression on his face and a tone in his voice that suggested he already knew that Freya and I were separated.

'You know, don't you?' I asked.

'Lucy told me everything.'

'What's this?' said Barney. 'Know what, exactly?'

'Freya and I have decided to separate,' I said, and hearing the words out loud still sounded strange and unfamiliar, like the time I tried learning Spanish on Duolingo.

'Oh, mate, that's monumental,' said Barney. 'Should I get shots? I'll get shots.'

'I don't think we need shots, mate. It is sad, but I don't think shots are the answer.'

'Sorry I didn't text or call. I thought I'd wait for you to mention it first,' said Stuart.

'No worries. Yeah, it's strange, surreal, and honestly, I still can't quite believe it.'

'But you've been having problems for a while, haven't you?' said Barney. 'I remember six months ago or more you mentioned something about going through a bit of a dry patch.'

'Well, that dry patch became a fucking desert, and now we're both just really thirsty. Unfortunately not for each other.'

'Lucy said you were still living together,' said Stuart, before he took a long pull of his pint.

'We're sharing the house until Dolly leaves for university because we didn't want to unsettle her while she's doing her A levels, and honestly, with the price of rent in Brighton, the idea of forking out for a flat didn't make a lot of financial sense.'

'That doesn't sound like a giant bag of fun,' said Barney.

'It isn't ideal, obviously, but we discussed it, and it's only six months. Then once Dolly is gone, we can sell the house, and, you know, start our new lives.'

I said 'new lives' as if I had some sort of idea of what that might look like, but the truth was I had literally no idea. Although, I'm sure before Dad met Juliette, the idea of living in France had never once crossed his mind. In fact, I knew it hadn't because he had never been there, thought baguettes were impractical for making sandwiches and, growing up, I remember him making several disparaging comments about the Channel Tunnel.

'What if you want to bring a woman home?' said Barney. 'What is it, student-house rules? A sock on the bedroom door and music to drown out the moaning?'

'Hardly, and I think the chances of me bringing a woman home are probably slimmer than you,' I said to Barney. Man banter, it always kept things from getting too real. We were good friends, but discussing anything too personal, too deep, was strictly off limits, and we all knew it. Keep it light and surface-level only. It was like the opposite of therapy, but equally needed to keep me sane.

'Actually, that's where you're wrong!' said Barney suddenly and with a great deal of excitement. 'I joined a new dating app, and I've been going great guns!'

'You're actually getting women back to your place?' said Stuart, slightly disbelievingly.

'I mean, define "back to your place"?' replied Barney.

'I think it's quite clear,' I said. 'You're getting women back to your flat for sex?'

'Oh, Joe, you're so base,' said Barney. 'The ladies I wine and dine aren't into me just for the physical. We're talking, debating, delicately navigating the early flushes of romance. It's a dance, a whirlwind of the unknown, the familiar and yet the new. It's complicated and yet simple. It's—'

'You're not getting any, are you?' said Stuart.

'No, not yet, but you know, one day,' said Barney, and we all laughed. 'It's all about PMA, gentlemen.'

'PMA?' I asked.

'Positive mental attitude!' said Barney as Stuart finished his pint and went to get another one, while Barney and I slowly finished ours.

It felt good getting outside and away from the house for a night. I needed the company of my friends to remind me that there was a life outside of my own. Stuart returned, and the conversation moved on from me and my marital issues, and Stuart told us about his boys and how well they were doing at cricket. The eldest, George, had been selected for his county, and Henry had just been made captain of the school team. Stuart was so proud of them, and then he spoke about Lucy's cold water swimming club.

'Lucy said that Freya had gone along to Cold Water Club.'

'Oh, right, she didn't mention it.'

'Said she loved it, and was going back again,' replied Stuart. 'I went once. Never again. It was so cold I didn't see my testicles for a week! Shocked into submission.'

'Sounds awful,' I said, wondering why Freya hadn't mentioned it, and then it was clear. She was moving on. She had her own life now, separate from mine, and it was something I had to get used to. The tangled web of our lives and friendship groups unfortunately overlapped, so there was no getting away from her completely, unless perhaps I moved out of Brighton altogether. Although with my income, the only place I would be moving anytime soon was a shit one-bed flat in one of the less trendy parts of Brighton.

We were standing outside the pub, three hours and five pints later, and ready to head off home. We were each going in different directions.

'I just hope you get yourself ready for the divorce,' said Barney.

'What do you mean?' I asked.

'Things can get ugly. An old buddy of mine in London just went through it. Absolute fucking nightmare. She wanted the house, there were custody issues with the kids, and it all got very ugly with solicitors on both sides, and they had to go to mediation, which sounded like bloody torture. Poor bugger almost had a complete breakdown, lost most of his money, and had to move to fucking Slough!'

'I think we'll be okay. Things aren't bad with Freya. It's amicable.'

'Yes, now,' said Barney. 'But wait until it's about deciding who gets what, how much money you each get, and how you disentangle your whole life. Plus, she's already working with solicitors. You don't think she's already thinking about it? Plotting who will get what?'

'Freya isn't like that,' I said, but even as I said it, I knew I didn't sound utterly convincing.

'I'm just saying, mate, get ready for it, that's all,' said Barney. 'Because you never know.'

'Okay, mate, I think that's enough scaremongering for one day,' said Stuart, jumping in. 'See you both soon? I have a busy few weeks with work and family stuff, but maybe after that?'

'Definitely,' I replied, but already I was thinking about what Barney had said. Was he right? Was I being naive? Should I already be thinking about the divorce and solicitors? Was Freya already thinking about it? She worked for a firm of family and divorce solicitors, so surely it was already on her mind. She knew the law and what exactly she was entitled to, and I had no idea. What if my new sitcom was commissioned, did well, was sold to America, and then syndicated, and made millions? Would she want some of that money? Could I stop her? Would I even want to? Or perhaps worse, if it didn't get commissioned and I had no income, I would need every penny of my share from the sale of the house, and what if she made that difficult? As I walked home, hundreds of questions were suddenly swirling in my mind, and I had to tell myself to stop it. Freya wasn't like that. I wasn't like that. We were still friends. Weren't we? We were going to have an amicable divorce, and discuss everything like adults, and put Dolly first. It's what Freya had always stressed. No, Barney was wrong, and everything was going to be just fine.

I walked up the stairs of the house towards my bedroom, definitely feeling a little tipsy. It was quiet downstairs, the lights were off, so I assumed everyone was upstairs, even though it wasn't that late. I really wanted to talk to Freya. Barney had freaked me out talking about divorce, mediation, and that I needed to be careful. I had to know she wasn't thinking like that. I walked up to her bedroom door, took a quick breath, knocked, and then opened the door.

'Freya—'

'Oh my fucking God! Get out!' screamed Freya, who was standing in the middle of the room completely and utterly naked. For a second I didn't know what to do, and so I just stood there and looked at her. I hadn't seen Freya naked in a very long time. 'Joe!'

'Oh, shit! Fuck!' I said, covering my eyes, but I had already seen too much. 'Sorry, sorry—'

'Out!' demanded Freya, as I backed out of her room, and then Dolly was suddenly on the landing.

'What's going on?' said Dolly. 'I heard shouting.'

I turned to face Dolly, my face red with embarrassment.

'I, umm, walked in on your mother, and she—'

'Is fucking livid!' said a very angry Freya, now in a dressing gown, her wet hair up in a towel. 'You can't just walk into my room like that, Joe. What's wrong with you?'

'I know, I'm sorry.'

'It's a bit pervy, Dad,' said Dolly. 'Just saying.'

I looked at Freya, who huffed in annoyance, gave me a look that I could only describe as 'hostile' and then walked back into her room and slammed the door shut. I turned to Dolly.

'It was an accident, Dolly. I didn't mean to—'

'That's what all the dirty pervs say,' said Dolly, turning around and walking back into her bedroom, leaving me on the landing, speechless, and feeling like I had just made things between me and Freya so much worse.

Chapter Thirteen

Freya

It was hard to pin down exactly when I had stopped doing things just for myself. When I looked back, I think it had happened so gradually I hadn't even realised it was happening. When I was younger, and even after Joe and I first got together, I liked to do things on my own. I had my own set of friends and I had hobbies. I used to fly to places on my own, I had interests, and then very slowly my whole life shrank down and all I had was Joe and Dolly. I was a wife and a mother and that seemed to be about it. Gradually over time, I made friends with Lucy, but I still didn't really have things that were just mine. I had even stopped reading when I used to be a voracious reader of at least two or three novels a month, but now I was lucky if I finished one a year. What had happened to me? Who was I? I was discussing this very point with the rest of Cold Water Club, while we waded into the sea at just after seven o'clock on a Friday morning.

'I know what you mean,' said Caroline. 'Before we had kids, I used to do all sorts. I ran half-marathons, did yoga, and me and a few friends hiked the West Highland Way for fun!'

'I used to go to dance classes,' said Debs with a whimsical smile. 'Without Steve, of course, because the useless bugger has two left feet. I did Latin, jazz, swing and flamenco!'

'That sounds brilliant. I can imagine you doing the tango!' said Lucy, and then we all stopped because it was time to submerge ourselves up to our shoulders and start swimming. I was getting slowly better and with each and every time I went into the sea, I felt myself getting stronger. The main thing I enjoyed, apart from how I felt afterwards and the energy it gave me, was the camaraderie with the other women. I loved how we all shared stories about our lives without apprehension or worry.

It was clear from day one that we each had our own ways of being in the water. Caroline was always the most physical and would start swimming, heading off in all directions, while Lucy would do her sort of half breast-stroke, half doggy-paddle around in circles. Debs and Helen walked about a bit, and Amy did a couple of breast-strokes before she stood up and looked off towards the horizon. I had decided that I definitely couldn't swim as bravely as Caroline but wanted to do a bit more than Debs, Helen and Amy, and so I joined Lucy in her swimming-in-circles routine. It felt like I was actually doing some exercise and it helped keep me warm.

Eventually, just as I started to feel like everything was numb, and knew it was time to get out, everyone came together and we slowly stood up and started making our way back towards the beach. I realised as we were walking that I hadn't yet mentioned my after-work walk home with Sam to Lucy, which was strange because I'd had plenty of time to tell her, and it wasn't like it was something I was trying to hide. Lucy and I told each other everything, and it felt odd I hadn't mentioned it.

'Sam walked me home from work the other day,' I said suddenly, and Lucy looked across at me.

'And you didn't tell me about it?'

'I'm telling you now, aren't I?'

'When? Where? Why? So many questions.'

'Last week, and only because he somehow knew about my separation, which I mean to ask you about—'

'I didn't say anything to him,' said Lucy quickly.

'You're sure?'

'One hundred per cent.'

'Then how did he find out?'

'No idea, but what happened?'

'He offered his support, and just wanted me to know that if I needed anything then I could lean on him.'

'I bet he did!' said Lucy with a salacious smile.

'What?' I said, as we reached the shore, and walked across to our stuff. I quickly grabbed my towel and started drying myself off.

'Recently divorced, handsome solicitor walks pretty, recently single paralegal home after work to offer his support,' said Lucy with a grin. 'It doesn't take much to imagine what sort of support he's offering!'

'Oh, Lucy, it wasn't like that,' I said, putting my towel down and reaching for my trousers and top. My skin was blistered with dots from the air. 'It was actually very pleasant.'

'I'm sure it was!' said Lucy, who had just zipped up her tracksuit top with a smile.

We sat with the rest of the Cold Water Club, drinking from our flasks of hot drinks. I had coffee because I had been tired when I woke up that morning, and needed a little pick-me-up. Caroline, who had obviously overheard our conversation, was the first to chip in. She was sitting next to me, taking sips from her flask, and she had made banana bread and was offering it around.

'Is this Sam fella handsome?'

'Bloody gorgeous!' replied Lucy immediately. 'I mean, if you like handsome solicitors, who ride folding bicycles, dress in expensive suits, and smell heavenly.'

'Sounds absolutely perfect to me!' said Helen, who was sitting next to Caroline, eating from a small lump of banana bread.

'But, and let's say for argument's sake that he did like me,' I replied, 'which he definitely doesn't, but imagine he had some ulterior motive, I'm definitely not ready to start dating.'

'Who said anything about dating?' said Debs, looking at me with a certain bluntness. 'Perhaps he just wants to have some fun.'

'Aye, maybe she's right,' said Caroline. 'If he wants you, then have some fun while you can! You're still young, single for the first time in two decades, and if someone wants to wine you, dine you, and you know the other one, perhaps it's time you started thinking about it. There's nothing wrong with saying yes once in a while.'

'But it isn't that easy,' I replied. 'He's a partner at work for a start. I can't just have a bit of fun with him. Plus, I'm not sure he's that sort of man.'

'Trust me,' said Helen. 'All men are that sort of man when it suits them.'

'I actually think Freya might be right,' said Lucy. 'Dating Sam would be far too complicated. He's lovely, handsome and very nice, but he isn't the sort of man you have a bit of fun with. Plus, he's her boss. It could make things very awkward at work if it doesn't go well.'

'Exactly,' I said.

'What about your husband?' said Amy, looking across at me. 'Do you think he's dating?'

'Joe?' I asked, suddenly feeling strange just thinking about the possibility of it. 'You think he's already plotting dates?'

'He's got a penis,' said Helen. 'Of course he is!'

It was the first time I had thought about Joe being with someone else. Obviously the idea of us dating other people had been discussed, and I'd had passing thoughts about it happening one day, but that one day had always been some distant, faraway date in the future when we had sold the house and moved on. I couldn't actually imagine seeing Joe with someone else in the same way I couldn't actually imagine being with someone else myself. It was too difficult to process, and it also meant admitting that my marriage was over. I knew the separation felt quite final, but admitting it was still difficult. The truth was, I hated the thought of Joe with someone else, even though I knew I didn't necessarily want him myself.

'He did walk in on me naked the other day,' I said suddenly.

'He did what?' said Lucy.

'The night he went out for a drink with Stuart and Barney. He came back a little drunk, barely knocked, before he walked into my bedroom. I was just out of the shower, and he saw everything.'

'What did you do?' said Caroline.

'What do you think I did? I told him to get the fuck out of my room. I was livid.'

'Do you think it was on purpose?' asked Helen.

'I don't. He apologised profusely and we had quite an awkward conversation the following morning over breakfast, and I don't think it will happen again,' I said.

'You know what you have to do?' said Caroline.

'What's that?' I asked.

'You need to get back at him. You need to walk in on him naked!'

'Oh my God, yes!' said Lucy.

We laughed, and then sat and finished our drinks and Caroline's delicious banana bread before we all had to head off home.

On our way back to our cars, I had a few minutes with Lucy, who filled me in on what was happening with her boys, and also on Stuart's new adventure. Stuart had spent the past fifteen years managing an English language school in Brighton, but wanted to branch out and start his own school. It would mean more work, longer hours, and he had mentioned the possibility of Lucy coming to work with him, too. If he was going to venture out on his own and create something wonderful from scratch, he would need Lucy's support. She was brilliant at administration, and the finer details of things, while Stuart was better at being the face of the school. It wasn't happening soon, she stressed, but the idea of not working with Lucy already made me sad. She was one of the best things about Becket, Godwin & Anderson, and without her my days would surely not be as fulfilling. It was also more change, and I wasn't sure I could handle any more upheaval given the last few months, and what was to come next.

Chapter Fourteen

Freya

On the way home from Cold Water Club, I stopped at Tesco to pick up a couple of things, before I drove home, ready to start my day. I was running a little late, and I still needed to have a shower, eat breakfast and get ready for work. I opened the front door, walked along the hallway and into the kitchen. I was hungrier than usual, and decided to have breakfast before my shower, but when I walked into the kitchen I saw Joe and Dolly sitting at the table and the air in the room was thick with tension. Something had obviously happened.

'What's going on?' I asked straight away, putting my shopping down on the floor. I had forgotten my bag for life *again*, and had to pay for another one.

'I got my letter from Durham,' said Dolly, and I immediately knew what this meant for her. Durham University was her dream. We had gone up for her interview, to have a look around the campus and to spend the night so she could get a feel for the city, and she had fallen in love. Ever since, she had become obsessed with going there and this letter would determine the next three years of her life, and perhaps the rest, too. Dolly stood up and then Joe followed.

'Are you going to open it then?' I asked, stepping closer to her so we were all huddled together in the middle of the kitchen.

'I'm too nervous,' said Dolly frantically. I had never seen her look so terrified before.

'I'll do it,' said Joe with an eager smile, taking the letter from Dolly's hand.

'Good luck, love,' I said, reaching out and holding Dolly's in mine.

'Thanks, Mum. Okay, I'm ready.'

'Here goes,' said Joe.

Dolly and I both looked towards Joe, who had the letter in his hand. He reached down and was about to open it when Dolly stopped him.

'I'll do it,' she said, taking the letter from Joe. Dolly took a deep breath, and then she slowly opened the envelope that contained the letter that might change her life. My heart ached in anticipation and I watched her face as she read the letter aloud. *Please let her get in.* With everything going on between me and Joe, this felt like the good news that might give us all a lift. She began to slowly read the letter.

'Dear Miss Wallace, we are pleased to offer you a conditional offer to read English Literature at Durham University. Oh my God, I got in!' screamed Dolly, and then Joe and I engulfed her and we were all huddled together, jumping up and down and squealing with delight. Our baby girl was going to read English at Durham and I couldn't have been prouder of her.

'Dinner tonight to celebrate!' I said, as soon as we had stopped jumping up and down like maniacs. 'Wherever you want!'

'Okay,' said Dolly, who already had tears in her eyes.

'Joe?' I said. 'Dinner?'

'I'm in,' he replied.

'Right, I'm really sorry, love, but I have to get ready for work. I'm so proud of you and I can't wait for tonight. Oh, should I invite Mum and Martin?'

'You mean Marmalade?' said Joe.

'Fine, should I invite Mum and Marmalade?' I asked.

'Yes,' replied Dolly with the biggest smile.

I leaned in and gave her one final hug before I had to dash upstairs and take a shower. I still hadn't had breakfast, but I would grab something on my way out. It had been a crazy morning, and I couldn't wait to celebrate later.

-

I was sitting on my bed, trying to decide what to wear for Dolly's celebratory dinner. Dolly had chosen Wagamama, her favourite restaurant, and she was meeting us there, along with Mum and Marmalade. After college, Dolly spent the rest of the day with her friend Maya, and I was excited to see her again to properly celebrate her success. If only I could decide what to wear. I was feeling a little under the weather, and not particularly attractive, and nothing in my wardrobe was singing to me, which was why I was sitting on my bed, in just my underwear with my dressing gown over the top. I could hear Joe moving about the house getting ready, too. For one man, he certainly made a lot of noise.

I was scrolling on my phone, when I went to Facebook for the first time that day, and the first thing that popped up was a video of Dolly and me. We were at the beach and she was about seven or eight, and she was so adorable and, before I knew it, I was deep-diving into memories of

Dolly from a toddler all the way up to her teenage years. Nostalgia soon got the better of me, and I was quickly an emotional mess, and with her off to university in a matter of months, I couldn't help but be incredibly sad. I wanted my little girl back. I knew it was impossible unless they somehow invented a time machine, or I was involved in some sort of accident and I woke up ten years ago, and got the chance to put everything right. But I wouldn't because this was real life and not a time-travel romcom film starring Lily James. Photo after photo of Dolly as a little girl popped up on my phone, and the more I saw, the more my heart broke and I couldn't stop the tears that soon rushed down my face. There was a sudden knock at the door.

'Freya? Are you okay? I heard crying,' said Joe.

'Yeah, I'm fine,' I replied, sniffling.

'But I definitely heard crying. Are you sure you're okay?'

I took a moment, stood up, made sure I was suitably covered up – especially after our recent naked indiscretion – and then I walked across and opened the door.

'I'm fine. I just saw some photos of Dolly on Facebook, went down a bit of a rabbit hole, and got a bit weepy, that's all,' I said, before turning around and walking back to sit on my bed. For a moment, Joe dithered by the door, before he slowly made his way across the room and sat down a good couple of feet away from me.

'It's hard to believe Dolly will be leaving for university soon,' said Joe.

'I'm just...' I said, and started sobbing again. Joe quickly got up and then returned with a handful of toilet tissue. 'Thank you.' I wiped my eyes and blew my nose. 'I'm just sad she's not our little girl any more.'

'I was thinking about her earlier. Do you remember the time when she was about nine? We'd bought her that new bike for her birthday, the one with the little basket on the front, and we had taken her to the park? She was so excited, but within a minute she had fallen off, grazed her knee, and she threw her helmet down and said she'd "never ride that horrible bike ever again".'

'She was back on it the following day.'

'After you bribed her with an ice cream,' said Joe with a smile. 'Do you remember when instead of shark, she would say shoke and instead of park it was—'

'Poke!' I said and we both laughed.

'They were the best days.'

'They were.'

'I wish we could go back and do them all over again.'

'Would you do anything differently?' I asked.

Joe turned and looked at me, and then he smiled a sort of soft, melancholy smile, and for a moment, I almost reached across and held his hand, but I didn't. Things were confusing enough and I was still just in a dressing gown and basically naked beneath, we were on my bed, and touching him, however innocently, felt like a step too far.

'I'd do a lot of things differently if I could,' said Joe after a moment.

'Me too,' I replied, and we sat in silence, neither of us, it seemed, sure what to say next.

Our relationship felt like it was constantly evolving and it wasn't always clear exactly where we were. Before the separation, being together had felt so difficult, almost impossible, but now we were separated but still living together, there was something new about us. Perhaps it was just the pressure of trying to make our marriage work that had made us both miserable, and maybe now being apart had given us the breathing space to see each other in a new light. I didn't want to forget about all the incredible moments we had shared over the years, and despite the difficulties of the past eighteen months and the complete breakdown of our relationship, it wouldn't erase all of the wonderful memories we had created together. Perhaps from the jumbled wreckage of our marriage, a new friendship was possible, and we would always have Dolly to bind us together. We were the only two people in the world with all those memories, and I knew exactly how much he loved her because I felt the same.

'I suppose we'd better get ready,' said Joe after a moment, gingerly standing up.

'Yes, right,' I said, standing up, too. Joe went to walk out but I stopped him. 'Thank you.'

'What for?'

'For checking up on me.'

'Of course. You're still technically my wife,' said Joe. He smiled at me, but it was definitely tinged with a little uncertainty, before he left me alone to get ready for Dolly's celebratory meal.

Chapter Fifteen

Joe

Karen was wearing a white shirt under a thin grey jumper, and despite it being June and with summer just around the corner, it was lashing it down outside, which created a gloomy atmosphere in the room. It wasn't the day for therapy.

'How are you?' said Karen brightly, which was somewhat jarring given the dampness of the day. I fidgeted in my seat. Why didn't she have a sofa? I would have loved a comfortable sofa. I had brought a coffee with me, and I took a sip. It was the day for warm drinks, comfy seating and jumpers. I longed to be at home.

'Umm, good, yeah. A few things have happened since my last visit.' She got herself ready, pen in hand to jot down notes. 'Dolly got a place at Durham to read English. We're obviously really proud of her. We went out for dinner to celebrate, and it was nice. We went to Wagamama, and, I don't know, but things with Freya felt good. Before we left, we sat on her bed and reminisced about the old days, and it was nice. I'm also working on a new script.'

'That's exciting,' said Karen, quickly writing something down on her notepad. 'Do you want to talk more about you and Freya?'

'Yeah, we're good. I don't know, we've had a lot of positive interactions lately. I suppose it's easier without the pressure of marriage. Although I did walk in on her naked, which definitely didn't go down well.'

'Sounds awkward. Do you want to discuss that?'

'Not really. I'd had a couple of drinks, made a hasty decision, instantly regretted it, apologised, and I think we're both over it now.'

'Right, that's good.'

A pause.

'But there's something else I need to talk about.'

'Go on,' said Karen, sitting up a little taller in her chair. The rain continued lashing against the window and it sounded like a thousand small gunshots.

'The thing is, my new sitcom, it's about me and Freya. I had a meeting with my agent and he thought the idea of a couple, separated but forced to keep living together, would make a great sitcom. It's modern, zeitgeisty, and yet it still has all the traditional tropes of a sitcom. At first, I was against it, but then I started making notes, sketching out ideas, and I just fell in love with it. It's the best thing I've written in years.'

A beat. More rain hammered against the window.

'But?' said Karen after a moment because she could obviously detect the uncertainty in my voice, and probably see it written clearly across my face.

'I haven't told Freya about it, and I know I should. It's so personal, and we're still going through it. It's happening right now, and I'm using it for laughs, but it's cathartic, writing the scenes we've already lived, and seeing things from her perspective has, I think, really helped me understand what went wrong. What I've written so far is probably the best stuff I've done for a while, and I love it. It's reminded me that I'm good at writing, that I can do this and be successful again, but a part of me knows I have to tell Freya. That I need to ask for her permission.'

'So why don't you? What are you so afraid of?'

A good question. What *was* I afraid of?

'I don't know. I think about telling her, but when it comes to actually doing it, I can't, and usually I just change the subject. I suppose I'm afraid of upsetting the apple cart. Like I said, we've been doing so well, and I don't want to jeopardise that. I suppose I'm also worried she might tell me to stop writing it.'

Karen looked at me from behind her glasses with a familiar expression. 'Would you?'

'Would I what?'

'Stop writing it if she asked you? Remember your homework from last time? I asked you to think about why your marriage ended, and if there was something you could have done differently.'

'I remember.'

'Do you think that this lack of willingness to risk confrontation had something to do with it? You have always lacked the ability to tell Freya exactly what you're thinking. When it comes down to it, you don't tell her your deepest, darkest fears, your worries, frustrations, and even now when you have separated, you're still afraid to tell her something even when you know you should. Where do you think this challenge with communication comes from, Joe?'

This was the sort of thing that made me hate therapy. I despised being put on the spot and questioned in such a practical, straightforward way, and yes, I knew she was right and had a valid point, but it wasn't something I wanted to address. I would rather keep things light and breezy. It was probably why I had ended up being a comedy writer. Nothing could get too deep when you were writing a sitcom, and if it did, you just chucked in a knob gag and you were back to laughter again because the thing about sitcoms was that people didn't really change. It was why audiences loved to watch them again and again because the characters, the situations, didn't change in the way that life did. Sitcoms were comforting because they were simple, uncomplicated, and always had a happy ending – or at least an ending. A whole storyline neatly wrapped up in a tight thirty-minute script. There was something incredibly beautiful about it.

I leaned back in my chair for a moment, running a hand through my rapidly thinning hair, and I didn't quite know how to reply.

'I'm not sure,' I said finally.

A pause. She looked at me.

'But do you agree your, shall we say, lack of communication effectively hurt your marriage?'

'I'm sure my inability to tell Freya how I'm feeling, and what I actually need or want, negatively impacted our relationship.'

'But where do you think it comes from? Sorry if I'm repeating myself, Joe, but I think it's important to get to the root of where this fear of confrontation comes from.'

There wasn't a neat, perfectly scripted answer for this question. The obvious answer was my parents, and more specifically my father, but was it that simple? Could everything I was, or wasn't, solely be blamed on the deficiencies of my parents?

'We've spoken about my parents before,' I eventually replied. 'And it's clear my childhood has informed much of my adulthood.'

'Agreed. But do you think there's something else at play here, Joe?'

'Like what?'

She took her glasses off and placed them carefully on her desk. I noticed her earrings because they looked new, and I hadn't seen them before. Long, silver, with pearls at the end.

'It seems to me you have a complicated relationship with failure that has led to many of the decisions you've made as an adult. You decided to go into a career with a high chance of failure—'

'Which I have largely succeeded at.'

'True, and it's incredible what you have already achieved, but even that success has been laced with some failures. You seem afraid of opening up to Freya in case you upset the apple cart, despite the fact you're already separated. I'm just speculating here, Joe, but do you think your desire to live on the surface, keeping everything light and breezy, is linked to your relationship with failure?'

'It's because of my fucking parents!' I said, slightly more aggressively than I intended. 'Sorry, I just meant—'

'No, it's good to get emotional, Joe. You need to explore that. Don't you see that you have a particular fear of letting go, of telling people what you think, and being honest with yourself in the process? Sometimes it's okay to let go. You can't control every aspect of your life.'

'You think I have a need to control things?'

'Do you?'

'Doesn't everyone?'

'Not necessarily. Sometimes people need control because they think it equals some sort of success. If you control everything, it gives you power, and that power will be rewarded. Some people need to control every aspect of their lives because they're afraid of letting go and revealing their weaknesses. It's a way of protecting themselves.'

'And which am I, Karen? Driven by success or fear?'

'Which do you think, Joe?'

I hated the way she never answered my questions and would often turn it around as a question for me. Imagine if I did that in everyday life? People would literally hate me.

'There was a boy at my school, Harvey Cooper, who purposely failed his GCSE exams because he didn't want to go to sixth form. His parents thought he was going to be a doctor, and he ended up working at Halfords. He was definitely driven by a fear of success. Although if you needed a new inner tube for your bike, he was the person to go to.'

'Why are you bringing up a boy from your school?'

'Perhaps for the same reason his first girlfriend dumped him. No, not a tiny penis, although there were rumours. She probably realised he wasn't going places and if she stuck with him, she would be stuck, too.'

'What are you saying, Joe?'

'That I'm driven to succeed because I'm terrified there's nothing else out there. Writing is the only thing I'm good at. The only thing that will stop me from ending up working in a shit job I hate that pays very little money,' I said, and then I added without thinking, 'and essentially becoming my father.'

'That's time today, Joe, but really good work. Let's hang on to that last thought and really delve into it next time, okay?' said Karen with a smile.

I couldn't believe we were leaving our session on a cliff-hanger like that. Perhaps Karen should write for television because she fucking nailed the ending on that one. Talk about good plotting. Of course it all came back to my fucking dad. He was solely responsible for my inability to communicate like a proper, emotionally well-balanced, functioning adult, and now, just as we were discussing it in therapy, he was fucking off to France to run a bed and breakfast with his French girlfriend. I hadn't even told Karen about that yet. No doubt she would have an absolute field day with that one. Talk about daddy fucking issues.

Chapter Sixteen

Freya

I wasn't wearing my usual hat and gloves combination, although I did have on my black waterproof boots because they helped with the pebbles, but it was warmer now, and as I walked into the sea I definitely felt a change. I didn't feel as cold as I had in previous weeks, but I was still exhilarated by it, excited at being in the sea with friends at seven o'clock in the morning once again. There was something about starting a new routine with new people that made me feel so alive.

'How are you doing?' said Lucy. We had waded out, and despite it being so much warmer, the initial cold of the water was still jarring – it wasn't the Caribbean yet!

'Good. Dolly got into Durham, so we're over the moon.'

'Oh, that's brilliant. She's a smart one.'

'She is.'

'What about things between you and Joe?'

'Umm, they're fine, I suppose. We had dinner at Wagamama to celebrate Dolly getting into Durham, and it was actually quite nice. We spoke, and it wasn't weird or tense, and it was the most normal we've been for a while. We even shared a moment when we talked about the past, and it was sort of, I don't know, it made me wonder.'

'Wonder what?' said Lucy, as we stopped walking, the water reached above our waists.

'Whether there's still a chance for us.'

'That's good, right?'

I hadn't had the time or perhaps the inclination to really think about it. I suppose the thing was, I didn't trust myself at that moment to make any sort of decision about Joe. We had separated after months of heartbreaking arguments and discussions, and just because we were now in a better place, it didn't mean we were close to or even thinking about some sort of reconciliation. Maybe being friends was exactly where we were supposed to be.

'Maybe. I don't know,' I replied.

'Whatever happens, at least it's amicable. It will make everything so much easier,' said Lucy, and then she looked across at the other members of Cold Water Club. 'Okay, ready?'

They all nodded, and Caroline said 'Aye' in her Edinburgh brogue, and then we all ducked down until the water covered our shoulders, and then we started doing our own thing. The water was warmer, and as I swam around I felt myself adjusting quicker. It was glorious being out in the sea so early in the morning. I looked back towards the beach, and saw a few runners, and the same dog walkers we saw each morning.

Eventually, we all came together again and started walking slowly back in towards the beach, and Helen was talking about a date she had gone on with a man named Simon. Despite being divorced for a number of years, Helen had only just jumped back into the dating pool, and it seemed, finally, she had made a splash.

'It was really nice, actually,' said Helen. 'Simon was charming, funny, and runs his own business setting up wedding marquees. Does very well, by the sound of it.'

'Are you seeing him again?' asked Caroline.

'I am,' said Helen with a smile, and even in the cold water it looked like she was blushing.

'I think it's wonderful,' said Amy. 'I wouldn't have survived chemo without Steve, so I know what having a great partner can do for you.'

'Agreed,' said Debs. 'And you've been single for long enough, Helen. We all have needs!'

'It has been a long time! I think I might technically be a virgin again,' said Helen, and we all laughed, and I was happy out there with Cold Water Club. We were bonding, sharing stories about our lives, and I felt connected with these women. It made me want to share my life with them, too.

'I know what you mean,' I replied. 'Before the separation, Joe and I hadn't had sex in at least six months, so it's been a while. Not that I'm a rampaging sex beast, but like you said, we all have needs. Although to be honest, I'd take a nice hug at this point.'

'I can give you a hug once we get out,' replied Lucy.

'Deal,' I said as we finally reached the shore, and we were soon back on the beach, drying ourselves, and getting into our warm clothes. I had brought along my flask of hot tea again, and we all sat on the pebbly beach for a few minutes, chatting about our plans for the rest of the day.

Lucy had cricket with the boys at a village near Haywards Heath, and because Stuart had to work, she would be busy with them all day. Debs and her husband Steve were taking their daughter into London to see the

Harry Potter play, while Helen was getting ready for her second date with Simon. Amy and her husband Ferguson were doing a big shop at Tesco, and she was cooking roast chicken with all the trimmings, before a night on the sofa watching a film. I was the only one with nothing planned, and it made me realise that I had a whole day ahead of me, and I needed something to do. I knew Dolly was going to the library to study, and then she was going to hang out with Maya. I couldn't exactly ask Joe what he was doing because that would be weird, and so once I had said goodbye to everyone I sat in my car and decided that I needed a plan, and that plan would probably involve Mum.

–

'There she is! Hello, darling,' said Mum waving, as I walked into the pub. The Preston Park Tavern was one of those lovely big pubs that had been decorated beautifully, and had a wonderful menu of delicious food, and was also where Mum and I were going to spend the afternoon. I had called her earlier and, as it turned out, Marmalade had a car show in Cheltenham, so she had the afternoon free. I had suggested a pub lunch, and the afternoon was supposed to be lovely, so we were going to spend a few hours in the pub garden eating and chatting about our lives. It was just what I needed.

'Hello, Mum,' I said, giving her a quick hug before I sat down opposite her.

The garden was buzzing with people and families enjoying the bright, sunny day. A couple of small children ran about giggling, and a dog sat obediently with its owner, hoping for some leftover scraps to come his way.

'Right, I'll get the drinks, and then I want to know everything that's happening with you,' said Mum excitedly, before she disappeared inside towards the bar, and I got myself settled.

It felt good to be out in the world and doing something different. After a few minutes, Mum returned with a glass of wine in each hand, and two menus tucked under one arm. I was actually quite hungry after my morning 'dook', and I quickly scanned the menu for something delicious to eat.

'So, how are you?' asked Mum.

'I'm good. I'm loving Cold Water Club.'

'Oh, yes, you mentioned that before. Something about getting in the sea every morning, right? I've seen it on television. Looks painful.'

'You should come along, Mum. We're always looking for new members.'

'Oh, I don't know if that sort of thing is for me. I'm too old.'

'Nonsense. Honestly, it will change your life,' I said, and Mum laughed.

'Maybe I'll come along one day.'

'That's all I wanted to hear. How are things with you, and Martin's bottom?'

'The bottom is haemorrhoid-free, which is good news for Martin and me, obviously. He's at a car show today. I can't stand the bloody things, talk about boring. I went once, never again, but he likes it and it keeps him out of my hair.'

'Out of your hair? Do I detect unrest?' I asked, browsing the menu.

'No, darling. Martin and I are fine, but we both need our own things. He has his old cars, and I have…'

'Yes, Mum, what do you have?'

'Plenty. I have the tennis club for a start, Pilates on Tuesday, the book club on Thursday, and Veronica, you know Veronica, she has the little Jack Russell with only three legs, we meet up at least twice a week. I'm very busy, darling.'

'It sounds like it. Now, what are we going to order? I'm starving.'

I ended up going with the burger and Mum got the fish and chips, plus another two glasses of wine, and eventually the conversation circled back towards marriage.

'How or when did you know your marriage was over?' I asked Mum, as I ate the last few chips on my plate, dunking them in small puddles of blood-red ketchup. I looked across at Mum expectantly because we had never really spoken in depth about her and Dad. I knew they hadn't been happy for a long time before they eventually separated, but I wasn't sure how long it had been. Mum put her knife and fork down and looked across at me.

'It was a different time then, darling. Do you know why I married your father?'

'No.'

'Because he asked. I was nineteen, living at home, desperate to leave, but with the pittance I earnt working, and how things were, the only way I was going to leave home was if I got married. You couldn't just live with a man then, darling. My parents were very traditional and living in sin would have been a bloody scandal! I met your father, he had some money, a decent job, and he seemed nice enough, so I did what I had to do.'

'Are you saying you and Dad were a marriage of convenience?'

'You could say that, but honestly, darling, it wasn't that uncommon back then. I loved your father, and I think he loved me in his own way, but I wouldn't say we were ever in love,' said Mum, doing actual air quotes around 'in love'.

'Wow, that's, just… I'm not sure what to say, Mum.'

'Look, it all worked out. We had you, the single greatest thing in both our lives. I'm happy with Martin, and I think your father is happy, too. Some people are lucky enough to marry their soulmate the first time around, darling, and for others, it takes time or doesn't happen at all.'

'What about me and Joe? Do you think he's my soulmate?'

Mum looked at me and she smiled. 'I can't answer that, I'm afraid.'

'Bugger. I was hoping for some sage advice.'

'I will say this though. I always liked Joe, and the fact you're still under the same roof and not killing each other says something. If your father and I had done what you're doing, I suspect that one of us would be serving life for murder!'

'You think that means something?'

'I don't know what it means, but it's all the sage advice I have. Unless you need something on haemorrhoids because I'm quite the expert these days!'

We finished our lunch in the sunshine, and all I could think about was that my parents had only got married because it served a purpose. They had never experienced true love together, and that was definitely something that Joe and I had. When it had been good, it had been great, and surely that was something worth hanging on to. I didn't know what that meant exactly, but one thing was certain, we were definitely a lot luckier than my parents.

Chapter Seventeen

Joe

Freya was sitting at a table in the corner of a quiet pub in Hove, and I walked across with our drinks, placing them down on the table. She had come straight from work and looked smart in a flower-print shirt and a navy skirt. Her hair was straight and tucked casually behind her ears, and despite everything, I still found her stunningly attractive. Physical attraction had never been a problem for me, although the slow death of our sex life suggested it was potentially an issue for her. The notion she had been more attracted to my sense of humour than my looks had popped into my head from time to time, but was it true? She had never been shy about telling me how handsome I was, even though clearly I was no Ewan McGregor or Jude Law. I think, in my eyes at least, she was out of my league, but I just happened to have the one thing she couldn't resist – jokes. The thing was, when all you had was one outstanding quality, when that stopped working, you were left with nothing else. Maybe our relationship had just run out of laughs?

'Thanks,' said Freya, taking a sip of her wine.

'You're welcome,' I replied, having a sip of my beer. 'I called this meeting, so I guess I should start.'

There were two things on the agenda that we needed to discuss. The first was our upcoming annual summer party we threw every year, which we hadn't yet cancelled, and the second was my sitcom. I had to tell Freya about it because it was going really well, and I knew I couldn't stop now. I had already written the first episode, outlined two more, and I thought it could really be something. I had an upcoming meeting with Carl and we were going to delve into it and so I knew it was time to tell Freya about it. I hated lying to her, and it felt wrong and duplicitous not to discuss something so important with her. Also, things between us had been going so well recently, I felt sure she would understand.

'Do you mind if I say something first?' said Freya.

'Umm, no, of course not.'

'I know we're here to talk about the summer party, and whether we should cancel or not, and I know it's going to be a little weird this year with everything going on, but I think we've been doing so well recently, Joe, and it's probably going to be the last one, so I think we should go ahead with it.'

'Oh, right. Okay.'

'Sorry, didn't mean to steal your thunder.'

'It's fine. Thunder not stolen. Although slightly curious. I was coming here to argue for going ahead because I thought you'd be against having the party, given our current sticky wicket—'

'Sorry, but do we have to call our separation and living situation a "sticky wicket"?'

'What do you want me to call it?'

'I don't know—'

'Let's go to VAR on this one. Yes, it does appear that "sticky wicket" is just on the wrong side of appropriate, and has been ruled out. The referee is pointing to, what's this? A new term for Joe and Freya's house-shared living arrangement, and it's… tricky sitch?' I looked across at Freya, who was shaking her head but smiling. 'Sorry, but VAR has ruled that "tricky sitch" has been accepted and will be used going forwards.'

Freya laughed. 'Still just a massive knobhead.'

'I take that as a compliment. So, back to the summer party, you want to go ahead?'

'I do. Plus, with Dolly getting into Durham, and us probably selling the house soon after, I think it will be good to have one last party there. Like a final goodbye.'

Just hearing her talk about selling the house was jarring. It really brought home that within the next year, all of this was going to be over. Freya and I living together, our lives still connected, living with Dolly, it would all soon be gone and we'd both have to forge new lives alone. How had it come to this? It felt like we were on a ride, and I wanted to say stop, I want to get off. I wanted to have a break and make sure I was actually on the right ride, but I couldn't because it had already started and was gathering speed. Was it that long ago that Freya and I were still trying to save our marriage? It didn't feel like it. When exactly did we give up and why? I still wasn't completely sure I knew all the answers. There had been times when I had sleepwalked through the turmoil of our marriage, and looking back now, I wasn't always proud of myself.

'What's happening with you?' I asked after a moment of silence.

It felt like weeks since we had really spoken at length, and I had no idea what was happening in her life. She excitedly told me all about the cold water swimming club she had been going to with Lucy. She explained about how incredible it felt afterwards, and how much she enjoyed the camaraderie she felt with the other women. When I asked her how painfully uncomfortable it was being neck deep in freezing cold water, she said it was worth every second of it, then she took a sip of her drink, looked at me, and said, 'What about you? What's new?'

This was the part of the conversation where I would have to tell her that I was writing a sitcom about the break-up of our marriage. That I was using the heartbreak, our 'tricky sitch' and Dolly's life to create a laughter-fuelled thirty-minute comedy that could potentially save my career. I played the conversations I'd had with Karen over and over in my mind – the therapist that Freya also knew nothing about. How had I woven so many lies into the fabric of my relationship with Freya, and why? I could do this though. I could tell her now and get everything out in the open.

'Oh, you know, just working,' I said tentatively.

'What are you working on? Is it still the one about the media agency?'

I had to just say the words. *Tell her.* It was time to man up!

'No, actually. That one didn't work out. This is just a family comedy thing.'

You absolute fucking coward. Why couldn't you tell her? You know at some point you will have to tell her and the later you leave it the worse it will be, right?

'Oh, okay, and does Carl like it?'

'Yes, he does. It's still really early on so, you know, we'll see.'

'Good luck with it,' said Freya with a smile.

'I just need to use the toilet,' I said, getting up quickly and walking off.

Since the beginning of my career, Freya had read all my scripts and she had been the sounding board for most of the work. She had been an integral part of my process because she would often give me feedback before I even approached Carl. Most ideas would bubble away in my head for months before I jotted down notes, ideas, and then Freya would get a first look at it. Now she was literally one of the lead characters in my latest sitcom, her whole life was the subject matter, and she had no idea. I didn't even need to go to the toilet, and so I washed my hands and looked at myself in the mirror above the sink. Middle-aged, on the verge of separating from my wife, my daughter on the cusp of leaving home, a vaguely successful comedy writer, and I still didn't have the balls to tell my wife the truth. Was I ever going to be a proper grown-up? I looked in the mirror and the old man that stared back at me was definitely veering dangerously close to fifty and surely should have his shit together by now. But then again, being a comedy writer since university definitely hinted at some sort of Peter Pan complex.

'I suppose we should discuss the details of the summer party?' I said, sitting down again.

'Then perhaps another drink?' replied Freya.

'Okay, I'll get these,' I said, and I was about to stand up when Freya stopped me.

'Joe, can I say something?'

'Of course. Unless it's something awful. Is my receding hairline getting worse because I've been thinking about using a cream I saw on Amazon, but do I want to be that guy because it's a slippery slope? You know today it's cream for male pattern baldness and then tomorrow I'm injecting Botox into my eyeballs.'

'No, Joe, it's not about your hairline, which is fine by the way, and do people inject Botox into their eyes? I don't think that's a thing. Anyway, I just wanted to say how proud I am of us. When we agreed to this house-share situation—'

'You mean the tricky sitch?'

Freya giggled. 'Fine. When we agreed to the "tricky sitch" I genuinely didn't know if we could do it. Whether it would be too much, and we'd end up constantly arguing. I know it's been a little uncomfortable at times, and it's required some adjustments, and I *really* wish you hadn't walked in on me naked, but I think we've done ourselves proud. We've been honest, open with each other, and I'm really thankful we've been so mature about all of this.'

'Wow, well, thank you?' I said, feeling an uncomfortable and yet familiar stab of guilt, that I was a lying piece of shit, creeping up and through my body.

'With that, let me get the drinks and we can finalise the plans for the party,' said Freya with a bright, warm smile, before she hopped up and off towards the bar.

Could I feel any worse? Freya was so proud of us for being honest, open and mature, and yet in the background I had been lying to her the whole time. If she knew about the sitcom and that despite refusing to see a marriage counsellor I was visiting a therapist on my own, she would go fucking ballistic. The only thing that Freya had done since our separation was take up cold water swimming. She was wholesome, perfect and mature, while I was literally the exact opposite. Watching her standing at the bar, looking so lovely in her work clothes, I had the sudden feeling that I didn't deserve someone as incredible as Freya. Perhaps I never had.

She returned to the table and we made our plans for our annual summer party. We agreed upon a smaller than usual guest list, I ran through my ideas for the menu, and Freya chipped in with some ideas of her own, until eventually we had everything in place. When it came to party planning at least, Freya and I were still a well-oiled machine.

'Do you think it's going to be weird?' said Freya when we were all done, and our glasses sat empty on the table.

'Oh, it's definitely going to be weird, but I think we can pull off weird.'

'I mean, *you* can definitely pull off weird,' said Freya, standing up, and grabbing her bag.

'I'll take that as a compliment,' I said, standing up, too.

'Even though you know it's definitely not a compliment, right?'

'It's all subjective,' I said, walking out behind her. 'Many of the best actors I've known over the years have been batshit crazy, and most of them are routinely on national television earning large amounts of money.'

'I guess defining weird is a bit of a tricky sitch,' said Freya, and I couldn't help but laugh as we walked out of the pub towards home where we would be soon hosting our summer party.

Perhaps things were looking up and maybe the party would bring us back together? Was that what I wanted? Was that what Freya wanted? I was proud we had somehow managed to patchwork our lives together without really fucking anything up, but sat there at the back my mind, lurking in the background like a giant fucking storm cloud, were my lies that seemed to be just waiting for their moment to explode upon us, and fuck every single thing up.

Chapter Eighteen

Freya

Our first summer party was ten years ago, and it had started off small, and gradually over the years it had grown and become one of the most important dates in our calendar. We always held it at the end of June, as a way of marking the beginning of summer. Obviously this year was going to be a little bit different, but I was still excited about it. We had invited everyone important in our lives so the guest list was Mum, Marmalade, Lucy, Stuart, Barney plus one if he had a plus-one, Joe's dad and his new girlfriend, Juliette, and lastly Dolly's friend, Maya. I had thought about inviting the rest of Cold Water Club, and I had invited people from work in the past and Joe had invited Carl and other comedy friends, but we wanted to keep the numbers down this year. We thought smaller and more intimate was the way to go, considering everything that had happened.

'Have you seen the bottle opener?' I said to Joe, who was in the kitchen creating a charcuterie board of various cheeses, meats, olives, pickles and crackers.

'Should be in the usual spot.'

'Obviously it isn't in the usual spot, Joe, because I looked in the usual spot and it wasn't there. Hence why

I am asking you where it is because you probably moved it.'

'I haven't touched it.'

'You definitely haven't touched it?'

'Definitely not.'

'Okaaay,' I said, knowing full well that he had definitely moved it. When it came to putting things in the wrong place, Joe had a lengthy rap sheet.

'Need any help?' said Dolly, suddenly appearing in the kitchen.

'Oh, you look nice, love,' I said, and she really did. She was in a long flowery dress with white trainers, she had curled her hair, done her make-up, and she looked beautiful.

'Thanks,' said Dolly.

'You can help me find the bottle opener that your dad definitely hasn't touched, even though we all know he moved it and just can't remember—'

'Actually, I used that,' said Dolly. 'Sorry, it's in my room. I'll get it.'

I immediately looked across at Joe, who gave me a smug, annoying smile.

'Shut it,' I said, before I went outside into the garden.

I had set up tables, and despite the forecast saying it wasn't going to rain, the clouds overhead were ominously dark. Obviously we could move indoors if we had to, but it was best to have it outside if possible, and some of our best summer parties had been held late into the night in the garden. Joe had started the barbecue in preparation, and was planning on cooking burgers, sausages and chicken outside. Dolly found the bottle opener, and she helped me get the garden ready and open a few bottles of wine in preparation. I was slightly nervous about how this year's party was going to go, but things with Joe had been really good recently, and even his father had agreed to come down from Colchester with his new girlfriend. For the record, in ten years of summer parties, he had been to just one summer party. Dolly was excited because Maya was coming, although I had sensed a nervous energy about her for the last few weeks. Perhaps she was tired from all the studying she had been doing or maybe it was anxiety about her upcoming exams. Life was suddenly hurtling towards us all at breakneck speed, and there was no doubt it was fucking terrifying.

'You okay, love?' I said to her, as we put some extra cans of drink into the cool box.

'Yeah,' Dolly replied. 'It's going to be okay, right?'

'What do you mean? Is what going to be okay?'

'You and Dad? It's not going to be weird, is it?'

I looked at Dolly, saw the look of concern on her face, and it made me so sad that she was worried about us.

'It will be fine, love. Promise,' I said with a smile, and I meant it. 'Now, can you be in charge of music? Although nothing too, you know, out there. Remember most of us are middle-aged or older.'

'What the hell is "out there"? I'm hardly into anything weird. Have you seen my Spotify playlists?'

'Just keep it mainstream,' I said, and Dolly gave me a sarcastic look before I heard the doorbell go, and it seemed our first guests had arrived.

The party was in full swing, and fortunately the weather, although still gloomy, had remained dry, and after serving all the starters Joe was now stationed at the barbecue in his 'The Grillfather' apron – a birthday present from Dolly and me for his fortieth. Dolly had been doing a great job with the music, and was currently playing ABBA, and everyone was in the garden, drinking, talking, and so far our annual summer party was going perfectly.

'Do you know where Joe got the sausages?' said Marmalade, while Mum stood next to him, sipping on a glass of wine.

'Umm, not sure,' I replied. 'Waitrose, maybe?'

'I shall have to find out. They're delicious. Have you tried them yet, Freya?'

'Not yet.'

'Oh, you should. They're so perfectly seasoned, and juicy, I imagine the meat ratio is probably quite high, although they're soft—'

'Okay, Martin, that's enough sausage talk,' said Mum. 'I see Joe's dad is here this year, darling. That's a real turn-up for the books, and is that the new French girlfriend?'

'*Oui*,' I said, looking across at Joe's dad and Juliette. She was lovely, had beautiful dark hair and spoke with a gloriously French/English accent. I had only said a brief hello to her, but she gave his father a proper glow. I didn't think in all the years I had known Joe's father I had seen him looking so happy and relaxed. It was clear he was genuinely in love. It was a shame that when he was finally happy, and perhaps with the chance of being more involved in Joe's life, he was moving to the south of France.

'She definitely has a little *je ne sais quoi*, doesn't she?' said Mum, as Lucy came bounding across, a glass of wine in one hand and a hot dog in the other.

'Lucy, hi, how's it going?' I said. 'You remember Mum.'

'Of course, hi,' said Lucy.

'Hello, again,' said Mum. 'It's been, what, exactly a year since the last party?'

'That's right,' said Lucy with a smile.

'How's the sausage?' chipped in Marmalade, getting a stern look from Mum.

'I've come to steal Freya away for a minute,' said Lucy. 'Do you mind?'

'Not at all,' said Mum, and Lucy and I started walking away, although before we were out of earshot, I heard Mum chiding Marmalade about the bloody bangers. We walked past Joe on the barbecue, and he was talking with Barney and Stuart, looking relaxed and happy in his favourite spot, a bottle of beer in his hand. Lucy and I walked inside and took a seat at the dining room table. I had no idea where Dolly was. The music was still playing, and it had moved on to Olly Murs, so she was definitely keeping it mainstream.

'How's it going?' I said to Lucy when we had sat down.

'Good. I just wanted to have a quick word,' she said, a note of trepidation in her voice.

'What's going on?'

'What do you mean?' She met my gaze with a look of apprehension.

'Come on, Luce. It's obvious something is going on with you.'

Lucy looked at me, frowned, looked unsure, and then she said, 'Well, you know I said that Stuart is going to start his own language school?'

I nodded.

'Well, it looks like it's going to be next year, and we'll be moving, too.'

'Oh, right, shit,' I said, feeling a sudden flash of disappointment rush through me.

'It's a huge endeavour, and we'll be risking a lot financially to make it happen, but he really wants to do it and

I want to support him. I know it's probably a shit time to be leaving you, and—'

'Luce, it's okay. I mean I hate it, obviously, and I'll never speak to Stuart again, but I understand,' I said, trying not to sound as devastated as I felt inside. 'It definitely won't be in Brighton then?'

'We're talking about the possibility of the Midlands. With house prices so high in Brighton, we could sell up here, put some of that money into the business, and Stuart has plenty of contacts near Leicester and at a few of the larger boarding schools in that area. We could buy a house there for almost half of what we'd get for ours in Brighton.'

'But the Midlands,' I said. 'It's so far away, and what about Cold Water Club?'

'It will go on without me.'

I looked at Lucy, reached across and held her hand, and I wanted to cry. 'Whatever happens, I'll miss you terribly,' I said.

'Me, too. Although it won't be until the beginning of next year at the earliest, so we have time. Plenty more Cold Water Club!'

'Then we'd better enjoy ourselves while we can!' I said.

I would miss Lucy so much. She was my person at work, and now we had Cold Water Club too, and post-Joe she was going to be one of the tent poles of my new life. If she left for the Midlands, I knew I would find it hard without her, but I wanted her to be happy and I would be excited for her and Stuart to start a new adventure together. It also, and rather sadly from my perspective, made me feel a little jealous that Lucy and Stuart were obviously still so in love, while Joe and I were getting nearer and nearer to the day when we might separate for good. I remembered so clearly when we all met, and it felt like the four of us would be best mates forever, but now with Joe and me breaking up and Lucy and Stuart moving, all those dreams of the four of us growing old together in Brighton were nothing more than that. It was how I imagined Paul McCartney felt when Yoko Ono arrived on the scene.

Lucy and I finished up with hugs, and I said I needed to pop upstairs because all I really wanted to do was cry. I needed a moment to compose myself before I rejoined the party.

I left Lucy and went up to my bedroom. As I walked past Dolly's bedroom, I heard her talking and giggling with Maya, and then I went into my bedroom and closed the door, before I went into the en suite. I sat on the toilet for a moment, trying to get myself together. My life over the past year had been all ups and downs, and all I craved was some normality. Lucy had said that they weren't moving for a while, but I couldn't imagine my day-to-day life without her, in the same way I couldn't imagine the house without Dolly in it, or my life without Joe. All of these things were changing, and it felt like I had no control over any of them. At least things with Joe seemed to be going well, and there was a small part of me that was beginning to wonder if we did still have a chance.

While I was on the toilet, I heard the bedroom door open and then two voices. It was Joe and his father. What were they doing up here in the middle of the party?

'We should be okay here,' said Joe.

'I just wanted a quick word,' said his father.

They obviously had no idea I was on the toilet, and it felt weird just walking out, so I had no choice but to stay where I was and listen.

'What's going on?' said Joe.

I heard them sitting down on the bed. A pause.

'I, umm, just wanted to say,' said Joe's dad. 'That I'm sorry.'

'Sorry? For what?'

'For everything. For being so distant when you were growing up. For not talking to you about anything, and mostly, I think, being so distant since your mum passed. Being with Juliette has really made me appreciate just how bad I was as a dad. I didn't always know it, didn't always want to think about it, but, and this is weird to tell you now, but the thing is, Juliette got me to see a therapist.'

'Yeah?' said Joe. 'That's great.'

'Yeah, yeah it is. I had lots of issues, Joe, more than I ever cared to admit, and I think for years I just didn't know how to deal with it all. Things with your mum. You. Me. Anyway, Juliette is a big advocate for therapy, she's been going for years, and it's really helped me see myself and the world in a completely new light.'

I couldn't believe what I was hearing. Joe's dad truly was a different man. The person I had known all these years was hard-headed, stubborn and terrifyingly old-fashioned. He said so little about his own feelings, I often wondered whether he even had any. Now he was dating a French lady and talking openly about his feelings and failures. Perhaps there was hope for Joe, too.

'Right, wow, that's great, Dad. I'm really happy for you, and thanks, it means a lot. You know, it wasn't just you though, right? I wasn't good about dealing with things, and Mum just let things fester and get worse without saying anything. We all played our part.'

'I just… a part of therapy was dealing with my relationship with you, and I wanted to acknowledge that, and say I'm sorry if I ever made you feel like I didn't love you because despite everything, I always did. I obviously didn't always know how to show it or say it, but I did love you. Still love you. That's what I wanted to say, son.'

There was a pause, a quietness, and I couldn't help but wonder if Joe was going to cry. Joe didn't really cry, wasn't prone to moments of emotional fragility, but such a confession from his father had to have made him feel something. It was perhaps the first time I had heard Joe's father call him son. He always referred to him as Joe like they were friends or, more likely, work colleagues. Then, after a minute, Joe spoke, his voice catching in his throat.

'There's something I have to tell you, too, Dad. It's Freya and me, we've separated.'

'Oh, right,' said his dad. 'Why? What happened? I always thought you two were great.'

It felt wrong to be listening in on their conversation, but I couldn't exactly walk out in the middle of it now, could I?

'We were, Dad, for so long we were, but the last year and a half, it's been, I don't know. I think with my career not going so well, it put a lot of pressure on us, and like you, I didn't always handle things well or know what to say,' said Joe, and it felt strange hearing him talk about us, and admitting his faults. There was a short pause, and then Joe said, 'Actually, Dad, and no one else knows about this so please keep it quiet, but I've been seeing a therapist too for about the last six months.'

There was a sudden quietness in the room, but in my ears I heard a roar as blood rushed through my head, as my whole body was suddenly overtaken with emotion – and that emotion was fucking rage. Joe had been seeing a therapist! The man I had begged to see a marriage counsellor to save our marriage, who had declined and called it pointless, was seeing his own therapist in secret. I couldn't believe it. I couldn't control myself and I immediately walked out, crashing the door of the en suite against the wall, and I stormed into my bedroom. Joe instantly saw me, knew what I had heard, and saw the look on my face. He jumped up.

'Freya, I—'

'Just shut the fuck up!' I said loudly, feeling tears begin to bubble up and into my eyes. 'I can't believe you. I can't believe you lied to me about this, after I fucking begged you to see a therapist with me. I'm so angry with you, Joe.'

'I'm sorry,' said Joe, but I couldn't be in that room with him. I couldn't stand to even be in the same fucking house as him, and so I dashed out with no idea what I was going to do next.

Chapter Nineteen

Joe

I couldn't believe Freya had overheard my conversation with Dad, and now she knew I had been seeing a therapist. I had never seen her that angry before. It was clear I had really hurt her and whatever progress we had made over the past few months was all down the fucking drain. Every inch we had gained, every piece of momentum was all lost because of one careless fucking conversation. I felt sick to my stomach.

'What happened?' said Dad, looking shell-shocked.

'She, umm, didn't know I was seeing a therapist.'

'Oh, and after she had wanted to see a marriage counsellor. Got it.'

'Yeah, look, Dad, I need to go and see her, but, thanks for this.'

'It's okay. Now go. Sort this out before it's too late, yeah?'

I took one last look at Dad, and then I left. I had been shocked by Dad's admission about seeing a therapist and, fuck, I wished I hadn't said anything, but how was I to know that Freya was hiding in the en suite overhearing every single word? My head was spinning, and as I walked quickly out of Freya's bedroom, I almost bumped into Dolly walking out of her room.

'What's going on, Dad?' said Dolly, and behind her I saw Maya in the background.

'Umm, it's nothing, love. Just stay up here, okay?'

'It's obviously not nothing, is it?' said Dolly, a sullen teenage angst in her voice.

'Your mother and I just had a disagreement, that's all. It's going to be fine.'

'Mum promised it wouldn't be weird.'

'It's not going to be weird. Please just stay in your room, and once it's all sorted out, I'll explain everything, okay?' I said. Dolly obviously didn't believe me because she just huffed, mumbled something under her breath about lying fucking parents, and then walked back into her room, slamming the door behind her. I hated her being so upset, but at that moment I just needed to find Freya and explain myself. I knew that this was critical because obviously what I had done would be difficult to forgive, but I had my reasons. I hadn't told Freya about the panic attacks. I hadn't explained how worried I was about my future, my career, our marriage, and how all of it had just been too much. I should have talked to her then, explained myself fully, asked for her help, but I hadn't. Instead I had lied and now she knew all about it and it was all so much worse.

I hurried down the stairs and through the kitchen, popping my head around the living room door to see if she was in there. I walked outside and the garden was full of everyone having a good time. Stuart was still manning the barbecue, Taylor Swift was supplying the music, and when I scanned the garden it took me a moment but eventually I saw Freya in conversation with Lucy. I also noticed the sky had become quite a bit darker since I'd been inside, and it looked like rain wasn't far away. That was the last thing we needed. I took a deep breath and walked towards Freya.

'Do you have any more burgers, mate?' said Stuart as I walked past. 'They're almost gone.'

'Umm, yes, I think there's one more pack in the fridge,' I replied, but I could barely speak; all I could do was keep my eyes on Freya.

'There he is,' said Freya's mum, who was drinking a cocktail next to Marmalade. 'Can you please talk to Martin about the sausages because he's driving me up the wall. I think he cares more about the bloody things than me!'

'In a minute, I just need—'

'I mean, bravo on the bangers!' said Marmalade. 'I was just wondering if you knew the meat content percentage off the top of your head—'

I waved my hand in Marmalade's general direction. I wasn't trying to be rude, but I had to talk with Freya. I finally reached her and Lucy, and they both turned to me with expressions of disgust on their faces.

'Go away, Joe,' said Freya coldly.

'Please, Freya, let me explain,' I said hopefully.

'Joe, I don't think now is the time,' said Lucy, taking a step towards me.

'Freya, I just want to tell you the truth.'

'The truth?' spat Freya, suddenly so much louder, and it was clear that everyone in the garden had heard her. Conversations were halted, and all we could hear was the music, and the low spitting noise of meat sizzling on the barbecue. A dark cloud moved ominously overhead. 'Please Joe, explain why you have been lying to me for the past six months, I'd love to fucking hear it!'

An audible gasp went up from the garden. *What the fuck has Joe done?*

I turned, looked around and, as I had suspected, everyone was looking at us, and then Dolly and Maya came walking into the garden, followed rather sheepishly by my father. Everyone in the garden was waiting for my retort, and yet I couldn't speak. I didn't know what to do or what I could possibly say to defuse the situation. I was a bomb-disposal officer without the proper training. Eventually, after a minute of agonising silence, Freya broke the horrible stand-off.

'Just as I thought, Joe, when it comes down to it, when the shit hits the fan, you still have the emotional maturity of a toddler.' She strode past me and back into the house.

I stood in excruciating awkwardness and I didn't know what to do. The party was clearly over and so was my marriage. Freya was right: when it came down to it, when the chips were down, I wilted. I couldn't cope when the pressure was turned up and, once again, when faced with a moment of truth I had failed to rise to the occasion.

'I'm sorry,' I said, turning to face everyone. 'Umm, just keep eating, drinking, and we'll be back soon. I hope.'

I started to walk back through the garden, past family and friends, Dolly – who gave me the deadliest of death stares – and Maya, everyone looking at me, and that's when the heavens opened and it started to rain, and not just a casual light summer drizzle, but an actual, proper, will-get-you-drenched-in-about-thirty-seconds downpour. Luckily, while I and everyone else seemed to be caught up in my argument with Freya, Stuart did what he did best and took charge.

'Right, everyone, grab what you can and get inside!' He turned the barbecue off, closing the top and grabbing whatever food he could as everyone ran for cover. The garden went from a lovely summer party, to the worst-case version of a wet Glastonbury Festival in about ten seconds. Freya's mum was trying to grab a plate of sausage rolls, while Marmalade attempted to immediately run inside, tripped on a chair and ended up face down in a flower bed. Dad and Juliette picked up the big tray of sandwiches I had lovingly prepared and took them inside. Barney was trying to help get some food inside, but was dropping more than he was saving, and Lucy was attempting to help Freya's mum with plates of food, but after a moment realised how wet she was getting, and just grabbed Freya's mum and they both made it inside, closely followed by a very wet and slightly muddied Marmalade. Dolly and Maya both grabbed a plate of food each, and I tried to get whatever I could, and finally we all made it inside, dripping wet, but all I really cared about was seeing Freya. I turned to Stuart.

'Can you sort everything out, mate? I need to find Freya.'

'Of course,' he said, and immediately started rallying the sodden troops, while I walked up the stairs to Freya's bedroom because I imagined she would be in there – the scene of the crime. I took a deep breath, opened the door to her bedroom, and there she was, sitting on her bed, her face as dark as the clouds outside. I could hear the rain battering against the bedroom window. So much for summer.

'Just fuck off, Joe!' she exclaimed as soon as she saw me.

'Freya, please let me explain.'

'No, Joe,' she said, the anger on her face suddenly replaced with sadness and tears. 'You lied to me. You made me feel like a fucking idiot. Just when I thought we were getting somewhere, that maybe you and I… it doesn't matter, we're done, Joe. We're—'

'I had panic attacks,' I said suddenly, walking across and sitting down on the edge of the bed. Freya looked at me, her face red and her eyes glistening. I took a second to compose myself before I continued. 'It's why I started seeing a therapist. The panic attacks started about eight or nine months ago when things were really bad between us, and I wasn't writing, and I felt this huge weight on me. That's when it happened. I felt like I couldn't breathe, like the whole world was closing in on me, and I needed help. I know, I should have told you, come to you, but I didn't and instead found a therapist. Her name is Karen and I go whenever I need to, and it's really helped me. I'm sorry I didn't tell you, and I'm sorry you had to find out like that, but that's the truth.'

I stopped speaking and turned to Freya. I had no idea what she was going to say. She was so angry with me and rightfully so, but all I could do was hope that maybe she might find a way to forgive me and perhaps understand. Finally, after a minute of silence, while we sat and listened to the rain outside, Freya spoke.

'But why wouldn't you go to couples' counselling with me? If you were already in therapy and knew it worked for you, why wouldn't you do the same for us?' She had tears in her eyes, her voice was drenched in despair, and I hated myself for doing that to her.

'Because I didn't think I could do it. It was hard enough talking to a therapist about my own shit, Freya. I didn't have the emotional bandwidth to admit to another therapist what a shit husband I had been to you, too. How I had failed you, failed us, and it all felt so overwhelming. I know it's fucking weak and you deserve better. I'm sorry.'

A pause, and the silence in the room was overwhelming.

'Then why didn't you tell me that? I would have understood a lot better if you had just explained and instead you let me think you didn't give a shit about saving our marriage.'

'I know. I'm such a fucking idiot, Freya, and I'm sorry. I really fucked up.'

'You did,' said Freya bluntly, before she added with a slightly softer tone, 'but I'm sorry about the panic attacks. It must have been scary.'

'It was,' I replied, and then we sat in silence, not saying a word to each other.

I don't know how long we sat there, but it felt like hours. Eventually, we both stood up, and slowly made our way downstairs without saying another word to each other. There had been some sort of agreement between us, and I wasn't even sure what the agreement was, but it had in some part been resolved or at least put aside for a moment. It was still pouring with rain outside, and when we walked into the kitchen, most of the tidying up had been done. Some of the food had been lost to the weather, but most had been saved and packed away in the fridge, or wrapped in cling film on the table. I couldn't thank our friends enough for helping, especially after everything that had happened. After a few minutes, when it was clear the party was definitely over, people started leaving.

'Sorry, son,' said Dad by the front door. 'I didn't mean to—'

'It's fine, Dad, it wasn't your fault.'

'But I feel responsible.'

'You weren't the one who lied to their wife about seeing a therapist, and thank you for what you said. It might have got lost in all the drama, but I appreciated it.'

'You're welcome, and I'm sorry about you and Freya. If you need to talk, you know where to find me. Right, ready?' he said, turning to Juliette. 'It's a long drive back to Colchester, and with the rain, the traffic on the M25 will be an absolute nightmare.'

'*Oui*, ready,' said Juliette, and I said how nice it was to meet her, and I apologised for all the drama, and the rain. 'The only thing worse than the English food, is the weather,' said Juliette, which I thought was stunningly accurate.

'You've got a good one there, Dad.'

'Definitely a keeper,' he replied with a smile, before they left and then one by one Freya and I said goodbye to everyone else. Freya's mum and Marmalade were some of the last to leave, and despite everything Marmalade insisted I give him the name of the sausages, which I duly did, much to Freya's mum's annoyance. I heard her muttering something to him about appropriate behaviour on the way out of the front door, before they dashed for their car.

Stuart and Barney both said a rather sheepish goodbye, and I said we should get a drink in the week, which was met with polite nods. Lucy wasn't so polite and gave me the cold shoulder, which was fair enough. Eventually everyone was gone except me, Freya, Dolly and Maya. We were in the kitchen, tidying up the last of the mess, when Dolly stopped, turned to us, and said, 'Mum, Dad, there's something I have to talk to you about.'

I was putting plates in the dishwasher, and Freya was emptying the bin. We both stopped what we were doing.

'I know, love,' said Freya. 'I'm sorry. I promised today would be fine and it wasn't fine.'

'It isn't that, Mum.'

'It's me, isn't it?' I said. 'I really messed up, Dolls, and I'm so sorry—'

'Dad, it isn't about you guys at all,' said Dolly, a frustration caught in her voice.

'Oh, right,' I said.

'Okay,' said Freya uncertainly.

Dolly was standing next to Maya, and then slowly Dolly reached down and held Maya's hand.

'I'm gay,' said Dolly. 'And Maya is my girlfriend.'

I honestly didn't know what to say. It had already been such an emotionally charged day and now this on top of everything else, and it felt like someone had reached into my chest and was squeezing my heart until it felt like it was going to burst. Something had to give, and that something was me, and quite unexpectedly, standing there in the middle of the kitchen, I started to cry.

Chapter Twenty

Freya

Joe and I were in the living room, waiting for Dolly, who was saying goodbye to Maya at the front door, and we didn't know what to say to each other. At least, I didn't know what to say to him and he was being strangely quiet. I think the thing was, the afternoon had been so much about my argument with Joe, but at that moment, it was only about Dolly. She was all I could and wanted to think about. I had to admit I had been completely shocked when she announced she was gay and that Maya was her girlfriend. For so many years, I had thought her lack of interest in boys was down to her diligent work ethic and that she was still quite young. It hadn't occurred to me that she might not be straight. After the initial tears – and so many from Joe that it was almost as shocking as Dolly's news – we talked and we said it was okay, we were just shocked but happy. Joe was at pains to explain to Dolly that he didn't know why he was crying so much, and that he was so proud of her, loved her, and then Dolly cried, too, and then struck with the emotion of the occasion, I cried, then Maya joined in, and we all ended up in a slightly damp, snotty hug.

'Joe?' I whispered across the room. I was on the long sofa and he was on the short one. He looked across at me. 'Did you have any inkling Dolly was gay?'

'No, you?' whispered Joe back.

'No, none. I feel bad, like I should have known or at least suspected.'

'Me too.'

'Are we terrible parents?'

'I don't think so, although—'

'Okay, Maya is gone,' said Dolly at normal volume, walking into the room and sitting down next to me. 'I suppose we should probably talk.'

I moved myself a little nearer to Dolly, placing a hand on her leg for support.

'I was just going to say,' said Joe. 'That I love you, support you, and that, as far as I'm concerned, nothing is different.'

'It's what, business as usual?' replied Dolly, and Joe and I were momentarily caught between laughing and responding, and so we did neither. Dolly's joke was met with silence. 'Sorry, bad joke.'

'No, love, it isn't that,' I said. 'I just, we just, want you to know that we support you, love you, and that it doesn't change anything in our eyes.'

'That's right,' said Joe.

'Okay,' said Dolly. 'Do you have any questions?'

Dolly was being remarkably mature about all of this. It was as if she was hosting an event, taking questions from the audience, and she was calm and in control. I had always been so proud of her, but perhaps just that little bit more after today.

'How long have you known?' asked Joe after a moment.

'Umm, not really sure,' said Dolly. 'Honestly, I didn't think much about it until probably the last year of secondary school. I think I always knew I didn't really fancy boys, but also, I hadn't fancied a girl either.'

'Right, okay,' said Joe. 'Are you and Maya serious?'

'Quite serious, I guess. It's not that old. We haven't been official for very long, but I've known her for ages, so, yeah.'

I looked across the sofa at Dolly, and I just wanted to hug her and never let her go. It felt like finding out she was gay right before she left for university was just another reason to love her. Another layer to add to the millions of layers of why I was so in love with her already.

'Why didn't you tell us sooner?' I asked, and Dolly looked across the sofa at me. I still had my hand on her leg. 'You know we wouldn't ever have cared, right?'

Dolly's face softened, and it looked like she might break down and start crying again. I could tell she was doing her best to keep it together, to stop herself from falling apart in front of us.

'It might sound silly,' said Dolly, and I gently squeezed her leg.

'Dolly, love, whatever the reason, I know it's not going to be silly,' I replied.

Dolly took a moment, a breath, and then she told us. 'The reason I didn't come out sooner was that I just wasn't ready. I needed time to process it myself before I put it out in the world because I thought that once it was out there, I couldn't take it back again. I needed to be sure.'

'Oh, Dolly,' I said, and I moved along the sofa and gave my daughter a hug. I took her in my arms and held her. 'I totally understand.'

'Me, too,' said Joe, who got up, walked across, and he put his arms around us, too, and everything between me and Joe, all of the drama, didn't matter because Dolly would always come first.

After a minute, we slowly pulled away from each other and returned to our previous positions, all with tears in our eyes, even Joe again – seriously, what had happened to him? Joe hardly ever cried, and yet he was suddenly a wobbly mess. Where had this vulnerability been for the past eighteen months when I had needed more from him? I stood up, went into the toilet and got us all some tissue so we could wipe our eyes and blow our noses, before we could continue with the conversation.

'It's been quite an emotional day, hasn't it?' I said. 'I tell you what, and this is just an idea, why don't you invite Maya over for dinner next week? Now we know she's your girlfriend, I'd like to get to know her better.'

'Definitely,' added Joe quickly.

'Yeah? You're sure?' asked Dolly.

I looked at Joe and he looked at me, and we both nodded at the same time.

'One hundred per cent,' Joe and I said in unison.

Chapter Twenty-One

Freya

Maya was arriving at seven o'clock, and I didn't know who was more nervous: Dolly, Joe or me. It had been my idea to invite Maya for dinner so we could get to know her, but it had quickly dissolved into a bit of a disaster on a few fronts. Firstly, as it turned out, Maya was vegan, so all of Joe's tried-and-trusted dinners were null and void. Secondly, Dolly quickly decided the idea was terrible, doomed to failure, and that we should cancel immediately, but Joe and I ignored her and ploughed on regardless. Lastly, since the summer party, things between Joe and me had been decidedly frosty. We had spoken more about it, Joe had apologised a hundred times, and I had sort of forgiven him, but the atmosphere between us had changed. All the previous successes and little wins of the past few months seemed to have evaporated and now we were back to square one – awkward, uncomfortable and not quite sure where we were with each other. Not great for hosting a meal for your daughter and her first girlfriend. So, as I walked into the kitchen to see how dinner was going, I wasn't surprised to get a rather negative response from Joe.

'Fucking vegan shit tastes like sick,' said Joe.

'Anything I can do?' I enquired sheepishly.

Dolly was upstairs getting ready.

'Making Maya not a vegan would be a great start.'

'Anything actually useful?'

Joe looked at me, sighed heavily, and then turned back to the stove.

'Get me a beer?' he said while poking the vegan lasagne with a fork like someone trying to see if something was dead or not. It did look like it had been hit by a car.

'Right. On it!' I said, trying to remain positive.

I wanted this to go well for Dolly. We had let her down at the party, and I didn't want to do it again. I had offered to help with dinner, but Joe had said it was probably better if he did it alone, and that he would be fine. There was a time when Joe and I would have cooked this together. We used to be quite the double act in the kitchen, and we had in the past whipped up more than one dinner party together and quite a few Christmas roasts. However, now we were separated and with the tension between us bubbling away, it seemed Joe preferred to work alone.

'Here you go,' I said, passing him a beer. 'Are you sure I can't help?'

'I'm fine,' Joe demanded with all the certainty of someone who definitely wasn't fine.

'I suppose I'll just get ready then.'

Joe ignored me and walked across to the fridge and took out a bag of salad, clearly not in the best headspace to greet Dolly's girlfriend. I walked up the stairs, and then poked my head around the door of Dolly's bedroom.

'You all right, love?' I asked.

Dolly was sitting on her bed, looking at her mobile phone.

'Yeah,' she replied, but much like Joe, it wasn't convincing.

I walked across and sat next to her.

'A penny for your thoughts,' I said, and Dolly looked across at me.

'Are you and Dad going to be all right tonight? I don't want tonight to be another summer party fiasco. Maya's had enough family stuff to deal with, and the last thing she needs is to walk into our house with you and Dad being all weirdly passive-aggressive.'

'I promise tonight will be better.'

'You promised last time, Mum. I'm sorry but I just don't trust you two at the moment.'

'Then we'll just have to show you how mature and perfectly charming we can be!' I said, and finally a smile broke out on Dolly's face, cracking through her stubborn teenage resistance.

'Okay, well, you'd better be,' said Dolly, and I gave her a hug.

'Just you wait. Tonight we'll be on our best behaviour.'

'Promise?'

'With a capital P! Right, I need to get ready,' I said, standing up. 'See you downstairs?' Dolly gave me a thin smile before returning to the security of her phone.

I went to our bedroom and quickly got changed, brushing my hair and putting it up, before I went downstairs. I needed to make sure that when it came to Dolly, Joe and I were on the same page. I needed him to realise that while things between us had been tense and uncomfortable, we couldn't be like that around Maya. It required a frank, straightforward conversation. It was time to be honest with each other because I wasn't sure how many more chances Dolly would give us – and how many more we deserved.

'The lasagne tastes like utter dog shit, but I don't have time to make anything else,' said Joe when I walked into the kitchen. 'So be prepared.'

'Can we talk?'

'About the vegan lasagne? I don't think any amount of talking is going to save it.'

'Not about the lasagne. Can we sit for a moment?'

I walked across and sat at the table, and Joe followed me with his beer. I would need a glass of wine soon if I was going to survive tonight. We sat for a moment, then Joe looked at me.

'What's going on?' he asked, taking a sip of his beer.

'We can't be weird with each other tonight. Dolly is worried it's going to be awkward for Maya, and with her own parents already divorced, the last thing she needs is us causing a scene. After the summer party, when I think we can both agree that neither of us were at our finest, we need tonight to be perfect. For Dolly.'

'I think we can handle one night together without having a raging argument.'

'I know, me too, but Dolly is worried we can't. I promised before the party that everything would be fine and look at what happened.'

'I have apologised to you and Dolly multiple times. We're okay now, aren't we?' said Joe, and he was right, we were okay, but there was definitely still an atmosphere between us, and I supposed it was up to me to make sure there wasn't.

'Yes we are and tonight is going to be great!' I said with all the positivity and enthusiasm I could muster. I felt like a secondary school teacher trying to get pupils on board with a particularly boring school trip. *Guys, this might look like just a small hill next to another slightly smaller hill but it's actually a super important neolithic site!* 'Let's try really hard to be, I don't know, normal, okay?'

Joe laughed. 'I'm not even sure what that is any more, Freya.'

'Me either, but we have to try.'

'Although no amount of smiling and polite conversation is going to save the lasagne, I'm afraid. It's basically roadkill in a fancy oven dish.'

'I mean, how bad could it be?'

Fifty-seven minutes later, we were all sitting around the dining table about to find out. Maya and Dolly were on one side, and Joe and I were on the other. We had all just taken a bite of Joe's vegan lasagne. We looked across at each other, and there was a moment when none of us knew exactly what to say. It really was awful. It somehow managed to taste bland but also absolutely horrible at the same time. It wasn't like anything I'd had before. I looked across at Dolly, who was trying not to screw up her face in disgust, and poor Maya didn't know what to say. I looked at Joe, and it was up to me to break the silence.

'Joe, you were right about the lasagne,' I said.

'Probably the most inedible, disgusting thing any human being has ever cooked?'

'That's right,' I said, and then I looked across at Dolly.

'Thank God you said something. Sorry, Dad, but it's really bad. Worse than Trifle-Gate two thousand and seventeen,' said Dolly before she turned to Maya. 'It's okay, you don't have to eat it.'

'I've actually had worse,' said Maya.

'I can't imagine how,' said Joe.

'When I first became vegan, Mum made a shepherd's pie that somehow tasted fishy, and not the good sort of fishy either,' said Maya.

We all laughed, and if there had been an air of tension or awkwardness, Joe's vegan lasagne had certainly broken through it.

'Shall I just order some pizzas?' I said.

'Now that,' replied Joe, 'sounds like a cracking idea. I'll put the vegan lasagne in the only place it belongs. The bin!'

After Joe's vegan lasagne disaster, dinner relaxed into a nice, easy-going affair, and once the pizza arrived, everything turned out perfectly. Maya spoke about her plans and what she might do after sixth form. She hadn't got into her first-choice university like Dolly and was thinking about taking a gap year and travelling. I did notice a look from Dolly while Maya spoke about her desire to head to Southeast Asia, and how her older sister had spent six months travelling throughout Asia, and then a year working in Australia. I wondered how Dolly felt about it because I knew she was set on going straight to Durham. Obviously, if Maya was going to be travelling for a year, it would put a strain on their relationship, and perhaps at their age it might be insurmountable.

After dinner, Joe served a delicious vegan apple crumble with vegan custard that more than made up for the lasagne. I served coffee, and afterwards, Dolly and Maya went upstairs to her room, and I helped Joe clear up. It had definitely been a success, and it had even brought Joe and me a little closer together again.

'That went well,' I said, on drying-up duty, while Joe washed.

'It did, despite the vegan lasagne.'

'Another beer?'

'Are you having another wine?'

'Fine, one more,' I said, before I put the tea towel down, got Joe a beer, and poured myself a small glass of white wine. I returned to help Joe finish washing up.

'Thanks,' said Joe, taking a sip of beer before he washed up the last few items. 'Just leave the rest of the drying up.'

'Yeah?'

'Let's sit down.'

We took our drinks and sat down at the dining table.

'What do you think of Maya?' I asked.

'I like her. Although I'm worried about what might happen when Dolly goes to university and Maya goes travelling. I'm not sure you can survive that much time apart at that age.'

'Right? I mean, they're only kids, but I'm worried about Dolly. It's her first relationship, and they're always the hardest.'

'I remember my first girlfriend,' said Joe, a hint of nostalgia in his voice. 'Helen Gibson. We went out for almost a year, then she dumped me on my seventeenth birthday at a McDonald's. It wasn't a very happy meal for me.'

'On your birthday? Ouch! I actually dumped my first boyfriend.'

'Of course you did.'

'What's that supposed to mean?'

'It's you, Freya. Overachiever, great personality, and always the best-looking girl in the room. He was never going to dump you, was he?'

I felt myself blushing slightly. 'You still think of me like that?'

'Just because we're separated, it doesn't mean I can't see what an incredible catch you are.'

'You, too,' I replied, and we both looked at each other, an atmosphere suddenly in the room that definitely hadn't been there before.

Years of moments like that shot through my mind, and it made me so sad that we wouldn't have that for much longer. And yet I also knew it was for the best because despite everything – and the warmth I still felt for him – it still didn't replace the last eighteen months. It didn't change all the nights we had stayed up until the early hours wrangling over where the passion had gone, and whether we might ever be able to find it again. It didn't change the fact he had lied to me about seeing a therapist.

After a moment, there was a sudden noise in the hallway and Maya and Dolly appeared in the kitchen. Maya was leaving as they both had college work to do, and Maya thanked us for dinner, and we said good night. Dolly and Maya kissed at the front door, with Joe and I spying from the end of the hallway, and then Dolly came through into the kitchen.

'Thanks for tonight,' said Dolly. 'It was really nice.'

'You're welcome,' Joe and I said in unison.

Dolly smiled before she went back upstairs to her room, Joe and I finished our drinks, and then we moved instinctively to our own corners of the house, back to our strange new reality.

Chapter Twenty-Two

Joe

I was in my bedroom looking out of the window, feelings of trepidation and nervousness sitting inside me like unwanted squatters. I had sent Carl over the first episode of *House Shared*, and we were about to jump on a Zoom meeting. I couldn't stop my leg from nervously bobbing up and down in anticipation. What if he hated it?

I had poured my heart and soul into *House Shared*, and I genuinely believed it was the best thing I had written in years, but that didn't mean Carl would agree. I knew he looked at my work from a different perspective than me. I only wore my creative hat, but he had his finger on the pulse of what production companies and channels were after, what was flavour of the month, what was already in production, and what was needed next. Like so many things, it wasn't always what was best, the funniest, or the most well written, but what could be sold and marketed. It truly felt like the success or failure of this project would determine whether I had a bright future to look forward to or whether I would end up a miserable failure, drunkenly lamenting to anyone who would listen in late-night pubs that I used to be someone.

It was a glorious day, and the sun was shining against the window and creating patches of warmth that lay across my room. I looked outside and saw the top of a bus go by, people in seats staring at their phones, and in the distance a plane flying against the sky, and I wanted to be on that plane. Any plane, actually, because it felt like it had been so long since I had been on a proper holiday abroad with sunshine, sandy beaches and exotic food. So many things I wanted, craved, and yet I felt it all rested on the potential outcome of this meeting. I waited for a moment, and then the screen changed, and Carl was suddenly in front of me, sipping a coffee in his office, looking as dashing as always in a smart shirt and tie. I did feel rather grubby in my old polo shirt and with my hair that probably needed a wash, a few weeks of stubble on my face that was turning greyer and greyer with each passing year.

'Joe!' said Carl loudly.

'Hello, Carl,' I replied, never quite sure of myself over the internet. I always preferred meeting in real life. Old-fashioned? Probably, but it just felt different. 'How are you?'

'Yes, yes, all good. Just back from a meeting at the mothership.'

'The mothership?'

'Broadcasting House. The BBC. The Beeb.'

'Oh, right. Did it go well?'

'Define well, Joe. Anyway, how are things with you? Still under one very awkward roof?'

'I am, although doing my best to make it work.' Obviously I didn't mention walking in on Freya naked and having a huge argument about me seeing a therapist in secret.

'Right, well, let's hope it doesn't impact the writing because, Joe, mate, I have to say that I absolutely loved the script. For a pilot it has everything. I think we can definitely tighten up a few places, tweak some of the jokes, but it's terrific. I thought the cold water swimming club was a stroke of genius – no pun intended. Very much on the money!'

'That's good to hear, Carl. So, you want me to write a full series?'

'Definitely. Crack on with it. I really think this could be something. In the meeting today they were asking if I had something like this. A multigenerational prime-time comedy series, and I mentioned it, explained the concept and that you were attached, and they thought it was a fabulous idea.'

'Blimey, right, I'd better get cracking then.'

'I'll send over the pilot to my contacts at the BBC and see what they think, get some early feedback, but if they love it as much as I think they will, this could really be something. Everyone loves a good comeback story, and this, Joe, could be yours! Now, have you told Freya about it yet?'

'Well, umm, not exactly.'

'Then you must because if this does get commissioned, I don't want any problems down the track. The last thing we need is to get the green light, and then the ex-wife gets pissed off, and the whole thing gets pulled because of the threat of legal action. Have the conversation, Joe.'

'Right, will do.'

'But otherwise, I'm all in and very excited. This has the feeling of a hit, and now with all the streaming platforms, plus all the old boys desperate not to get left behind or miss the boat on something, there's more chance than ever of something like this getting made. It's bang on the zeitgeist, Joe, and you know how much I love the fucking zeitgeist!'

I couldn't believe how positive he was about it. Carl was an agent, and it was his job to blow smoke up the bottoms of creatives like me, and wine and dine the people who bought scripts like the BBC. Carl knew how to work people and how to get what he wanted, but he was also a realist and he hated wasting anyone's time, especially his own. He knew giving me the green light to go ahead and write a full series of six episodes would mean a serious chunk of time, and if he didn't think it was good, he would have told me. He knew how to make things sound better than they were, but he also knew when something was never going to work, and he would tell you straight. I had pitched him numerous ideas over the years that he had told me weren't strong enough. He would tell me to come back with something better, bigger, funnier, more dramatic with a higher concept. He didn't blow smoke up my bottom because he knew we didn't have the time, and also we had worked together for so long, he knew I didn't need the smoke.

'There is one thing I want you to focus on going forward,' said Carl with a slight note of caution in his voice.

'Right.'

'The daughter. I think her story needs more layers, Joe. At the moment she's just a little, err, one-dimensional, you know. A bit of a clothes horse. Any ideas?'

Fuck. I had already thought about using Dolly coming out as gay in the show, it was gold, but I couldn't. It was bad enough that Freya didn't know I was writing a sitcom about the break-up of our marriage, the last thing I could do was use my own daughter's sexual awakening, too. I already knew I was on thin ice with Freya after the whole therapy argument, I couldn't risk losing Dolly as well. Whatever I did with the character, it just couldn't be that.

'Leave it with me, Carl. I'll think of something.'

'Because I think you've nailed Kate and Dan, but it feels like the daughter is a little too, you know, pointless. She needs an edge. Find the edge, Joe!'

'Right. Got it. Find the edge!'

'Good man.'

Carl and I spoke for another twenty minutes on the show, and his ideas going forward, and a possible timeline of future episodes, before we said goodbye. I promised Carl I would have some more scripts for him soon. I would deliver each episode after it was done, and he would offer editorial advice, script changes, ideas, and together over the next few months we would craft the first series. Perhaps if the BBC really loved it, we would get into meetings with them soon.

One thing Carl said before he left was that he wanted to get this done quickly because he felt like we had a window of opportunity. At that moment, there was nothing else like it in production, and if we could get it ready for meetings as quickly as possible, it stood a better chance. All I heard was: *Start writing and don't stop until it's done because your whole bloody future depends on it!* The biggest issue was that I needed to tell Freya about it and soon.

After the dinner with Maya, things with Freya had been marginally better. It really felt like having that night together had somehow connected us again, and I didn't want to ruin it by telling her about the show. On the other hand, surely the longer I waited, the more difficult it would become, and I didn't want that either. Plus, there was the constant guilt that moved around inside of me like a computer virus, shutting down apps and causing involuntary glitches. I was caught between a particular jagged rock and a very hard place, and I wasn't keen on either.

After the Zoom meeting, I went downstairs and popped the kettle on. I would get my tea, and then head back upstairs to work. I needed to find some additional layers for the daughter, which definitely couldn't be that she was gay. Perhaps an abusive boyfriend? No, too dark for a sitcom. Recently dumped and heartbroken? Perhaps but a little cliched. I obviously needed to spend more time on this. She needed an edge, and I had to find it. Perhaps the success or failure of the whole project depended on it.

I trudged back up the stairs, my cup of tea in hand, thoughts swirling through my mind. A deluge of ideas and things I had to do. I had never been particularly good at multitasking and now I had so many thoughts carefully balanced one on top of the other, I had the notion that I needed to be careful, or they might all come toppling down one after the other, and I would be left in a messy heap. It wasn't the first time I'd had that thought recently, and it was slightly unsettling because there had been times in my life when I had been so clear-thinking, focused and completely in charge of my life, but perhaps these complications were good because they were at the very heart of *House Shared*. Love was more straightforward when we were younger, at the beginning of life, but as we got older, our lives were full of baggage, and maintaining love became harder and harder. My marriage had started out as this beautiful, wonderful thing that had come to me so easily like the world's greatest gift, but it had been inflicted with the intricacies of middle age, and crumbled under the weight. This was what I was writing about, and so I had to embrace the carnage because that was life and truth, and surely life and truth could both be fucking hilarious.

Chapter Twenty-Three

Freya

I had been to Cold Water Club, showered, had breakfast with Dolly, and I had finally arrived at work, full of energy and purpose. Since dinner with Maya, my relationship with Dolly had significantly improved to the point where this morning we actually laughed together over breakfast, and had an interesting and in-depth conversation about Extinction Rebellion. Luckily Joe wasn't involved because he hated Extinction Rebellion and thought they were quite annoying. The last time we had spoken about them he had said, 'I just don't think pissing everyone off and destroying great works of art is the way to get your message across.' Dolly and I didn't share that view. It was lovely to have breakfast with my daughter where she wasn't glued to her phone and we actually chatted.

I was in the kitchen at work making a coffee, and preparing myself for the day ahead, when Sam walked in. I had just put the milk back in the fridge, and I was stirring my coffee, when Sam was suddenly next to me. He looked ever so handsome in a slim navy suit, a crisp white shirt with a cutaway collar, a knitted navy tie and his usual delicious aftershave that hit my nose, sending waves of dopamine and serotonin coursing throughout my body.

I had no idea how much his aftershave cost, but surely it was worth every last penny.

'Morning,' said Sam.

'Morning,' I replied.

'How are you?' said Sam, getting himself a pod for the coffee machine, and grabbing a mug from the cupboard. They had twenty or so white mugs with the Becket, Godwin & Anderson logo stashed away in cupboards for us to use.

'Good. I went to Cold Water Club with Lucy this morning.'

'Ah, yes, she mentioned that to me before. You take a dip in the freezing cold sea at some ludicrous hour of the morning, I believe.'

'Yes, that's it. It's actually very liberating, and it makes you feel incredible afterwards.'

'Sounds bracing but I think I'll stick to my usual morning routine, thank you very much.'

'What would that be, exactly?'

'Well,' said Sam, popping his pod in the machine and pushing it down, before he slid his mug beneath. The machine started to rumble and whirr. 'I usually rise at six.'

'Six? That's early.'

'Early birds, worms, etcetera. I've always been an early riser since boarding school.'

'What's next?'

'I normally go for a run, then I shower, shave, before it's breakfast and the newspaper.'

'Let me guess… *The Times*?'

'Shit, am I that obvious?'

'Depends,' I said with a smile, as Sam finished making his coffee. 'Let me see if I can guess what you eat for breakfast?'

'Go on then. It's pretty much the same three things on rotation, if that helps.'

'Right, let me see,' I said, pondering. 'One has to be soft boiled eggs and soldiers. You seem like the soft boiled eggs and soldiers type.'

'Correct. Although is there a type for that?'

'Definitely. Porridge?'

'Two out of three. I'm getting concerned I'm either that predictable or you're stalking me.'

'Last one. I was thinking something posh like kedgeree or perhaps an old staple like a bacon sandwich, but I think I'm going to go with toast. Everyone likes toast, and I'm thinking Marmite?'

'Seriously, Freya, do you have a spy camera inside my kitchen because that's three out of three?'

'I'm just very good at reading people.'

'You'll make a bloody good solicitor one day.'

'Hopefully,' I said, and we both picked up our coffees. 'Have a good day, Sam.'

'Yes, you too, Freya,' said Sam, smiling at me, and I smiled back, and I definitely felt something pass between us. I wasn't sure what it was exactly – an attraction perhaps? – but it was definitely something. How had I never noticed it before? Surely it hadn't just appeared the moment Joe and I separated? Hadn't we always got along, and hadn't I always found him attractive? I started feeling guilty that perhaps I had harboured secret sexual feelings for Sam Becket even while Joe and I were more happily married, but then I realised it definitely wasn't the case. I had always appreciated the fact he was good-looking, and we had always got along as friends and colleagues, but that part of my brain that allowed attraction to blossom had been turned off. It was like walking past a restaurant where the food smelled incredible, but you were already full. It was just a nice idea if the situation was different.

The message arrived at just after two o'clock:

Fancy a drink tonight?

It was from Sam. I couldn't help but smile when I read it. I really had no idea what this meant or what it might lead to, if anything, but I was curious. Was it just a friendly drink or a drink and perhaps something more? Was I even ready for something more? The answer came swiftly and with startling clarity: DEFINITELY FUCKING NOT! It would be nice to have another friend though, and someone I could lean on if needed, and who understood the world of law, too. If it just so happened that he was also quite handsome, surely that was just a bonus. I replied:

Sure. Straight after work?

Yes. A few of us are going out.

A few of us. I had clearly misread everything. It was office drinks. I was just another body. I had to admit that the surge of euphoria when I had thought he was asking me out for a drink had felt rather exciting for a moment.

Sounds great. Is Lucy going?

I believe so.

You can count me in.

Wonderful! See you later.

My finger hovered over my phone screen and I was pondering replying with something a little flirtatious like 'Looking forward to it!' with maybe a kiss afterwards? Just one of those casual kisses, like the sort you might add without a thought on a birthday card. However, after a moment, I decided against it and put my phone away.

I was disappointed that my initial thought it was a drink just with Sam was wrong, and it was merely an invitation for a work event. However, as I got back to work, I realised it was all very silly because when I had thought it was just us, my first reaction, after a slight initial thrill, had been complete and utter horror. How could I even think about another man when I was still under the same roof as Joe and still so unsure about my feelings towards him and whether our marriage really was inoperable. Was it worth the last-punt surgery in the hope we might make a full recovery?

The place they had chosen for drinks was a lovely old pub just around the corner from work that Lucy and I occasionally frequented, usually on the warmer summer months when we could sit outside. It was a large open pub that had been stripped back with comfy leather sofas, old wooden floors and lots of greenery. It was there that the very best and brightest from Becket, Godwin & Anderson had congregated for after-work drinks.

'I have a confession,' I said quietly to Lucy as we started on our second glasses of wine. I'd had quite a light lunch at my desk, and already after one glass I was feeling a little tipsy. My mind had certainly decided it was going to be a little less inhibited than usual.

'Interested. Go on,' said Lucy, who was standing next to me at the bar.

I had a brief look around to check that no one from work was within earshot. The partners – Sam Becket, Brian Godwin and Claire Anderson – were sitting around a table together in deep conversation, while the two other paralegals, Emily and Tom, were at the next table, and Lucy and I were at the bar. We were safe.

'Earlier when Sam texted me, and asked if I fancied a drink, I got a bit excited because I thought it was just going to be us.'

'Oh my God, Freya, that's...' replied Lucy with a huge smile on her face without finishing her thought. Perhaps she was feeling a little tipsy, too. 'So, you think if he was interested you might be ready to go on a date?'

'That's the thing. When I initially thought it was just us and he was asking me out, I was terrified and immediately shot the idea down in my head, but then when I realised it was work drinks, I was disappointed. What the fuck does that mean?'

'I think it means you're starting to think of a life beyond Joe.'

'You think so?'

'I know so, but, wait, heads up, a hot partner at a local law firm is on his way!' said Lucy, and when I looked across I saw that Sam was walking towards us, a smile on his face, and I felt my cheeks immediately redden – and it definitely wasn't the wine.

Sam had already slipped his jacket off – it was lying over the back of his chair – so was just in his shirt and tie. I had to admit he looked bloody good in it. Despite not caring to go into the sea at seven o'clock, obviously his morning runs were doing the trick. He was holding a half-empty glass of red wine in his hand, so obviously didn't need another drink yet.

'Hello, ladies,' said Sam with a dashing smile, and I was feeling rather self-conscious. Could he detect that we had just been chatting about him, and could he see the obvious heat and redness that was emanating from my face? Surely I looked like I had just returned from a week in Greece, and I'd forgotten to pack the sun cream. The word lobster sprang to mind.

'I just need to pop to the loo,' said Lucy with an obvious note of *I'm going to leave you two alone* in her voice that Sam definitely picked up on. To be fair, Lucy wasn't particularly subtle, especially after a glass or two of wine.

'Was it something I said?' asked Sam, filling the space at the bar where Lucy had been.

'I don't think so,' I replied, having a quick sip of my wine to try and settle my nerves. Why was I acting like a silly teenager lusting after the hottest boy in school? I was forty-five years old, surely I was too old to behave like that. 'I think she just really needed a wee.'

Great save, Freya.

Sam leaned against the bar, and smiled at me, which really didn't help settle my nerves. 'So, Freya, how are you?'

'Yes, yes, all good.'

I noticed his tie had been loosened slightly, and the top button of his shirt had been undone. Was this Sam letting his hair down? I couldn't even imagine Sam in weekend clothes. I took another sip of wine, and my head felt fuzzy. I should definitely have eaten something before I started drinking, even a packet of crisps or some nuts would have sufficed.

'I, umm,' said Sam rather uncertainly. 'Just wanted to say that after my, umm, divorce, it took me ages to get back out there again. I had been married for the best part of twenty years, and the prospect of dating, of meeting new people, felt like the hardest thing in the world.'

'I totally understand. Just the thought of it sends my mind into spirals of anxiety and fear.'

'I also know that eventually it gets better with time,' said Sam with a smile. 'And being alone, or the idea of being alone for me, at least, felt harder than actually moving on.'

'So you're saying that in two or three years, I'll be so desperate and lonely, that I'll be on as many dating apps as my phone can handle?'

'That's not what I'm saying at all,' said Sam with a chuckle. 'What I'm trying to say, and failing badly at, apparently, is that it's hard moving on and I've been on a few dates, and anyway, Freya, what I wanted to say was that, gosh, this is much harder to say than I thought—'

'It's okay, just say it,' I said, desperate to know what it was that Sam was trying to convey, and gosh, didn't he look even more handsome when he was nervous.

I noticed out of the corner of my eye that Lucy had returned from the toilets, and was heading towards the paralegal table. She was clearly leaving us to it.

'What I wanted to say was that maybe, one day, and I know you're just coming out of a difficult break-up, and I'm prepared to wait for as long as it takes, but Freya, I think that you are really lovely, and whenever you are ready, maybe, I could ask you out?' Sam stopped speaking and looked across at me, and I honestly didn't know where to look. I was suddenly even hotter than before, and my heart appeared to have fallen into the pit of my stomach, which was suddenly like a washing machine on its fastest spin cycle. OMG! Sam Becket wanted to ask me out!

I really didn't know what to say to him. I was flattered and intrigued that perhaps one day something might happen between us, when I had finally got over my separation from Joe – could I even imagine that? – but all of that felt so far in the future. It felt like trying to understand the size of the universe and, the more videos you watched on YouTube, the more it blew your mind. Obviously Sam and I dating one day wasn't as complex as how many trillions of galaxies there were in the universe, but still, it was a bit of a head fuck. And yet, I was also excited at the idea of it. How could I not be? Sam was a catch, and for some reason, he thought I was, too. With the complete absence of anything else to say, I said the only thing I could think of.

'Would there be any issues with work? With us dating, I mean.' When in doubt, bring it all back to law.

'Not really. Just some paperwork to fill out. If we're completely transparent from the beginning then it's not a problem. At least from a legal viewpoint. Are you worried it might make things awkward though?'

'A little, and it's not like I'm anywhere near ready to even think about dating. I'm flattered, Sam, really, and if you're still interested when I'm like fifty, then I think a date sounds lovely.'

'It's a date,' said Sam with a smile.

'Wow, you're prepared to wait five years just for a date. That's impressive,' I said, and Sam laughed, and I could feel droplets of sweat sliding down my back. My whole body felt like it was on fire! Imagine going on an actual date with him? It would have to be in the middle of winter or perhaps somewhere near the Arctic Circle. *Fancy a date, Sam? Where? Oh, you know, I hear far-north Sweden is lovely in December.*

'I'm sorry if this is weird or overly presumptuous,' said Sam. 'But I was listening to a podcast the other day, and they spoke about vocalising your desires and dreams, and how when we say things out loud, put it out in the universe, so to speak, they become more of a reality. So, I just wanted to put it out there.'

'It's, honestly, one hundred per cent fine,' I replied, and I couldn't deny the feelings that were suddenly crashing their way through my body at that moment. A blast of dopamine and other related romantic chemicals that were suddenly shooting through me causing a surge of giddy euphoria that I hadn't felt since my early twenties. The idea of dating was terrifying, but somehow the idea of perhaps dating Sam one day didn't seem so utterly awful. It was complicated, and we both had a lot more baggage than probably either of us would care to admit, but it might be a shot at love the second time around. Sam was divorced from his wife, had three grown-up children, and I was separated and had Dolly, and blending our lives and families would no doubt be a challenge, but that was love and relationships when you were both on your second trip around because the first hadn't worked out how you'd thought. It was scary, and it would no doubt be a long road ahead, but a difficult, uneven road ahead with Sam was surely better than trying to walk it alone. Right?

Chapter Twenty-Four

Joe

'So, Joe, how is your relationship with Freya at the moment?' said Karen.

It was a beautiful day outside, and I felt a warmness that spread across the room, enveloping me in its grasp. Sunshine flooded through the window and dust mites danced in the air. I had been sitting in Karen's office for a good fifteen minutes already, and after a few brief conversations she had asked me that question. My initial thought was that it was far too complicated a question to answer. There were layers to our relationship. What was the word they always used on *The Great British Bake Off*? Oh yes, lamination. The layers that were created by repeatedly folding and rolling butter into dough, and that was how I felt about my relationship with Freya. We had spent so many years creating the perfect lamination, folding and rolling the dough that was our relationship, that now it was just hundreds and hundreds of complex super-thin layers that couldn't easily be pulled apart. Every layer gave it structure, meaning, and trying to somehow deconstruct it felt practically impossible without causing a massive fucking mess.

'It's complicated.'

'Relationships, even the good ones, are complicated, Joe. Every relationship has layers, and it's only when we peel back those layers that we discover what's beneath. The truth is often hidden, but it's there if we look hard enough.'

I had been in a strange mood all morning, and perhaps it wasn't the best day for therapy. I had been feeling more and more anxious about *House Shared*, and more specifically about telling Freya about it. It consumed my mind, and I knew I just needed to do it, but it terrified me – especially after how she had taken to discovering I was seeing a therapist. I also couldn't think of a storyline for the daughter in the show, other than her being gay, and that would be a terrific storyline, but I couldn't use it. It was impossible, right?

'The truth is, I haven't told Freya about the sitcom yet. I know I need to do it, but the idea of it scares me to death.'

'Why does it scare you, Joe?'

'Because when she found out I was seeing you, she went ballistic. Rightfully so, obviously, but we're just starting to put our relationship back together after that and I'm afraid telling her about this will put us all the way back to the start again. It's like snakes and ladders. You almost get to the end, it's right there, you can almost touch it, and then you hit a fucking snake and you're all the way back at the bottom again. I can't go backwards with Freya again.'

I looked across at Karen, and she gave me a thin, sympathetic smile.

'I understand but from what you've said, it sounds like she's going to find out at some point.'

'If it gets commissioned then, yes, she would have to know.'

'So wouldn't it be better to do it now? Get everything out in the open so you can deal with it, and then move on? Maybe she will be more relaxed about it than you think.'

The truth was I was worried she would tell me to stop writing it because it was all I had in my life at that moment. If I couldn't write *House Shared*, I would have nothing, and if I went against her wishes and did it anyway, then our relationship would probably be over. It felt like I was trying to balance on an impossibly narrow beam and either side the drop-off would kill me, but trying to stay steady, keep my balance, was exhausting, and I couldn't keep doing it forever.

'Maybe.'

'Do you think there might be another reason why you might be scared to tell Freya about the sitcom?' said Karen, and then she did what she often did, and just looked at me because she wanted me to go deeper, really reach inside myself and pluck something profound from within the depths of my psyche. I, of course, had no idea what to say when confronted by such a request. My hidden depths were so well hidden, it would take a crack team of highly skilled experts in a variety of fields to come together like one of those action films for a special operation – a rogue group of retired specialists for one final mission.

'I don't know, but if there is, I have no idea what it might be.'

'You're writing a sitcom about your marriage you can't confess to your wife. You're terrified of moving on, of being a failure, whatever that term means to you. Perhaps this fear is you holding on to the past. Do you think that on some level you don't want to separate from Freya?'

I didn't know what to say. Was there something to it? Did I still want to be married to Freya? I looked across the room and at the old wooden sash window. I had always loved the older houses in Brighton, the Victorian and Georgian properties, because of the character they gave the town that seemed to almost underpin everything else. I liked the stability of it, and maybe that was also why I was having a hard time letting Freya go, too. She had always been my stability. She had grounded me and given me the support I needed when things weren't going well. I wouldn't have been able to have any sort of career without her, and now if we actually divorced, I was terrified of what it would mean for me. It seemed logical that a part of me was still holding on to our marriage, but I also knew it was over. We'd had the conversations, the arguments, and we'd had the final meeting and concluded that, yes, the verdict was in and it wasn't good. Surely, despite whatever reservations I had, the consensus was that my marriage was done, and I had to find a way to move forward on my own.

'I mean, you have a point, obviously, but you can't just hold on to something that isn't working because you're afraid of whatever is next.'

'True, but this week, I want you to really think about what it is you're holding on to, and what you're afraid of because it seems to me, Joe, that at the moment you're sort of trapped in this place between the past and the future. Perhaps your living situation is perpetuating that, but you need to begin the process of moving on, of beginning the next chapter of your life, and you won't be able to do that unless you understand what it is you're letting go of. Make sense?'

I nodded, and after a few more questions and discussions about other topics, we said our usual goodbye, before I left and headed outside.

Dolly was at college, Freya was at work, and so I had no reason to rush home. I probably wasn't going to get much work done for the rest of the day. I stopped at the Marks and Spencer in town and got something nice for dinner. I fancied pushing the boat out and making Dolly and Freya something a little bit special. I browsed the meat aisle and ended up getting a nice leg of lamb, and I was going to roast that, make a red wine gravy, some mashed potatoes, and I got some broccolini, too. I also bought a nice bottle of red wine we could share, all the while thinking about what Karen had said. I was trapped in a state of limbo, unable to properly move on while I was still living in the past, and while I couldn't do anything about our living situation until Dolly moved out, I could do my best to control it. I could make it the best version of itself, and maybe that might help me – and perhaps all of us – transition a little easier.

I got home, and after making some brief notes on my morning's work, I started on dinner. I put on a Spotify playlist of my favourite Nineties songs, and began cooking. When Freya and Dolly got home, we would sit down together and share a nice family meal. My relationship with Freya was complicated, but she was also someone I could rely upon when things were rocky.

The lamb was just coming out of the oven, and I was going to let it rest for thirty minutes under a sheet of tinfoil, when I heard the front door open and then close.

'In the kitchen!' I shouted.

I heard footsteps, and then Freya walked into the kitchen, dumping her handbag on the dining table.

'Something smells nice,' she said.

'I thought we could have a nice family dinner. I made a roast leg of lamb with a red wine gravy, mashed—'

'Dolly texted and she's going to Maya's after college.'

'Oh, right.'

'But I'm here for dinner.'

'Great. Good. We can have a nice dinner.'

'I'm just going to jump in the shower first,' said Freya. 'Fifteen minutes?'

'Sounds good. I'll plate up,' I said, and there was a slight moment of nervous tension between us as we realised we were going to sit down for a meal together without Dolly. She was the buffer, and we could point most of the conversation towards her, but without her we would have to talk to each other, and although things between us were so much better than they were directly after the summer party, it was still awkward. I also had the sitcom secret I knew had to come out at some point. Would that be tonight? And if so, how would Freya respond? I heard the shower being turned on upstairs, and I began getting the food ready and plating up.

Ten minutes later, Freya came walking into the kitchen, drying her damp hair with a towel.

'That feels better and this looks lovely.'

'Glass of wine?'

'Sure, why not?'

I poured us both a glass of wine and placed them down on the table, before I joined Freya with my own plate of food.

'Cheers,' I said, lifting my glass up. Freya chinked her glass against mine, said cheers, and we tucked into our food. This would be the perfect chance to tell her about the sitcom. We were alone, eating a delicious dinner, and I could explain myself calmly and give her the appropriate time to respond. I just needed to pluck up the courage to do it. Maybe Karen was right and she would take the news better than I expected, and then we could move on. Surely it was best to get everything out in the open and then just see what happened, right?

'Joe?' said Freya after a moment.

'Yes?'

'I don't want to cause a fight or anything, and I'm not being petty, but have you cleaned the bathroom this week? It just looks a bit, you know, messy. Sorry, again, not trying to be difficult or anything.'

I couldn't believe it. There was me, having just cooked her a slap-up dinner, and perhaps about to tell her about the sitcom, and she was picking apart my fucking cleaning skills.

'Oh, right,' I replied, not sure what to say. 'I, umm, actually now that you mention it, I haven't cleaned it this week. I've been busy with work, and—'

'It's fine, honestly. No need to explain,' said Freya, and immediately I felt defensive and like I had to explain. In all the years we had been together, she had never mentioned anything about my cleaning, and there had been times when I was busy when I hadn't always kept things up, and she hadn't said a word. Now, apparently, I was being monitored. It was an issue.

'I will do it tomorrow. I've just been busy with work, and I had a meeting with Carl—'

'Like I said, Joe, no need to explain, and you have the lion's share of the housework, so—'

'But you mentioned it, so obviously it's an issue, Freya,' I said, popping some mashed potatoes in my mouth.

'I'm sorry, Joe, honestly,' replied Freya quickly. 'I shouldn't have said anything.'

'Okay.'

'Good.'

'Right then.'

We continued eating, but the air between us that had started out so smoothly was suddenly rattled with some minor turbulence that didn't exactly toss us around the cabin and cause some of the overhead baggage to begin moving, but we definitely fastened our seat belts a little tighter.

'There was something else I wanted to talk to you about,' said Freya, after a minute of silent eating.

'Okaaay. Sounds serious.'

'It's not serious, it's just something and I'm telling you because I want to be honest with you, Joe, and I don't know, let me have some wine first,' said Freya, taking a long sip of her wine. I was suddenly nervous about what she had to say. What else had I forgotten to do? Separate our washing? Water the indoor plants? Dust? I took a sip of my wine, too. We both put our glasses down at the same time. 'I went out for a drink with work the other day and Sam—'

'Sam your boss? Partner Sam?'

'Yes. He's divorced, and knew I was getting separated, and wanted to offer his support and friendship.'

I bet he fucking did, I thought. *I can't believe he barely waited for the paint to dry on our marriage, before he started putting his socks in my sock drawer. I bet he's the sort of person who pairs them together then rolls them up in neat fucking balls like what's her name again? The Japanese lady who had a show on television about how to organise your life, and tidying up so everything has its place. Oh, yes, Marie fucking Kondo. I imagine Sam Becket's whole life has the Marie Kondo seal of approval.*

'Right,' I said, feeling pangs of jealousy begin to stretch throughout my body, creeping up my throat, and entering my mouth, desperate to escape and say something. 'That was nice of him.'

Freya gave me a look, as though she wasn't quite sure what to say next. 'And,' she added, 'while we were having a drink, he did mention that maybe, one day in the future, when I was ready, we might go on a date.'

And there it fucking was. Of course, the bastard boss was just waiting for me to get out of the way before he moved in. The feelings of jealousy were now more like full-scale road rage and I wanted to get out of the car and shout expletives at someone for not using their indicator properly, but I couldn't be that man. I couldn't show her how I really felt because we were separated, and she had every right to go for drinks with other men, and there was nothing I could do about it. She could spend the rest of her days organising drawers neatly with Sam Becket, and none of it was my business.

'And what did you say?' I said, trying to keep the voices in my head quiet.

Keep everything inside and push it all down. Put it all in boxes and store it far away so you don't have to think about it. Sam Becket might be the fucking GOAT at organising his life and underwear drawers, but he has nothing on me when it comes to compartmentalising feelings.

'That I wasn't ready for anything like that, but I… the thing is, Joe, it made me realise that this sort of thing is going to happen to me, and to you, too, and I want to be honest with you. After what happened at the party, I realised that if we're going to work, if we're going to separate amicably and still be friends, then we have to be open with each other. Nothing is happening with Sam right now, but it might in the future. That's all I wanted to say.'

I looked across the table at Freya and I didn't know what to say. Obviously the thing I should have told her about was the sitcom, but I couldn't. Something was still holding me back, and instead I smiled, thanked her for being so honest, filled up our wine glasses, and kept everything inside because letting it all out felt like opening the largest can of fucking worms in the world.

Chapter Twenty-Five

Freya

I was lying in bed, tossing and turning, unable to sleep, and all I could think about was how Joe had taken my news earlier. When I had told him about Sam and the possibility of a date in the future, I'd honestly expected a different reaction. Not that I wanted him to be full of jealous rage, cursing me and full of expletives for Sam, but I thought it might stir up some semblance of emotion within him. Not that I told him just to make him jealous, but he was far calmer than I had imagined. In fact, he barely said anything at all, and instead we finished our dinner and I tidied up, while Joe said he had to get some work done. I don't think I fully understood where we were any more. Perhaps just living together in this house had changed our relationship and now new and slightly confusing branches of it were beginning to grow, but what did it all mean? Anything? Nothing? Something? And why had I mentioned the stupid bathroom? It wasn't that bad, and honestly, in all the years we had been together in that house, he had never been the greatest cleaner and it had never bothered me before. Was I trying to cause an argument and, if so, why?

I finally sat up in bed, frustrated with myself that I couldn't sleep, and reached across the nightstand for my phone. It was almost midnight, and I had Cold Water Club in the morning. I would need to be awake by six fifteen at the latest, and so if I fell asleep now that would give me six solid hours of sleep. That was fine. Six hours was good. I could definitely survive the day on six hours of sleep, but that was if I could fall asleep right away and the signs weren't looking promising. I quickly checked Dolly's location on my phone and she was at Maya's house where she was spending the night. Then I went to X and started scrolling through that, checking the latest news, and what ridiculous things were trending and how many of them I would even understand or know about, before I got annoyed with myself because everything about falling to sleep said to never go on your phone. It was chapter one of the big book of being an insomniac: *Stay away from your phone, stupid!* Then I had to go pee.

Why had I told Joe about Sam? I was on the toilet thinking about it and outside I heard a car going past, and then a couple of people, obviously drunk, talking loudly and jarring against the peace of the night. I'd just wanted him to know. I was being honest, open, and yet, if that was the case, why was I disappointed in his reaction, or lack of a reaction? Did I want to make him jealous? I didn't think so, but when I looked at the facts, scoured the evidence, it definitely appeared to be the case. But, if that was true, why? What good could come from making Joe jealous? What would it achieve? Was I trying to get back at him because he had lied about seeing a therapist? Was I that petty? I didn't want to believe I was, but we all had the darker corners of our minds where we didn't like to go, but which we knew were there. The crap drawer where we kept all the things we were embarrassed to leave out, and so we shoved them away, hidden in cupboards away from the prying eyes of any visitors.

I washed my hands, and then stood in the en suite for a moment, the light on, looking at myself in the mirror. I looked tired, in an old T-shirt, a small round stain just about level with my belly button, no bra, hair a mess, and obviously with no make-up. We'd had a little bit of sun recently and so that meant my freckles were out in full force. I had always hated them, and especially so when I was a teenager. Joe had always loved them though. He had told me on so many occasions that he preferred it when I didn't wear make-up, and it made me think about the future and about being with someone new. At least Joe knew everything about me: the good, the bad and the downright ugly. He had seen me naked, and knew about the stretch marks that hadn't gone away despite me applying cream to them constantly during my pregnancy. He didn't mind that I only had the occasional trim 'down there', and after watching *Naked Attraction* together, and realising that pretty much every single female on the show was completely shaved or had the 'landing strip', it made me appreciate how much Joe didn't care. What if I started dating Sam, or anyone else for that matter, and they were used to only well-shaved vaginas? What if the cellulite on my bum and legs was on the wrong side of off-putting? Then there was the impending fear of what the menopause might do to me in the near future, and what sort of cliff I might fall off after that.

So many questions flew through my head, and this was the trouble with being awake in the middle of the night. My brain was in full-on spiral mode, and now I was hungry, too. It was now just past midnight, I was wide awake, and now I had to eat. Fuck!

I padded down the stairs in the dark, avoiding the step that made the awful squeak. There was always something quite strange about being in your own house in the middle of the night, like you were trespassing. Everything felt different, a little scarier, a touch more psychological thriller when during the day it was more romantic comedy. I turned the kitchen light on, went across to the cupboard and took down the box of Crunchy Nut. Not the healthiest midnight snack, but not the worst. I got a bowl and filled it up, before pouring over some milk. I made a mental note to buy more milk as we were low. Perhaps after Cold Water Club in the morning, if I made it.

I sat at the kitchen island and ate, scrolling through Instagram on my phone. Photos of the celebrities I followed, all living their best lives, and then friends posting photos from holidays, children's birthday parties and family gatherings. I hadn't posted anything on Instagram for several months. My last post was a picture of Dolly on the beach near the pier. She looked absolutely beautiful, her windswept hair across her face, looking at my phone over her shoulder with the biggest smile. That was taken in February, right before Joe and I had decided to separate. Was it that long ago? It felt like a different lifetime now. Was I even the same person? It was the beginning of July now, Dolly was done with her exams, and headed into her last summer before university, and time felt like it was moving too fast. I wasn't ready for any of the changes that were coming, and yet I couldn't do anything about them. I wanted to stop life for a moment and get off. I could use a break. Perhaps a holiday.

I walked back up the stairs, making sure to avoid the squeaky step, and then I walked past Joe's room. I stopped for a moment, hearing the low rumble of him snoring. It was funny, over the years I had hated that snore, tried a variety of things to help him stop snoring, with little success, but now my room was so quiet, I missed it. Just having that noise had helped me sleep, and when I'd woken up in the middle of the night, turned over and listened to him, I'd known I wasn't alone and I would slowly drift off again to the melodious sounds of Joe.

I clambered back into bed and looked at my phone for the last time. It was just after twelve thirty, and I needed to sleep. I should have brushed my teeth again after the Crunchy Nut, but I couldn't be bothered. I was tired. I just needed to close my eyes and eventually I would fall asleep. It was our nineteen-year wedding anniversary soon. I didn't know why that little fact popped into my head but it did. It would feel strange to acknowledge it, given the current state of our union, but it would also feel odd to ignore it, too. We were still married, and this would be the last year when we would be living together and able to perhaps celebrate – was that the right word? – our mostly happy relationship. I didn't know. It was late and my mind was moving quickly from one thought to the next. Where would I live after this house? What might it be like dating Sam? Should I get my vagina waxed now in preparation because what if it looked awful and needed time to grow back? Why couldn't I stop thinking about my marriage to Joe? Did I still want it to work? Did he? Was I spending enough time with Dolly, considering she would soon be leaving? My mind slowly began to stop, and I drifted off, my eyes closed, and I felt myself floating, dreaming, and then finally, I was asleep.

Chapter Twenty-Six

Joe

'Fancy going to the pub tonight?' I asked Freya over breakfast on the morning of our anniversary.

'Why?'

'I don't know. It's our wedding anniversary, probably our last under the same roof, and I thought that maybe we should have a drink to celebrate? Commiserate? I don't know, it felt weird to not even acknowledge it.'

Freya looked at me across the kitchen, she was buttering her toast, and she smiled at me. 'All right then.'

'Yeah? It won't be weird?'

'I mean it will definitely be weird, Joe, but still, you're right. Probably our last chance to do it.'

'Say seven? The Cow?'

'Sounds good,' said Freya, and that was that.

I had known our anniversary was coming up and I had been thinking about it for the last week or so. Would it be weird to do something together or perhaps weirder not to? Surely it was more difficult to ignore the elephant in the room than to just acknowledge that, yes, actually there was an enormous fucking creature blocking the view out of the window.

We arranged to meet in The Cow pub, the nearest to our house, at seven o'clock, and it had me on edge all day just thinking about it. It was hard when you had a wedding anniversary not to feel pangs of nostalgia, and especially so given our current circumstances. I had a tradition with our anniversaries in the past that I would wear the same outfit, and the same aftershave. It had started on our first wedding anniversary, when for a joke I wore the same outfit I wore on our first date. It was a pair of dark blue Levi's boot-cut jeans, a pale blue shirt from Ted Baker, a pair of brown leather shoes from Russell & Bromley, and my classic L'Eau D'Issey by Issey Miyake. I had worn the exact same outfit and aftershave on nearly every wedding anniversary since. It had been something of a nostalgia blast, and I was also proud of the fact I could still wear the same clothes I had worn in the early Noughties. Admittedly, now the jeans were quite tight, so my stomach puffed up like I had a child's semi-inflated swimming ring around my waist, the shirt was definitely a size too small, so I couldn't button it up and had to wear it *casually open* with a fashionable T-shirt beneath, but at least the shoes fit. I stood in front of the full-length mirror at home for about fifteen minutes and debated wearing something more contemporary – that actually fit – but in the end I said, 'Fuck it,' and went with it.

Freya was going straight from work as she had to stay late, and so I met her at the pub, although when I walked in ten minutes late, she was already there.

'I can't believe you wore it!' said Freya with a smile.

I walked across, doing a little fashion catwalk spin on the way.

'Of course. It's still our wedding anniversary.'

'Well, you still look good in it, Joe. Although I don't recall the T-shirt addition, and aren't the jeans just a little—'

'Drink?' I said quickly.

'I'm okay, I already have a glass of wine.'

'Right, won't be a sec,' I said, and then made my way to the bar to get myself a lager. I had to admit that wearing the outfit and being in that pub we had been in so many times before, it wasn't as strange or as awkward as I thought it might be. There was still something between us that made it okay. I got my beer and headed back to the table. Freya was in a grey work suit, with a white shirt, unbuttoned a few buttons, so I could see the top of her chest and the necklace I had bought her with the white-gold love heart pendant. She still looked gorgeous.

'How was your day?' said Freya.

'Good, yeah. Just writing, mainly.'

'Mainly?'

'I had to get ready for tonight. You don't look this good without the effort,' I said, and Freya giggled, although as I was sitting down, I realised I needed to loosen my jeans as they were definitely on the snug side, so I covertly unbuttoned the top button without Freya spotting me.

We both took sips of our drinks.

'I can't believe Dolly is done with sixth form,' said Freya.

'It's crazy how time flies.'

'It is.'

'It doesn't feel that long ago we had just moved to Brighton, Dolly was a year old, the second series of *The Mornings* was on, and you and I were, what, ridiculously happy?'

'I would say so.'

'It makes all of this even sadder when I think about how great we were because we were fantastic, Freya.'

'We were, Joe. The very best.'

I didn't want to make the night weird and go down the rabbit hole of why it all went wrong because we'd had those conversations over and over again. We had dissected our relationship on too many occasions already. We didn't need to go back over it again when surely the point of tonight, if anything, was to try and enjoy being together again while we still could. We needed to find that thing that had made being together fun in the first place.

'Do you remember our first anniversary in Paris? That was perhaps my favourite,' I said.

'It was. Although you have clearly forgotten you got monumentally pissed on the second night and ended up puking up in the en suite. I bought that expensive piece of lingerie for nothing!'

'I still claim it was food poisoning. There was something dodgy about those oysters.'

'The only thing dodgy, Joe, was the amount of vodka you drank. Seriously, we were in the most romantic city in the world and you passed out on the bathroom floor!'

'You're hardly one to talk, Freya. Glastonbury two thousand and ten?'

'That wasn't my fault and you know it!'

'You projectile vomited midway through Stevie Wonder! Stevie was singing "Signed, Sealed, Delivered I'm Yours", and you were chundering onto my shoes. A brand-new pair of Adidas Sambas, and they didn't survive the weekend!'

'Lesson learnt though. Never accept home-made cider from strangers.'

'I did make up for Paris though. Remember that gorgeous cottage I rented in Scotland?'

'That was lovely.'

'Although you had terrible morning sickness the whole weekend.'

'But still, it was a perfect weekend. Right on the coast just outside of St Andrews, if I remember correctly.'

We looked at each other and smiled. A thousand more memories like that were sitting in my mind, and it felt like one of the most difficult things about the break-up of a marriage to know that the one person who had shared so much of your life wasn't going to be a part of the rest.

'How's the new script going?' said Freya suddenly, her words jarring against the backdrop of nostalgia.

'Sorry?' I said quickly, feeling a heat suddenly rise up inside of me. I had a nervous sip of my lager.

'The new family comedy you told me about?'

It was definitely time to come clean about *House Shared* and explain everything to her, but we were getting along so well, I didn't want to ruin it. I knew she would hate the idea, but Carl loved it, and it was coming along nicely. I was already on episode four, and I had outlined ideas for the rest of the series. Stopping it now just wasn't an option. Perhaps once I had finished it, and got the green light from Carl, then maybe telling her would be easier. Plus, it would be more difficult for her to say stop when it was already a done deal. I knew it was duplicitous, and underhand, but I really felt like I had no option at that moment.

'Yeah, umm, good.'

'What does Carl think? Is he happy with it?'

'He likes it. He took it to the BBC, and he said they loved the idea, so fingers crossed.'

'Definitely,' said Freya, crossing her fingers in front of me. 'It would be great to see something of yours on television again.'

'It would. Right, more drinks, methinks!' I said like someone in a Christmas pantomime, getting up quickly and marching off towards the bar before she could ask me any more questions about *House Shared*. I got myself another beer and Freya a glass of wine, before I returned to the table.

I moved the conversation along to easier topics, and more moments of nostalgia, and we kept drinking, until it was time to head home. We'd both had quite a few drinks by that point, and as we staggered out of the pub into the fresh air, I felt the alcohol hit me. Freya was definitely a bit drunk, too, and as we walked home I felt her knocking against me, and I had to put my arm around her to keep her stable.

'I think I'm a little tipsy,' said Freya.

'Me, too.'

'I have Cold Water Club in the morning.'

'Oh, yes. Ladies-get-freezing-cold-in-the-sea-at-ridiculous-o'clock club. How's it going?'

'It's going great, actually, and surprisingly, once you get used to it, it isn't that cold.'

'Oh, okay,' I said disbelievingly, and Freya gently punched me on the arm.

'Whatever. I love it.'

'I actually think it's brilliant. You shouldn't have waited so long to join.'

'I know. I think I put a lot on hold because of us and Dolly.'

'Well, I'm glad you aren't any more. You seem happier.'

'I am. And what about you, Joe? What's your Cold Water Club?'

'I don't think I have one. Maybe once I'm done with this script, I'll have time to find a new hobby.'

'What about lawn bowls?'

'Surely I'm too young for lawn bowls, Freya?'

'Tennis?'

'I'm awful at racket sports. Hand-eye coordination issues.'

'Fishing?'

'Boring as fuck. Have you ever been fishing?'

'No,' replied Freya.

'It's shit. Worse than lawn bowls.'

'Then I give up.'

We kept walking, meandering through conversations until we got home. I struggled to get the key in the lock, which made Freya giggle, and then when I did finally get the door open, we stumbled into the house. Dolly was staying at Maya's overnight, so we had the place to ourselves. Freya said she'd put the kettle on, and I made us some toast – an old habit after nights out drinking that hadn't gone away. I put in four slices of white bread and retrieved butter from the fridge, and marmalade and Marmite from the cupboard, while Freya focused on the tea. Once done, we ate our toast and drank our tea in the kitchen, reminiscing about nights gone by when we had done the exact same thing.

'I'm really going to miss this house,' said Freya, looking at me across the table.

'Me, too,' I replied, eating the last corner of my toast.

'We've put so much work into it and it's perfect. Now someone else is going to enjoy the fruits of our labour, and what, we're going to have to move into a flat or something and start over from scratch?'

'I already have nightmares about moving into a one-bed flat or, worse, a bedsit! What exactly is a bedsit, anyway?'

'It's a room in a shared house. You have a kitchen in the flat but you share a bathroom.'

'Oh, God, it sounds awful. It will be like being twenty again and broke. What's next? I'll have to sign on, and move somewhere cheaper like, I don't know, Darlington.'

Freya laughed. 'I think you're being a bit melodramatic, Joe.'

'Am I?' I said, and then I smiled at her. 'Fine, perhaps Darlington was a little far.'

'I'm just sad we have to leave our beautiful home,' said Freya after a moment, and I looked across at her, and we both smiled a sad, reflective smile. The sort of smile that said something like: *What the fuck are we doing with our lives?*

Eventually, it was time to head off to bed, the alcohol being slightly mopped up by the toast, and we stood on the landing, Freya heading off to our old bedroom and me to my room.

'Happy anniversary, Freya,' I said.

'Happy anniversary, Joe.'

Instinctively, I leaned in to give her a kiss on the cheek, but slightly misjudged it, and it landed on the side of her mouth.

'Sorry,' I said, pulling away slightly, but Freya just looked at me. She didn't say a word. I didn't know why, or what was pulling me towards her, but I leaned in and kissed her properly this time, and she kissed me back, our lips coming together with more passion than we'd had in years. A confusing mixture of nostalgia, alcohol, and the thought that suddenly filled my mind was that we had never had a 'last time'. I mean, there had been a last time, but we hadn't known it was the final time when we were doing it.

'What are we doing?' said Freya, her voice full of passion.

'I don't know,' I replied, still with my arms around her, looking into her eyes. 'But I think I want this. We never had a last time.'

'I know.'

'Do you want to do this?' I asked, and she didn't say anything, and then she took my hand, and we walked slowly into her bedroom in the darkness, closing the door behind us.

Chapter Twenty-Seven

Freya

I was sitting in the car at almost seven o'clock, still in shock at what had happened the night before. I had left Joe in bed, crept out, grabbing my clothes from the floor, and leaving the house at just after six thirty, my head pounding from the early signs of an impending hangover. I couldn't believe that after everything, all the fights, the conversations, the break-up, the horrible fucking awkwardness, we had slept together again. What did it mean? We had both said, admittedly in our drunken states, that we wanted to have one last time, and maybe that's all it was. It was drawing a line under us. It was goodbye sex. Thanks for the memories. But was sex ever that straightforward? In my experience, the answer was always a big, fat NO.

It was the first time we'd had sex in a long time, and I had to admit, it felt good. Really good, actually. It was the thing with Joe, despite everything, it was familiar and enjoyable in the way it was to rewatch old episodes of *Friends*, and in bed we were full of passion and we both knew what the other liked. There weren't any massive surprises, and I liked that. When I thought about the possibility of having sex with someone else, it was exciting, but also, what if they did something weird, were into something kinky, or what if it was just really shit?

With Joe nothing mattered because we had grown up with each other. He had seen me in my twenties, my thirties, and now my forties, and we knew every square inch of each other. Despite the separation, and everything else that had happened, the sex was still good because we knew what worked. It also still meant something, too, and that was perhaps the only surprising thing about it. We had, for the want of a better word, connected again.

Lucy and the rest of Cold Water Club all pulled up in their cars and got out, and I slowly joined them. It was gradually getting warmer with each passing week. Lucy told me I had joined at exactly the right time because December through February were brutal and I had missed them, and we had all of summer to look forward to.

'Morning, Frey. You look a little…' said Lucy, before she added, 'peaky. Big night?'

'Something like that,' I replied, as we walked towards the beach.

Helen was regaling us with stories about her and Simon, the man she had been dating, and it was wonderful to see her so happy and excited. My stomach definitely felt a little queasy, and my head had a dull pain: the early signs of a headache that would no doubt make an appearance at some point during the day. I couldn't take alcohol the way I used to.

'What's the sex like?' said Caroline, and we all looked towards Helen as we stood on the beach in our swimsuits, facing the sea. 'Sorry, is that inappropriate? You don't have to answer—'

'No, it's fine,' said Helen, a smile on her face. 'It's so different from my ex. With him it was always very physical, almost a fight, but with Simon it's tender and, fuck me, the orgasms! I hardly ever had actual orgasms during sex before, but with Simon it's been nearly every time!'

'That's brilliant,' said Debs. 'Steve and I have been doing it for so long, it's like painting by numbers. You follow the numbers, and when you're all done, the picture looks nice, but it's never going to get into an art gallery, is it?'

'Not us,' said Caroline. 'Mark and I are pretty adventurous in bed. Always have been.'

'Oh yeah?' said Lucy. 'Details please.'

We all started walking slowly into the sea.

'Mark has always liked a wee bit of dress-up,' said Caroline, and we all laughed.

'Wow!' said Lucy.

'Nothing wrong with a bit of old-fashioned role play,' said Amy.

'Although not always so old-fashioned,' said Caroline with a wink and a smile.

We continued walking out into the sea until we were waist deep, and then it was time to slowly drop down until the water came up to our shoulders. I already felt the effects of the cold water and my whole body was energised and so much more awake. My head was still very much in a spin about Joe though. Eventually, we were all in the sea with just our heads protruding out, and I knew I needed some advice from my cold water ladies, before we started swimming.

'I slept with Joe last night,' I said suddenly without warning.

'What?' said Lucy incredulously.

'Jesus!' said Caroline.

'I thought you were separated?' asked Amy.

'We were. Are. It just sort of happened,' I said, and then Lucy asked me to start at the beginning and explain exactly what had happened, and so I did. 'Then I woke up this morning with a headache from hell and wondering what the hell had happened. I felt like a teenager again, sneaking out of the room, the walk of shame downstairs, and slipping quietly out the front door.'

'Do you think it might change things between you?' said Caroline.

'I honestly don't know. Last night we both said we wanted one last time, so maybe it was just goodbye sex.'

'Can I give you some advice?' said Helen.

'Of course, please,' I replied.

'After my divorce, it took me a long time to really discover who I was again. I needed time to just be me and sit with that. I'm not saying you shouldn't date or shouldn't get back with Joe if that's what you want, but make sure you take some time to just be you, too. I know it's a cliché, but date yourself for a little bit.'

'Such good advice,' said Debs.

'One hundred per cent agree,' said Caroline.

'I definitely will,' I replied. 'Whatever happens with Joe, I feel like I'm at a point in my life when I need to start doing things for myself. I've spent so many years being a wife and a mother, it's like I've forgotten what it's like just being a woman.'

'I know what you mean,' said Caroline. 'I've been desperately trying to organise a holiday away or something. I need a break.'

'Me, too,' said Lucy. 'Between ferrying the boys backwards and forwards all across Sussex for cricket, and balancing Stuart's insane work schedule, it feels like all I get for myself is this.'

'It sounds like we need to organise something,' said Debs.

'Like a holiday away?' replied Lucy, and we all looked at each other, smiled, and the seed had been planted.

We started swimming and moving around in silence, and then after about ten minutes we waded back to shore, battling against the waves that were stronger than usual and seemed desperate to push me over. I managed to get back to the beach without injury, and we all dried off and had our hot beverages. I had a strong coffee, which was much needed, but as I headed back to the house I felt a lot better than when I had left. My mind was clearer, my body stronger and ready to face the day, and my hangover all but gone. I was dreading seeing Joe again though. Would he even be up? It was only eight o'clock. Perhaps I would have time for breakfast first, and another cup of coffee before I would have to face up to the repercussions of the night before.

I opened the front door, wondering if I would see Joe straight away, but as I closed the door and walked into the hallway, it seemed to be quiet. I poked my head around the door of the living room, and he wasn't there, so I walked along the hallway into the kitchen and saw Dolly sitting down at the dining table. Immediately, I knew something was wrong.

'Dolly. You're home from Maya's early?' I said, walking across. Dolly was eating a bowl of cereal, but stopped, and then immediately burst into tears. 'Oh, baby, what's happened?' I said, and she fell into my arms. I squeezed her tightly against me, and she wept into my shoulder.

'It's Maya and me, I think we've broken up,' she said eventually.

'Oh, Dolly,' I replied, slightly relieved that was all it was, although obviously I knew that at her age, and with Maya being her first girlfriend, it probably felt like the end of the world. First loves were always one of the hardest. 'I'm sorry, love. What happened?'

'You know she's going travelling now instead of uni?'

'Yes.'

'Well, now she's going travelling with Faith.'

'Faith? Who's Faith?'

'A girl from college, who has fancied Maya for ages. She's the worst, but now she and Maya are like best friends. I was over Maya's house last night, and suddenly Faith turned up, and all they spoke about all night was travelling. Where they're going to go, what they're going to do, the best beaches in Thailand, and getting working holiday visas for Australia, and Maya couldn't give a shit about me. All she cares about now is travelling, and Faith, apparently.'

'I'm sorry, love.'

'We had a huge argument at midnight last night. I was going to come home, but her mum told me to sleep in the spare room. I didn't even see Maya this morning, and I came straight home. I think I'm over her, Mum. I mean, we can't really keep dating once I'm at uni anyway, and she's going travelling for a year. It's really shit because I thought we had something special.'

I looked at Dolly and my heart went out to her. I remembered having my heart broken for the first time, and it was awful, and so I knew the pain she was going through. I was also so proud of her because she was mature enough, despite how much she liked Maya, to realise it was over. It took a strong mind, and someone secure in themselves to recognise when it was time to move on. It had taken Joe and me a long time to have that conversation.

'You think it's definitely over?'

'I do,' said Dolly, and I could see more tears in her eyes, and in that moment I knew exactly what she needed.

'Fancy a morning on the sofa with Harry Potter?' I asked because she had been a massive Harry Potter fan growing up. She had read every book at least five times and watched the films multiple times. Over the last couple of years, her interest had waned slightly, but sometimes when we were feeling down it was nice to be reminded of what it felt like to be young again. Nostalgia always had a way of making you feel better.

'That would be nice. Thanks, Mum,' said Dolly with a fragile smile.

'Okay, you get it ready. I just need to have some breakfast, and I'll bring it through.'

Dolly walked off towards the living room to get the film ready, and I tidied up her bowl, and then I made myself a bowl of muesli, and put the kettle on for a cup of coffee. I assumed Joe was still asleep because I hadn't heard any noise from upstairs. I would deal with him later, but at that moment I just wanted to watch Harry Potter with my daughter and make sure she was all right because, when it came down to it, nothing mattered as much as Dolly. She would always come first, no matter what.

Chapter Twenty-Eight

Joe

When I awoke, the first thing I realised was that I was alone in Freya's bed, and then all the moments from the night before began cascading through my mind one after the other. Freya and I had slept together, and it seemed inconceivable after everything that had happened between us, but it was true. We'd had sex, and if I remembered correctly, and I was sure I wasn't that drunk, it had been fucking fantastic.

I sat up, rubbed my eyes and reached for my phone. No messages, and twenty-seven emails, of which twenty-six were spam, and one was from Carl following up on an email I had sent him about the script. I put my phone down and looked around the room. My old bedroom. Our old bedroom. How had I ended up there again, and what did it mean? Apart from the pain in my head, the early signs of a certain hangover, the main feeling was one of absolute confusion.

We had spoken the night before about needing one last time together, and perhaps if it had felt like the last turgid comeback of a once famous pop star, desperately trying to get his career back on track, then I would have been happy to let it go, but it wasn't. The sex had been the best we'd had in years. It didn't feel awkward and hackneyed, as if we were just going through the motions, and instead it felt really, really fucking good. And it wasn't just because I had been starved of sex, it was genuinely fantastic, and the sort of sex that made you stop and think.

I sat up, the noise of life already happening outside, and downstairs I heard the television was on, and I started wondering whether there was still some hope left for us. Yes, things had been shit for a long time, and we would need to rebuild our relationship from the ground up, but it was possible, wasn't it? Karen had asked me what it was I was holding on to, and perhaps it was hope. Hope that Freya and I might actually be able to get back to the 'us' who had been so happy, but was it possible or just some ludicrous dream, like the time I thought that despite being in my thirties I could start skateboarding? That had ended up painfully at A & E with a fractured wrist, and maybe that's all my relationship with Freya would be, too. A painful reminder that sometimes in life, we were too old to go back again.

I eventually got up, made my way back to my own room, and got dressed. I went to the toilet before I went downstairs, and I was actually a little nervous about seeing Freya again because I had no idea what she was thinking about our night together. When I reached the hallway, I realised that someone was watching a film in the living room, and when I walked in I saw Freya and Dolly together, under a blanket, watching the first Harry Potter film together.

'What's happening here?' I asked.

Dolly paused the film, and she and Freya looked across at me.

'Having a Harry Potter day,' said Freya.

'Oh, right.'

'Want to join?' said Dolly, patting the empty space on the sofa next to her.

I could tell from Dolly's face, the puffiness around her eyes, the redness in her cheeks and the tone of her voice that she had been crying. Something had obviously happened. It had also been a few years since I had seen Harry, Hermione and Ron on the television in the living room, when for years before it felt like they had hardly left.

'I just need to get some breakfast. Coffee?' I said to Freya.

'Can you give me a moment?' Freya said to Dolly, pulling the blanket off herself. Dolly immediately reached for her phone, and Freya stood up and walked with me into the kitchen.

There was definitely an air of something between us. A frisson. Not an awkwardness, exactly, but tantalising unspoken questions and things left unsaid dancing in the air between us, while fleeting memories of the night before, our naked bodies entwined as one, groaning and moaning in passion, filled my head.

'It's Dolly and Maya, they've broken up,' said Freya when we were in the kitchen.

'Shit. How's she doing?'

'Not great, hence the Harry Potter marathon.'

'Good old Harry Potter,' I replied, but still, despite Dolly's relationship problems, I wanted to at least make a pass at discussing what had happened last night.

'Poor thing's had her heart broken, and really needs our support. I'm going back in. Will you join us after breakfast?'

'Umm, yes, will do.'

'Okay, right,' said Freya with a hint of a smile, and then she left and walked back into the living room to join Dolly for a Harry Potter marathon, leaving me alone in the kitchen, completely unsure of everything.

–

It was Sunday evening, and Dolly was in her room, deep in conversation with Maya on the phone, and Freya and I were in the living room, and it was finally time to have the conversation. Yesterday we had spent the day with Dolly, trying our best to keep her mind off Maya, and we ended up watching five Harry Potter films, and I dashed out and got us fish and chips for dinner. Freya and Dolly eventually fell asleep on the sofa, and I put a blanket over them and left them to it. This morning, Freya went to Cold Water Club, and then she took Dolly out for lunch, and now, finally, Freya and I had some time alone.

'Freya?'

'Yes, Joe.'

'Can we discuss what happened the other night?'

'The night we slept together?' said Freya, and I nodded. 'What's to discuss? We both wanted one last time together, it was our wedding anniversary, and I think it was lovely.'

'It was lovely.'

'Did it confuse things for you, Joe?'

She turned and looked at me. She was being rather glib about it, wasn't she?

'It didn't confuse me, exactly, but it did make me think.'

'About?'

'I don't know, Freya. Perhaps it made me wonder whether we're giving up too soon. We definitely still have something in the bedroom.'

'But Joe,' said Freya, her face slipping slightly into a frown. 'Have you forgotten about the last year and a half, and how awful it's been? The arguments? The distinct lack of sex? The conversations where we both realised that despite how great our marriage had been, it just wasn't any more, and it was best to go our separate ways?'

'I haven't forgotten.'

'It's just like you to romanticise things, Joe. You always have.'

'I don't think I do. Do I?'

Freya laughed. 'Oh, Joe, how are you so unaware of yourself? You've always been a bit of a romantic. Remember the holiday to Greece?'

'Of course. We met that couple from Essex. Oh shit, what were their names again?'

'Kelly and Liam. They were from Basildon. He was an IT recruiter, and she was a nurse.'

'We had a great time with them. That was the height of our sex life prior to Dolly.'

'Yes, you're right, but do you also remember what happened on that holiday?'

I thought back to that time and tried to think about what might have happened because, in my mind, I only had fond memories of that holiday. It was 2005, and I had just signed the deal for the first series of *The Mornings*, and to celebrate, Freya and I booked a last-minute package holiday to Greece. All I could remember was seven days of incredible food, sunshine, meeting Kelly and Liam, and having lots of sex with Freya. That wasn't me romanticising anything, it was fact. Those things actually happened. Right?

'We had an amazing time and nothing bad happened at all?' I said, knowing I was clearly wrong about something.

Small slivers of negativity had clearly slipped through the net.

'You see, this is the problem with you, Joe, you only remember the good bits. You don't remember the second night of that holiday when I got food poisoning, do you?'

'Oh, yes, of course,' I said, as it came shooting back into my memory. That was bad. Both ends until the early hours.

'And the day we both got badly sunburnt.'

'I mean, would you call it badly sunburnt?'

'We spent the entire night applying aftersun to each other in the shower, Joe. And do you remember what happened on the penultimate night?'

Admittedly, I had forgotten about the food poisoning and the sunburn, but surely nothing else awful had happened that I had completely forgotten about. I racked my brains, but nothing untoward came back to me. I remembered a day trip on a boat, lots of lying on the beach, and again, more sex, and delicious food, but nothing that could be constituted as bad. I got drunk with Liam one night, which ended with me being sick in the toilet after some shots of a local and quite potent raki.

'Nothing is coming back to me, Freya.'

'Kelly and Liam had that huge argument by the pool, he stormed off, and she spent the entire night crying in our apartment.'

'Oh, right, that,' I said, although I had literally zero memory of it. Was it possible she was making it up to prove a point? 'But that wasn't awful, and it didn't ruin the holiday, did it?'

'It did for poor Kelly. Liam vanished, and she ended up flying home alone, still mostly in tears. I kept in touch with her, and it turned out that Liam had slept with one of the local waitresses, and he was going to move out to Greece! They were due to be married the following year, and she'd already put a deposit down on the venue. Poor Kelly was bereft, and yet all you remember about that holiday is sun, sand, sea and sex! All I remember is food poisoning, sunburn and one heartbroken girl crying in our apartment. You don't see a pattern here, Joe?'

'That I like to remember the good times, and conveniently forget the bad? Is that such an awful quality to have? Also, and I'm not trying to be purposely argumentative, but is it possible that as much as I only remember the good, you seem fixated on only recalling the bad?'

I looked at Freya, and she seemed to squirm because I had obviously hit a nerve. For a moment her body stiffened up, before she relaxed and looked at me square in the face.

'I just think that when you're deliberating whether to save a marriage that was considered dead and buried, you can't romanticise it just because we had one great night of sex.'

'A great night of sex?' I said with a smile. 'Would you also say mind-blowing sex?'

'Right now our daughter needs us, and we have to focus on her,' said Freya, with a certain frankness that left me in no doubt that the conversation was over, the words 'mind-blowing sex' being left unanswered in the air between us.

-

It was Monday morning, and I was home alone working on *House Shared*, when the doorbell rang. Dolly was out with friends, although it was clear that whatever she was doing, Maya wasn't involved. The telephone summit in her bedroom had resulted in them breaking up for good, and now Dolly was doing her best to move on. She had drawn a line under Maya and said she was going to try and enjoy her last summer before university. Things with Freya were still much less resolved, as far as I was concerned. She had claimed I was looking at our marriage with rose-tinted glasses, and perhaps she had a point, but I wasn't ready to give up on our marriage yet.

I walked down the stairs, opened the front door, and standing there was a man in a suit. He was probably selling something. He was tall, and had dark hair and glasses.

'Mrs Wallace?'

'I mean, obviously not,' I replied, and the man smiled at me.

'Sorry. I'm here to see Freya Wallace about a house valuation?' said the man.

'Sorry? A house valuation?'

'I was asked to appraise the house. See what it's worth before going on the market?'

'But the house isn't going on the market. Sorry, who are you again?' I said, my mind suddenly free-falling with a hundred questions.

'I'm Daniel Masters from Brunswick & Co Estate Agents. Mrs Wallace called us and asked for a house valuation. Are you Mr Wallace, by any chance?'

'Right, okay. Can you give me a moment?'

'Yes, of course,' said Daniel with a bright but slightly uncertain smile. I saw him glance at the front of the house again, checking he had the right number.

I pushed the front door until it was almost closed, and then I walked into the living room, retrieving my phone from my pocket. I was absolutely fuming. I couldn't believe Freya had gone behind my back and arranged to get the house valued. There I was, pondering whether our marriage could be saved, if there was still some tantalising hope left, and she was already planning on selling the house. It was obvious that no matter how I felt, she had already moved on. Our night together had obviously meant nothing to her. I rang her mobile and waited.

'Joe? You okay?' said Freya casually.

'No, I'm not fucking okay, Freya!' I yelled. 'Why didn't you tell me you'd arranged to get the house valued?'

'Oh shit, I forgot about that. I'm sorry, Joe. I was just trying to get things done.'

'So, that's it, is it? There was me thinking that maybe there was still a chance. Perhaps after our night together it had changed something, and you've already got the house on fucking Rightmove!'

'Joe, please calm down. I was just being practical.'

'Practical! Don't make me laugh. You were being cold, Freya. Fucking heartless.'

'Jesus Christ, Joe. Don't turn this into something it isn't,' said Freya, sounding suddenly angrier. 'We need to know what the house is worth. That's it.'

'Typical fucking solicitor! What happened to you?'

'Stop it, Joe. You're just being rude now.'

'Whatever. I guess we're done. That's clearly what you want, so guess what? You can have it. Sell the fucking house and throw me out on the street for all I care!' I yelled, and then I hung up the phone because I couldn't take it any more. She was done with me, and so I supposed I was done with her, too. Our marriage was definitely over, and despite the man waiting outside, I sat down on the sofa and immediately started to cry. This wasn't the first time I had wept recently, and clearly I was starting to feel the emotional pinch. What next? Would I start sobbing at *EastEnders* or soppy adverts featuring dogs that needed homes? Breaking down at the sight of an old photo of Dolly or an online story about a child being able to see because of the wonders of medical science? I was suddenly a proper emotional mess, and it had me wondering: *Where is it all going to end?*

Chapter Twenty-Nine

Joe

Freya and I first discovered Devil's Dyke a few months after we moved to Brighton. Someone had mentioned it in passing and told us we had to get up there because the views were to die for, and so one day we went on the bus, and brought a picnic with us. From that first time we were hooked. We stood at the top and admired one of the most stunning views in England. It felt like you could see all across West Sussex, with the undulating fields, small outcrops of trees, villages with church spires, and hedgerows that looked like they were drawn in to add definition and clarity. It was the most English of landscapes, and Freya and I had returned again and again, each time as Dolly got older, it seemed like a way of defining how we were all changing. The view never altered and so we were the variable, and I liked that juxtaposition. Today, as Freya and I stood looking out over the view we had looked at so many times before, I hated the variable we had become. Of all the versions of us that had stood in that exact spot so many times before, it was by far the worst.

'I don't know where to begin,' said Freya, before she turned and looked at me. 'How did we get here?'

‘I don’t know,’ I replied. My voice sounded unlike my own, and I felt a hollowness in my chest, a numb ache that had been there since I had shouted at Freya on the phone.

Freya had asked me up to Devil’s Dyke so we could clear the air. Things had been incredibly tense for the past week and we had barely spoken, just perfunctory words about practical things when we bumped into each other at the house, but it couldn’t go on like that, and Freya wouldn’t let it. I was happier to keep wallowing, and moping around the house, ignoring her and pretending that nothing had happened, but Freya wasn’t like that. She couldn’t pretend and had to get it all out in the open. It was one of our biggest differences as people. She loved to talk about our feelings, had to discuss ‘us’, and she needed to resolve issues as they came up, while I was generally happy not to. My ethos had always been to let things go for long enough that eventually they would just blow over. Perhaps it was why we had reached that point, standing at the top of Devil’s Dyke, because I had stopped talking, and she had stopped asking me to.

‘I wasn’t trying to hurt you, Joe. The house valuation was just something practical to do, so I knew exactly what I was dealing with in terms of money. For both of us. I know I should have told you, and I’m sorry, but it wasn’t intended to piss you off, or make some sort of statement. I simply just forgot.’

‘I know, and I’m sorry I went off on you like that.’

‘But what you said, Joe, did you mean it? Do you still think there’s a chance we could get back together? Are you really holding out hope?’

She looked at me, and I had to say something. She needed a decent response, but the truth was, I had no idea what I thought about us any more. I was so drawn into the narrative arc on the show I was writing, it was hard to distinguish between fact and fiction. Sitcom or reality? It felt like I was watching episodes of *Made in Chelsea.* You knew they were somewhat scripted but also reality, and so the line between what to actually believe or not was blurred. I knew the night we'd had together was magical, but it was only one night, wasn't it? And Freya had been right about one thing: whether I cared to admit it or not, I was a hopeless romantic.

Even being back at the top of Devil's Dyke, I had so many feelings coursing through my body, it was hard to know what was real and what was just whimsy on my part. I preferred living in the small space between where my sitcoms lived and where real life began because there was safety in that. Sitcoms by their very nature were nice places, and they always, without fail, had happy endings. If only life were that straightforward. If only every relationship ended like Ross and Rachel in *Friends*, but therein lay the problem. When *Friends* finished, Ross and Rachel were finally together but they were only in their mid-thirties. They still had the rest of their lives together. We don't know what happened to them, whether they made it, were happily married for the rest of their lives. What if they had another break? What if one of them had an affair, got sick, or they just fell out of love? We wouldn't ever know, and it didn't matter. In our hearts and minds, Ross and Rachel would always be that Ross and Rachel at the end of the show.

'I don't know,' I replied. 'Some days I can't imagine a life without you, and some days, I can't imagine staying together. I wish we could be as happy as the first time we came up here.'

'Me, too, but we can't. That us is long gone.'

'I know.'

'We can't go back to those people because they don't exist, Joe.'

'I just… the night when we were together again, it felt right. I felt that old spark between us, and it confused me and made me think about us and the future.'

'But it was the last time. We said we needed it.'

'I know, and I meant that, but in the morning when I awoke in our old bed, I thought what it would be like to wake up like that again. I wondered if it was possible.'

Freya looked out towards the view, and I knew she was thinking. She needed a moment to collect her thoughts, and I needed a moment to collect mine, too. I needed to tell her about the show. I needed her to know I was writing a sitcom about the break-up of our marriage. How could I keep writing it without her blessing? But I also couldn't do it because I was worried she'd resent me for using our pain for my gain, so as much as I knew I needed to tell her, the words just wouldn't come.

'The thing is, Joe, it wouldn't be like that, would it? That night was like a holiday, a momentary pause from actual life, and we, I think, both pretended we were those people again. The ones who had stood up here and been happy together. But the reality is that if we said, fuck it, let's get back together, we would just be this version of us. Slightly old, battered, bruised, and starting a marriage over again when it had already failed once before, hoping that by some miracle, we could get the magic back. Do you really think we'd have a shot, or would we just be dragging out the inevitable?'

Her question hung over me, and I didn't know the answer. How could I possibly know what might happen in the future, when even the past eluded me?

'The honest answer, Freya, is that I don't know,' I said with an uncertain smile. 'Sorry.'

'No need to apologise. I don't know either, but I do know if you look back over the last eighteen months, it wasn't any one thing that broke us up. It was a hundred little things, a thousand tiny moments that compounded, and we ended up here. The failure of our marriage is complex and difficult to put into words, and so I think even harder to put back together. It's like a giant jigsaw puzzle that I know is missing a hundred pieces, and no matter how hard we try, no matter how many pieces we put back, it will never be complete again.'

I reached down and held her hand, and we kept looking out at that view that was unchangeable, reliable, and would be there long after we were gone.

Freya and I sat down on the grass, she pulled her knees into her body, hugging them, and I stretched my legs out in front of me. I felt the grass between my fingers, and fragments of memories sat in my mind. The day was slightly blustery but warm, the large cerulean sky with soft clouds that looked like brushstrokes of eggshell-white paint were overhead where birds soared, and near us a dog ran with its owner, then barked excitedly for her to throw a ball.

'I booked a trip to New York with Lucy and the rest of Cold Water Club,' said Freya.

'Oh yeah?'

'The middle of September, just before Dolly leaves for university.'

'What prompted this?'

'We were talking, and for different reasons all needed a holiday, and so we thought, bugger it, why not? A girl's trip to the Big Apple might be fun.'

'When you get back, and Dolly is in Durham, we're really going to sell the house?'

'I suppose so.'

'It will be hard.'

'It will. What about you, Joe? Will you stay in Brighton or move back to London?'

A question I had asked myself countless times already, and I didn't have a definite answer yet. The truth was that I loved the idea of living in London again, but whether I could afford it was something else. I also loved living in Brighton. I had so many happy memories there, friends, and the idea of leaving and starting over scared the shit out of me.

'I'm not sure yet.'

'Really? I thought you'd be straight on the train once Dolly was gone.'

'I don't deny that I've missed London, but I've been here for a long time, too. I think I'd find it hard to leave, actually.'

'Okay. Well, whatever happens, I hope we can still be friends.'

'Of course, and we'll always have Dolly to think about.'

'Always Dolly,' said Freya with a tender smile.

'Oh, did she tell you that Stuart offered her a job at the language school?'

'No.'

'She's starting tomorrow. She's going to be an activity leader. It will give her something to do over the summer holidays and a bit of money in her pocket.'

'That's good. After Maya, I think she needed something to do.'

'That's exactly what I said.'

We sat on the grass for a while, and then decided to head back to Brighton. When we got back, Dolly was in the kitchen making herself something to eat, and Freya put the kettle on and made us tea, and all I could think about was how normal it all felt. We were all going along with this normality, almost pretending it was going to last forever, even though we all knew that in a few months it would be gone for good. Freya was going to New York with her friends in September, and it felt like that was her drawing a line under us. We were done, it was official, and however I felt about it wouldn't change a thing.

The only bright side to that realisation was that I had something else to add to the script. It was coming along nicely, and I had almost finished the entire first series. Carl was excited to see it, but I had an issue with the ending of the last episode. It was a sitcom that demanded something of a happy ending, or at least a cliffhanger to take us into a second series. The thing was, I had no idea how it was going to end yet, and that was something I really had to decide sooner rather than later.

Chapter Thirty

Freya

It was difficult to put into words what Cold Water Club had given me. I went at least four times a week and I simply couldn't imagine my life without it. There were mornings when my alarm was going off at six fifteen when I wanted to stay in bed, and some days I almost pulled the duvet back over me, but when I got up, had a quick wake-up coffee and got outside and into the sea, I never regretted it. The lasting effects of it on the rest of my day were undeniable. I was definitely a converted cold water swimmer. Today was different though because we had brought along someone who definitely wasn't ready for it.

'Oh my actual fucking God!' trilled Mum, who hardly ever swore, before we were even in the water. 'I'm not sure I can do this.'

'Give it a chance,' I said. 'I was the same as you at the beginning, Mum.'

'Hardly the same,' said Mum. 'You're in a thermal one-piece with the little boots. I'm in the old swimming costume I bought when you were learning to swim in the mid-Eighties, darling! It's amazing it still fits me, but it was bargain basement then, now it's barely holding everything in!'

'I did tell you to bring a hat, Mum.'

'Well, I forgot, didn't I, because it was so early, and Martin was faffing around with his new air fryer. He loves it so much. It's like he's got a woman on the side!'

'We just got an air fryer,' said Debs. 'Absolute game changer.'

'Yeah?' said Caroline. 'I was thinking about getting one.'

'Do it,' said Debs. 'I literally cook everything in the air fryer now.'

'Everything?' I asked.

'Pretty much,' said Debs. 'And the best bit is hardly any clean-up.'

'That does sound great,' said Caroline.

'Maybe I'll have a look, too,' said Lucy. 'My boys eat so much. Anything to make my life a little easier.'

'Right, can we get this over with before I freeze to death?' said Mum, as we stood by the water's edge. To be fair, it was the coldest morning we'd had in weeks, and there was a slight drizzle in the air and the wind was getting up.

'Ready everyone?' said Lucy.

Everyone said 'yes' except Caroline, who said 'aye', then we slowly walked into the water. Mum was holding my left hand for support, and when I looked across at her I could see the pain on her face. She grimaced and tightly squeezed my hand. Luckily she hadn't been there in March when the water was considerably colder. It was August now and I had noticed how much the sea had warmed up. I wouldn't call it a bath, exactly, but the biting chill I had first experienced was definitely gone.

'It gets better, Mum,' I said optimistically.

'That's what Martin said about classic car shows, and let me tell you, they don't!' said Mum, and we kept walking forwards, one careful foot in front of the other. 'I can't do it any more,' said Mum when we stopped walking and were preparing ourselves to squat down. 'I can't feel any of my extremities.'

'Try breathing deeply,' said Lucy. 'In through your nose, and then slowly out through your mouth. In slowly and then out slowly. In slowly, and—'

'No!' said Mum with a great degree of conviction, before she started wading back towards the beach. 'I never signed up for hypothermia! I'll be on the beach where I belong!'

We watched as Mum slowly made her way back to the beach and then we ducked down into the water. I had been doing it long enough now to know that it wasn't quite so shocking. Lucy said that by the end of September, it would feel barmy, almost tropical, which was hard to imagine. It was incredible to me what the body could endure and how, over time, we could get used to anything. Perhaps it was how I would eventually feel about my marriage. At the moment, it was still incredibly painful, still causing me so much trauma, but in time and with the right mindset, it would get easier.

I sat in the water, and I enjoyed the peace and quiet for a moment, before I followed Lucy's lead and started swimming around in wide circles. A few birds flew overhead, and as I swam I looked off towards the old pier, and then back towards the shore where I saw Mum drying herself off. Caroline was swimming away, fiercely thrusting her arms through the water, and kicking her feet, while Debs and Helen did their usual walking around a bit and having a natter. Amy was soon done with her breaststroke, and then we congregated back together and started walking in.

'Is everyone excited for Cold Water Club's first, and hopefully annual, holiday to New York?' said Lucy.

'Very,' I replied, and the rest of the ladies agreed, before I turned to Lucy. 'Although if you end up moving away to start a language school, surely it won't be annual for you?'

'It better be!' said Caroline quickly. 'You'll be coming back, right?'

'Of course!' said Lucy. 'Whatever happens, I'll always be back now and then for Cold Water Club, and if you ladies plan a holiday in the future, you'd better make sure you invite me!'

'Definitely,' said Debs.

'One hundred per cent,' said Helen and Amy in unison.

'There wouldn't even be a Cold Water Club without you,' said Caroline. 'You're a certified lifetime member, wherever you live.'

We eventually made our way back to the shore, where I found Mum sipping on a flask of hot tea, a blanket over her legs. Perhaps she really wasn't cut out for Cold Water Club. If she couldn't handle it in summer, she would be useless in the autumn and winter.

I asked how she was doing, and because she could barely speak, I just sat next to her in silence. I was feeling so calm as I sat there, the waves gently lapping against the shore, and sipping my coffee in peace and quiet. One by one, all the other members of Cold Water Club said their goodbyes, until eventually it was just me and Mum, sitting on the beach together. It was actually quite nice because we didn't spend much time just sitting in silence. We definitely never came to the beach together. Eventually, after about ten minutes, Mum spoke.

'I don't know how you all do it. I thought I was going to die. I already imagined the segment on the news. *Silly old woman dies of hypothermia on Brighton beach.*'

'Oh, Mum. You're fine, and it does get easier in time.'

'That's what Martin said about yoga.'

'Martin does yoga?' I said incredulously.

'He's surprisingly sprightly. He could downward dog for Crufts, darling, and you should see his chaturanga. Textbook.'

'Blimey.'

Mum and I sat looking out at the sea, sipping our drinks, and I felt for perhaps the first time in a long time a sense of calm about the future. Maybe it was the endorphins from being in the water or just sitting there with Mum, but I genuinely felt a real sense that everything was going to be okay, when for so long it had felt anything but. Maybe it was talking with Joe at the top of Devil's Dyke, but something felt different between us. He had been so angry when I had arranged to get the house valued, and surprisingly, and despite being annoyed at him for being so petty, it was nice to hear him being so passionate. Then at Devil's Dyke he had admitted he thought we had a chance of getting back together, and, I don't know, it got me thinking, too.

The night we had together was incredible, and living in our house, and being involved in each other's lives, I had seen a change in him. He was more open, honest, and he was seeing a therapist. Joe Wallace of 'What the fuck was that emotion?' fame was seeing an actual therapist. He had been great with Dolly when she came out and even when I had confessed what happened with Sam, he hadn't been horrendously jealous like I imagined he might. Maybe he was growing up and finally becoming the Joe I had actually needed for the past eighteen months. Perhaps we had both just needed a massive jolt to get our relationship back on track again.

'How are things with Joe?' said Mum suddenly, as though she could read my thoughts.

'Quite good, actually.'

'That's great, darling. It's better to be amicable heading towards divorce. By the end your father and I hated each other.'

'I didn't know it was that bad.'

'We hid most of it from you, darling, but after you left for university and it was just us, it was bloody hell. If you and Joe can stay friends, it will make everything so much easier.'

'That's the plan,' I said. I thought for a moment about asking her whether she thought Joe and I still stood a chance, but decided against it. I didn't even know myself, and it was all just jumbled-up thoughts rattling around inside my head.

'Right,' said Mum, standing up. 'I should get home. Martin is cooking American-style pancakes in the air fryer.'

'You can do that?'

'According to Martin, there is literally nothing you cannot cook in the air fryer. Jacket potatoes, biscuits, cakes, steaks, mac and cheese—'

'Mac and cheese in the air fryer?'

'Martin predicted that within the next year, we could stop using the oven all together. We will see. He also predicted Brexit wouldn't last six months, Scotland would vote for independence, and that I would pick the winner of the last Grand National.'

'Did you?'

'They fell at the first fence.'

'Oh.'

Mum looked down at me and smiled. 'I'm proud of you, Freya.'

'Why?' I said, a little shocked, and then standing up, too.

'Because you're doing cold water swimming, you have a career, and you're dealing with a messy divorce a hundred times better than I did,' said Mum, and then I saw the beginnings of tears in her eyes. She reached down and held my hands for a moment. Mum wasn't always the most effusive parent in the world and so when she was, it was always a bit of a shock. Maybe the sea water had temporarily affected her emotions. 'I'm just so proud of you, darling, because you're you. You're doing it all and making it work. Good for you!'

'Thanks, Mum,' I said, feeling tears settle in my eyes, too.

'I really had better get going before Martin sends out the search party. See you soon, darling,' said Mum, giving me a quick hug and a kiss on the cheek, before she walked off towards her car. I decided to keep sitting on the beach for a little while longer. Dolly was working at the language school, and I didn't know where Joe was, but it was a Saturday and I had nothing to go home for. I had been looking into returning to university and finishing my studies to become a full-time solicitor, and I could start in the autumn. My life would soon be significantly busier then, on top of potentially selling the house, and starting a whole new life on my own. I was going to enjoy sitting on that beach in peace and quiet because for one reason or another, it felt like the calm before the impending storm.

Chapter Thirty-One

Joe

I had finished the last episode of *House Shared*, sent it to Carl, and I knew it was something special. I had felt it the whole time I was writing it. It had that magic something, an alchemy that was intangible and couldn't be created but happened from time to time when I was writing. Maybe it was because the subject matter was so close to my heart, or because it was happening while I was writing it, I didn't know, but the words flowed from me and it was funny, emotional, dramatic and it really felt like a hit. The only other time I had felt like that was when I had handed over the script to *The Mornings*. The only problem now, of course, was telling Freya about it because I had used her life, her problems, and I had essentially written a sitcom about us. I knew that without her blessing there was no way the project could go ahead, no matter how much Carl wanted it or whatever money was involved. It terrified me because I needed this to work, but it relied on Freya giving me the green light. Then there was the daughter in the show and what I had decided to do with her. It had been a hard struggle, but I had finally found the edge Carl had demanded.

I had arranged to meet Stuart and Barney at a cafe in Hove called Fika. It was something of a local for Stuart, who explained they had wonderful coffee, and excellent breakfast sandwiches. I hadn't seen Stuart or Barney for a while because I had been working so hard on *House Shared*, but now it was done and I was waiting for Carl's response, I could focus on a life beyond my writing room. Writing was an erratic profession, and I would often find myself losing months of the year holed up in my office, but once it was over, I would have weeks where I did nothing at all. I was feeling nervous because, despite it being a Saturday, I was waiting to hear from Carl. He'd had a meeting at the BBC yesterday, and I wanted to find out how it had gone. Hence the breakfast with Stuart and Barney to take my mind off it.

I walked into Fika, where Stuart and Barney were already sitting at a table, sipping on coffee. Fika was one of those fantastic cafe/coffee shops that Brighton and Hove did incredibly well and always seemed to be in demand, no matter how many suddenly popped up. Stuart was in a pair of beige chinos and an old polo shirt with his language school logo on, and a pair of slightly battered brown boat shoes. Barney was dressed in a pair of smart navy trousers, dark leather shoes, a crisp white shirt, and over that he had on a light linen jacket. Barney always dressed up just in case he met his future wife coming out of a local Tesco Express. 'You never know!' he always said. I had to admire his optimism and perhaps he had a point, and when I looked down at my own ensemble of old jeans that were probably due a wash, white T-shirt with a small hole in the left shoulder, faded blue Oxford shirt I'd had for years and scuffed Adidas trainers, it was clear I definitely didn't look my best. I also hadn't shaved in weeks and so had quite a healthy beard that was veering very dangerously close to being more salt than pepper. If I met someone new right now, they would probably imagine I had fallen upon hard times. There was definitely a fine line between 'bohemian writer' aesthetic and just 'scruffy old bastard'.

'Morning, boys,' I said, walking across and sitting down.

'Ah, Joseph!' said Barney. 'Morning, sir.'

'Morning, mate, coffee?' said Stuart.

'It's all right, I'll get it. I'm starving. What's good?' I asked.

Stuart ran me through the menu quickly and suggested a few things, and I ended up getting a flat white and a fried chicken breakfast sandwich. We all took a few minutes to order before we settled down into conversation. I really wanted to tell them about *House Shared* because it was the first time I'd written something and not spent hours talking to Freya about it, and I was desperate to share it with someone other than Carl. When something lived solely in your head for months and months, it needed to get out from time to time.

'I just finished my latest sitcom and sent it off to my agent,' I said.

'Well done, mate,' said Stuart. 'Is this the one about the couple sharing a house after they separate?'

'The one based on you and Freya?' chipped in Barney.

'Well, yes, and that's the sticking point. I still haven't told Freya about it.'

'Ouch,' said Barney.

'Definitely a bit of a sticky wicket,' said Stuart.

'We prefer "tricky sitch" actually,' I said, and Stuart and Barney both looked confused so I continued. 'Anyway, I just don't know how to bring it up and I'm worried Freya will put the kibosh on the whole thing, and I need this. It's literally all I have.'

'What do you think she'll say when you tell her?' said Stuart as our food and my coffee arrived, and it smelled incredible. I hadn't eaten much the night before, and it was already later than I would usually eat breakfast, and my stomach was growling. I took a bite of the chicken breakfast burger before having a sip of my flat white.

'Honestly,' I said to Stuart, 'I literally have no idea. She might be fine with it, or she might hate my guts, force me to stop writing it, and never speak to me again.'

'A bit overdramatic, don't you think?' said Barney, who had just taken a bite of his sandwich and had some runny egg sliding down his chin. 'It's just a TV show.'

'But it's a TV show about us, which I didn't ask for her permission to write. The thing is, well, Freya and I slept together—'

'What? As in sexual intercourse?' replied an incredulous Barney.

'Yes, Barney, as in sexual intercourse. I take it you already know?' I said to Stuart.

'Actually not, mate,' said Stuart. 'The girls kept that one quiet.'

'So what happened with the SI?' said Barney, and Stuart and I both looked at him, wondering what the hell he was talking about, forcing him to explain. 'Sexual intercourse.'

'Oh, right,' I said. 'It happened the night of our wedding anniversary. We'd had a few drinks, one thing led to another, and you know the rest. Anyway, afterwards, I genuinely thought that maybe we had a chance of getting back together, but she wasn't interested.'

'Sorry, mate,' said Stuart.

'Anyway, rightly or wrongly, I ended up putting that in the show, too, or a scene like it, and I'm beginning to wonder if perhaps I went too far.'

'You mean, is it a sitcom or more reality TV?' said Barney.

'Something like that. My agent Carl had a meeting at the BBC yesterday, and I'm waiting for news, but I'm worried that if it's good, and I have to confess everything to Freya, it will all blow up in my face. Plus, there's Dolly, too. There's a daughter in the show, and there are obviously crossovers with her and Dolly. I don't know, it's all such a fucking mess.'

'If you want my advice,' said Barney.

'Depends. Does it involve the use of the term SI?' I said, and Stuart laughed.

'No,' said Barney. 'Although feel free to use that in the show if you like. My advice to you, Joseph, is to come clean about the whole thing. From my experience, the pain of keeping a secret is often worse than the secret itself.'

'Surprisingly sage advice,' said Stuart.

'Yes, Barney, very wise,' I added.

'I saw it on an Instagram post, but, you know, I think it works,' said Barney, before we got back to our breakfast sandwiches and coffee.

It was clear that wherever he'd got the quote from, it was solid advice. I had been holding on to this secret for such a long time that it had become bigger than the secret itself. The fear of what might happen when Freya found out had become so monumental in my head, so intrinsically linked to any sort of future happiness, it had paralysed me. Doing nothing had become easier than doing something, but the trouble with doing nothing was that nothing changed.

'How's your dating life, Barney?' I said after a minute.

'I've actually been seeing a woman from Bristol,' said Barney tentatively.

'From Bristol or does she actually live in Bristol?' asked Stuart.

'Lives in Bristol,' said Barney.

'That's a bit of a commute for a date,' I said, not imagining such a long-distance relationship would be easy.

'We've been on five dates already, and it's looking really, you know, promising.'

'Where do you go on these dates? Does she come here? Do you go there?' I asked.

'Actually,' said Barney. 'Our last date was at Chieveley service station. It's a bit nearer to her, but sort of in the middle. They have a lovely outdoor seating area, and we got a Costa coffee, shared a Cornish pasty and a packet of Percy Pigs.'

'That sounds sort of romantic,' I said.

'Do you think it has legs despite the sizeable distance between you?' asked Stuart.

'I do,' said Barney with a grin. We asked him about her, and his whole face lit up. 'Her name's Phoebe. She's forty, a novelist, so perfect for me, has never been married, has a dog called Wilf, used to live in London but now calls Bristol home, and she's just really lovely.'

'Oh, mate, you sound like you're in love,' I said.

'Stop it,' said Barney, blushing wildly.

'I think he might be right,' said Stuart with a broad smile.

'I'm just seeing how it goes. We FaceTime every day, and I'm seeing her tomorrow.'

'Have you, you know?' I asked, nodding my head so he knew exactly what I was talking about. Stuart and I both looked at Barney expectedly, and he was still blushing crimson.

'Perhaps,' said Barney after a moment. 'Although that definitely didn't happen at Chieveley services!' We all laughed, and for a moment the looming cloud of having to confess everything to Freya was forgotten.

We chatted while we finished our food, all got another coffee, and we slowly worked our way through a few different conversations. Stuart spoke excitedly about starting up his own language school within the next year, probably somewhere near Warwickshire, and that they would probably be moving. It would be a real blow if Stuart moved because I didn't have that many friends in Brighton, but I understood his need to branch out and start his own business. I would miss him, although at that moment I had no idea where I would be a year from now either. I thanked Stuart for giving Dolly a summer job, and he said she was doing great. A real natural, Stuart said, and he would hire her every summer if he could. I had seen a real upsurge in her happiness levels since she had started working. Gone was the gloomy teenager, who had just had her heart broken, and now she was up at seven o'clock in the morning, and not home until ten or eleven in the evening if she came home at all, and she was happy, talkative and like a different person.

After about thirty minutes, we had all finished our coffees and were getting ready to leave, my phone rang and when I looked down at the caller, I saw Carl's name staring back at me. He must have news about his meeting with the BBC.

'Fuck, it's Carl!' I said. 'This is it.'

'Good luck, mate,' said Stuart.

'Best of British!' said Barney.

I stared down at the phone. This could be the moment. The phone call that might change the rest of my life because, if it was good news, it could save me from being penniless and potentially homeless, but if it was bad, then I was back to square one, and I couldn't face the prospect of it – it was snakes and ladders all over again. I stood up and walked outside before I answered.

'Carl,' I said hopefully.

'Joe!' said Carl, as exuberant as always. It was always hard to tell if he had good or bad news. 'How are you, mate?'

'Yes, not bad. Just having breakfast with a couple of old friends. How are you?'

'Yes, yes, good, good, and right, you know why I'm calling.'

'I do,' I said, my heart beating rapidly in my chest. I couldn't stand it. It was the part of the job I had always hated the most. Waiting for success and fearing failure because they were always one moment away from each other. Sliding doors.

'So as you know, I had a meeting at the mothership yesterday, and I gave them the scripts, and we talked about the show for over an hour, Joe, and they loved it, but they had to go away and talk about it. You know how these things go. Anyway, I literally just got off the phone with Peter Darcy-Hopkins, head of comedy and drama, and he wants to get you in for a meeting ASAP.'

'You're being serious? They want a meeting?' I said, a flood of emotions engulfing me.

'More than a meeting. Obviously there's lots to iron out, hurdles to get over, these things are never straightforward, you know that, but they love the show and they want you back at the BBC where you belong. Congratulations, Joe, it looks like *House Shared* is going to get made!'

I had to take a moment to compose myself and get everything straight in my mind. The BBC wanted to make my show, and I knew, like Carl said, that it was never straightforward and so many things could go wrong, and even when they went right there was no guarantee of success, but they wanted the show. I was going to make some money and hopefully, if it did go well, I might see my series on the television. It was overwhelming and I didn't quite know what to do with myself, other than cry, which seemed to have become my default setting over the past month.

'Carl,' I eventually said. 'I can't thank you enough for sticking with me through the lean years, and we've had plenty of those, and just, I can't believe it's actually happening.'

'Save your speech for the BAFTAs. For the moment, I'm trying to get us into a meeting as soon as possible. I'll reach out once I have a date and a time. You have told Freya about it, yes, and she's okay with it?'

Ah. Freya.

'Well, actually, now that you mention it—'

'You haven't told her, have you?'

'No, not yet. I was sort of waiting to see if we even had a chance, but I suppose—'

'You need to tell her now, today, because we can't have any issues, Joe. Promise me you'll tell her today?'

'I will.'

'Good, right, well, that's it. Enjoy your weekend, and I'll be in touch next week.'

'Okay, and thanks, Carl, again, really, it means the world to me.'

'To me, too, old boy, me, too.'

We hung up and I stood there for a moment in complete disbelief, and two very distinct feelings suddenly took over my body. The first was complete, unabridged and overwhelming joy that I was going to get a television show commissioned on the BBC again, and the second was complete, unabridged and overwhelming fear that I had to tell Freya about it.

Chapter Thirty-Two

Freya

I opened the front door, and walked into the hallway, wondering if Joe was home. Maybe we could have breakfast together. I knew Dolly was already at work, and so I called out Joe's name, but when nothing came back except silence, I knew I was probably home alone unless Joe was still asleep. I wanted to have a shower before breakfast, and so I skipped up the stairs, quickly checking Joe's room, but the door was open, the bed was made, and so I assumed he must have gone out, before I walked into my room.

I got undressed, and turned the shower on in the en suite. I wasn't sure where it had come from, but I had this overwhelming feeling of optimism and joy as I stood in the shower, and I found myself smiling. Having a warm shower after Cold Water Club always felt incredible, and I really made sure to enjoy it today. I washed my hair, my body, and scrubbed my face, and then stood under the lovely warm water for an extra few minutes, letting it cascade over my head and then down my back. Eventually I got out and stood in front of the sink in just a towel, brushing my teeth, and then my hair before I put it up in a loose ponytail while I got ready. I applied some moisturiser to my face, neck, arms, and I was about to put on some deodorant when I heard the front door open and then close.

'Freya?' I heard Joe say from downstairs.

He was home. I imagined perhaps having breakfast together or just a coffee, and talking. No drama, no deep conversations about *us*, just a nice, normal chat and spending time together. Was that possible? I quickly got myself dressed and made my way downstairs. The hallway was empty, and so I walked into the kitchen, where I found Joe sitting at the table.

'Oh, hi, morning,' I said with a bright smile. 'I'm glad you're home.'

'You are?' said Joe, and I could see that he had an edge to him. His face was never very good at hiding his feelings, which I always felt was sort of ironic because the man who had such a hard time expressing his emotions also couldn't hide them.

'Is everything okay, you seem a little flustered?'

I looked at Joe and he looked back at me, and he was definitely looking more and more uncomfortable.

'Maybe you should sit down,' said Joe.

I walked across and sat at the table, and now I was starting to get worried. I literally had no idea what he was going to tell me, but I hoped it wouldn't destroy my good mood. In fact, I hoped it wasn't going to mess up our entire lives. Had someone died? Was Dolly okay?

'There's no good way to say this and so I'm just going to say it,' said Joe, his face teetering on the edge of complete and utter collapse. He looked so uncomfortable, so completely and utterly terrified of whatever it was he had to tell me. 'I had a phone call with Carl this morning, and the BBC wants to get me into a meeting about the new show I've written. Carl thinks there's a really good chance they want to commission it.'

I wasn't expecting that. It was good news. Really, really good news, which begged the question: *Why does he look so scared?*

'That's brilliant, Joe, I'm so happy for you,' I said, and I wanted to get up and give him a hug, open a bottle of champagne and have a Buck's Fizz for breakfast, but he still looked quite sombre. 'But why do you look so sad?'

Joe took a deep breath and then he looked at me. 'There's something I have to tell you, Freya.'

'Okaay, I'm getting worried now. What is it?'

'The umm, script.'

'What about it?'

'It's all about us. When I went to see Carl months ago, just after we had officially separated, we talked, and I mentioned our situation and he thought it was a great idea for a sitcom. At first I wasn't sure, but after I started working on it, and I wrote the pilot, I knew it was good. It's called *House Shared*.' Joe stopped talking and just looked across at me.

'Wait. You're telling me you wrote an entire show about the break-up of our marriage without thinking to at least tell me about it? Without asking if it was okay?' I said, a flurry of anger suddenly filling my mind. My good mood was wiped away in a second, like a tidal wave crashing through a small village.

'I'm sorry. It was wrong of me, Freya. I wanted to tell you, but I don't know, I was worried you'd hate the idea and I was already committed to it, and I had nothing else, and—'

'For fuck's sake, Joe, what's the matter with you? How could you use our pain, our sadness for cheap fucking laughs? I just, I don't know what to say,' I said, standing up and pacing around the kitchen, rubbing my forehead with the tips of my fingers. Trying to massage the pain and the confusion away.

He was a writer, and I had made my peace years ago with the idea that he would occasionally use something from our life in a show. He had borrowed dialogue from conversations we'd had, stories I had shared with him, and he had definitely taken characters from real life and put them in a script, but to actually use something that was so heartbreaking and turn that into a whole show was something else.

'I didn't mean not to tell you, Freya. I just started it, not knowing what it would be, what it would become, and then Carl loved it, the BBC loved it, and—'

'So you traded success for our marriage?' I said, turning to look at him.

'No,' said Joe, standing up, too. 'I would never do that. I loved you, still love you, Freya, and this, it just sort of happened—'

'Like you seeing a therapist without telling me about it just sort of happened?'

Joe looked at me, his face contorted and screwed into confusion, and I could see his sadness, his pain, but the thing was, he had caused it. He had made the choice not to tell me about his therapist and his sitcom. Everything he had done had been on purpose and with intent, and it was hard for me to see beyond that. He had intended to deceive me and he had lied to me, and that wasn't the man I had married. I suddenly felt tears sting my eyes.

'I'm sorry,' said Joe. 'Really, really sorry.'

'And what about Dolly? Is she in the show, too?' I said, looking at him, and without a second passing, I could see from the expression on his face that he had something else to tell me. 'What did you do, Joe?' Then it came to me in a blinding flash. 'Please tell me you didn't use her coming out as gay in the show. You didn't, did you?'

I couldn't believe Joe could be that cruel. Despite what he had done to me, to us, I knew how much he loved Dolly. He wouldn't use our daughter's sexuality in a fucking sitcom without discussing it with us first. It was one thing to lie to me, but to use our daughter like that would be truly unforgivable. He looked at me, an expression on his face like a child that had been caught with his hand in the sweet jar or perhaps something far more serious.

'I won't deny I thought about it, Freya. I actually discussed it with Carl and he thought it was a brilliant idea, but when it came to write it, I couldn't do it.'

'So you aren't a complete fucking monster then.'

'I couldn't do it because I knew it would mean that any chance we had of working things out would be gone, and I couldn't do that. I had to know that you and I were still on the table.'

'Yet, when it came to writing about us, you had no such problem. Fuck, Joe, I can't believe this,' I said, feeling another flash of anger burst inside of me like fireworks cracking against the dark night sky. 'I know you have always used things from our life in your writing, but I always thought there was a line. I thought this would have been the line.'

I looked at Joe and I had never been angrier with him. He had lied about seeing a therapist, but at least once he had explained about the panic attacks I understood. Despite the disappointment of finding out he'd been seeing a therapist in secret, I could sympathise with him, but this wasn't that. He had purposely lied, used the pain of our separation, the story of the break-up of our marriage, and was going to serve it up to the world in a thirty-minute sitcom. If trust was one of the key pillars of any good marriage, then Joe had just burnt that pillar to the ground. Joe stood up and walked towards me, a look of desperation on his face.

'Freya, I'm sorry. I know what I did was wrong, but—'

'What did you use in the script?' I said suddenly, and he stopped and looked at me.

'What do you mean?'

'What exactly did you use in the script? How many of the conversations did you turn into jokes? What about you seeing a therapist or everything that happened with your dad? Did you use all of that great material, Joe? Did you use the night we slept together?' I said, and when I said it, I knew I had hit on something. A momentary expression of guilt flashed across his face. 'You did, didn't you?'

'I, umm—'

'Fuck!' I shouted at him. 'No, Joe. You aren't doing this. You aren't going to parade our whole fucking life on the television for cheap laughs, and I'll take you to fucking court if I have to!' I was so angry at him, and also at myself for not seeing what sort of man Joe had become. Success at any cost, even if that cost was our marriage. 'You know, Joe. After we slept together, and after our chat at Devil's Dyke, and even this fucking morning, I did think that maybe there was a chance for us. I thought we might be able to salvage our marriage, but now… I don't know you. I can't even be around you.'

I took one last look at him, and then I walked out. I didn't know where I was going, but I knew I couldn't be in that house with Joe for a second longer. I grabbed my coat, my hair was still wet, but I didn't care, I just had to get out, and I felt tears rushing down my face as I opened the front door and then slammed it behind me. I had never felt so much anger before. Joe had betrayed me, and he wasn't the man I had married.

I walked away from our house, and I just kept walking. I had nowhere in mind, I just had to keep moving, get myself further and further away from him. I walked, cried, unable to believe what had just happened. How could he have used our marriage like that? I knew how much he loved me, or at least said he loved me, and yet he was prepared to use our pain for some sort of professional gain? I was dumbfounded the man I thought I knew had turned out to be someone else entirely. A man who had turned our marriage into a fucking comedy, and maybe he was right, because it seemed that, after everything, we were nothing more than a fucking joke. Joe and I were done. Our marriage was over, and Joe had been happy to burn it to the ground, just to keep his dwindling career afloat. At that moment, I never wanted to see his face again.

I finally stopped walking, wiped the tears from my face, and took out my phone. I was going to call the one person I probably shouldn't have called at that exact moment, but I didn't care. Joe had hurt me in ways I didn't think were possible, and I was going to hurt him, too. The phone rang and then after a moment was picked up.

'Hello, Sam,' I said. 'Are you busy?'

Chapter Thirty-Three

Joe

Karen was sitting across from me, and today she was in a white linen dress, she'd had her hair cut shorter, and she had on a little more make-up than usual. Perhaps she had a date straight after work or something, but I wouldn't know because I was never allowed to ask her questions about herself. It wasn't how therapy worked. I wasn't allowed to know anything about her, and she had to know everything about me. It was very much a one-sided relationship, which made me a little uncomfortable, but that was the deal for better mental health. Although with everything that had happened with Freya, it was hard to see how any amount of talking could fix it.

'So, Joe, tell me what happened.'

I explained everything that had happened in the past forty-eight hours from the conversation with Carl about the show to telling Freya about it, and how that conversation had ended with Freya walking out on me. I was still reeling from it, and I hadn't seen Freya since. Dolly was working at the language school, and barely made it home these days, and Freya had, I think, been staying with her mum and Marmalade. I had tried texting her but she hadn't replied. I understood how Freya felt, and she was entirely justified in how she responded, but I couldn't believe I had let it get to that point. I should have told her sooner because now I had truly fucked everything up, probably for good. When I finished speaking, Karen took a moment before she responded. She was obviously carefully constructing her response. I imagined it would be difficult to just say: *It's clear you've been a massive fuckwit, Joe, and Freya has every right never to speak to you again, you complete and utter arsehole.*

'What do you think about it now?'

'I think Freya has every right to ignore me. I can't believe what an enormous idiot I've been, and I just want to fix it.'

'Do you think that's possible?'

'I don't know but I have to try. Freya is my wife, and she deserves better than I have given her. Dolly, too. I'm meeting Dolly for lunch today and I'm going to tell her everything.'

'How do you think she'll take it?' said Karen, jotting something down in her notepad.

'Honestly, I have no idea. The thing is, I'll change the show if I have to. I'll rewrite the whole bloody thing if it means making Freya and Dolly happy. I just can't stand the thought of losing them.'

'What if Freya asked you not to make the show at all? To scrap it completely. Would you?'

This was the hardest question because clearly Freya and I were headed for permanent separation and eventually divorce, and if that was true, what was I going to do? I needed this show to work because I needed the money. It felt like when it came down to the nuts and bolts of the issue I had little choice.

'I don't know,' I finally said, after thinking about my answer for a minute or more.

'Just remember, Joe, that sometimes life can often feel like it's either/or. It's either this or that, but often, if we spend a little time thinking about it, there's another option staring us in the face.'

'What would that be?' I asked hopefully, and she looked at me and smiled.

'That isn't for me to say, Joe.'

We sat and talked for another thirty minutes before our time was up, and it felt good to just chat to her about everything. She didn't always offer up actual solutions to problems because her thing was that we talked, opened up our feelings, and from that discussion solutions would emerge or at least ideas. She had explained to me once that therapy was like planting a tree. You started with a seed, you watered it, gave it time, let the seasons pass, and eventually with some patience, it would grow. When she had first said that, I had brushed it off as wishy-washy nonsense, but I finally understood what she meant.

'You look nice today. Going somewhere?' I said as I stood up to leave.

She smiled at me. 'Thank you, but you know I can't discuss that.'

'Just testing the water.'

'See you next time, Joe,' replied Karen, and then I left, walking outside and readying myself to meet Dolly for lunch.

It was a gorgeous August day with a royal-blue sky, and it felt like one of those perfect summer days when living by the beach really paid off, and I would miss it if I moved back to London. The beach itself was packed with tourists, especially by the pier, and every fish and chip shop would be busy with punters desperate for some classic seaside grub while trying to fight off the notorious Brighton seagulls, who would happily snatch food right from your hand. I was meeting Dolly in a cafe near her language school, and I was dreading it. I had already ruined my relationship with Freya, and I couldn't stand the thought of losing Dolly, too. As far as I knew, Freya hadn't told Dolly about *House Shared*, and she knew nothing about our argument.

I found a table and sat down, perusing the menu while I waited for Dolly to arrive. It was a lovely new cafe that had popped up just before summer, and they had a wonderful range of sandwiches, plus great coffee. I had popped in a week ago and had been impressed with my flat white, and so when I asked Dolly to meet for lunch, I had suggested it. I waited for about ten minutes, until Dolly finally came bounding into the cafe, apologising for being late but her morning activities had run over. I stood up and gave her a hug before she sat down. She had her hair in pigtails, and she was wearing a pink language school polo shirt, and a pair of denim shorts. She looked beautiful, happy, and I was ever so proud of her. The dark cloud of her break-up with Maya was definitely gone.

'You look cheerful,' I said, and she gave me a huge smile.

'I am. Work is awesome and the people are great,' said Dolly, picking up a menu.

'Order whatever you want, Dolls. I think I'm going to go with the New York pastrami on rye sandwich, and a flat white.'

'Oh yeah, that sounds good, me, too.'

I walked up to the counter to order our food, and while I waited in a short queue, I looked back at Dolly, who was staring down at her phone. I couldn't help but be overcome with a nostalgia for the past when she was just a little girl. I imagined her sitting there but ten years younger, eagerly waiting for lunch, looking around because she didn't have a phone yet, and I felt that feeling all parents get when faced with the reality that their child was all grown up. A bittersweet sadness, a longing for the past, but also a deeply profound pride in how their child had turned out. Dolly was about to head off to university, and I was excited at all the wonderful things she was going to experience, but also terribly sad at the little girl I had to leave behind.

I ordered our food, sat back down again, and Dolly put her phone away.

'How's work?' I asked, because I had barely seen Dolly since she had started.

'Brilliant, so much fun. It's hard work, obviously, and the hours are long.'

'Is that why you stay over so often?' I replied, and she grinned, and looked a bit sheepish. 'What? Spill the beans, young lady.'

'I've met someone.'

'Oh, right.'

'Her name's Elle, she's from Nottingham, and she's going to uni in Newcastle.'

'That's great, Dolls. She obviously makes you happy.'

'She does,' said Dolly with a huge smile, and then our food and coffee arrived. The waitress put it all down on the table, and it looked delicious. I took a sip of coffee, and Dolly quickly tucked into her sandwich. I had a bite of mine, too, but all I could think about was how happy Dolly was, and I hoped I wasn't about to ruin everything.

'So, Dolls, I have something to tell you,' I said, as she took a sip of her coffee.

'Okay.'

'Have you spoken to your mother the last couple of days?' I asked apprehensively.

'No. Why? What have you done now?'

'Why do you assume I've done something wrong?'

'Daaad?'

'Fine. Look, here's the thing. This is the thing—'

'Please, just get to the thing.'

'You know I've written a new sitcom, right?'

'Yes. I mean, vaguely. You mentioned it, but I'm not sure what it's about or anything.'

I just had to rip the plaster off.

'It's called *House Shared*, and it's basically about the situation your mum and I found ourselves in. A couple with a daughter, on the verge of breaking up, but staying under the same roof until their daughter leaves for university.'

'Blimey, Dad, that's a bit close to home. How does Mum feel about it?'

'She wasn't happy when I told her, but I spoke with my agent, Carl, and he had a meeting at the BBC and they love it. It's probably going to get picked up.'

'Wow! That's brilliant news, Dad,' said Dolly, taking another bite of her sandwich. 'I mean, not the bit about Mum, obviously, but the part about the BBC.'

'Yes, it is,' I said, before I paused and then I said. 'I also wanted to tell you that there is a daughter in the show, and there are some elements of you in there.'

'What sort of elements?' asked Dolly, taking another sizeable bite of her sandwich.

'Well, she's smart, funny, quite sarcastic—'

'Hey! I'm not sarcastic,' said Dolly.

'She's independent, strong-willed—'

'Gay?' asked Dolly suddenly.

'Actually not gay. I did think about using your coming-out story in the show but it felt wrong, so actually, in the show, the character of you is a little bit of a Harvey Cooper.'

'Who the hell is Harvey Cooper?'

'A boy at my school who failed his GCSEs on purpose because he didn't want to become a doctor.'

'So she, my character in the show, fails her A levels on purpose to do what?'

'Follow her dreams, Dolls,' I said, and she smiled at me.

'I like that.'

'Yeah?'

'Yeah,' said Dolly.

'So you're okay with the show?'

'I think it's cool, Dad, but you need to fix things with Mum.'

'I know.'

'Because if you don't, it doesn't matter what I think about it.'

Dolly and I sat and finished lunch. She asked a few more questions about *House Shared*, and I did my best to answer them. I had toyed with the gay storyline for the daughter in the show, but when it came to actually writing it, I knew I couldn't do it. I couldn't cross that line. It took me a while to come up with something else, and that's when the Harvey Cooper story came back to me. A daughter, destined to get great marks and head off to a top-tier university, chucks it all in to work in a cafe and follow her dreams of being a writer. It was the edge Carl had wanted and he was happy with it. Plus, it meant the daughter wasn't heading off to university, and could stay in the show, along with her loser, hippy boyfriend, Rat – actual name Roland Mumford. I asked Dolly more about

Elle, and she glowed with a brightness whenever she spoke about her. Elle was obviously special, and I said I wanted to meet her soon. Eventually, Dolly had to head back to the language school, and I wanted to head home.

'Love you, Dolls,' I said, as we stood on the pavement.

'Love you too, Dad.'

'Thank you for being so understanding about the show.'

'Just remember, if it becomes a huge hit, you owe me,' said Dolly with a smile and then a laugh. I would miss that laugh so much when she left for university. 'And I don't mean like symbolically owe me, I mean literally with cold, hard cash.'

I laughed. 'I promise,' I said, and then Dolly turned around and started walking away.

I watched her for a moment until she was out of sight, and then I started walking back towards home. It was a gorgeous day and perfect for a stroll through town, and then home to do some work. Everything was finally out in the open, and maybe it had broken Freya and me, but it had, perhaps, made my relationship with Dolly even stronger, and that was something worth hanging on to. Now I just needed to find a way to make up with Freya – or at the very least, get her to speak to me again.

Chapter Thirty-Four

Freya

We were sitting around the kitchen table and the atmosphere was definitely a little fraught. At least, it felt fraught to me. I was on one side, holding my cup of tea in my hands for comfort, and opposite me were Joe and Dolly. I hadn't seen Joe since the argument because I had been staying with Mum and Marmalade, which had brought its own challenges. Mainly Mum constantly asking if I was okay, and Marmalade asking me every five minutes if I wanted something air fried. It was an incessant barrage of concern and air-fried food, but I was home now, and Dolly had news.

'I got three As! I'm going to Durham!' said Dolly jubilantly, breaking through the tension and in a second the entire energy and atmosphere in the room changed.

'Oh my gosh, Dolly!' I said, getting up and walking around the table to give her a hug. 'I'm so proud of you! Three As, that's incredible!'

'Dolly, darling, that's amazing!' said Joe.

We both gave Dolly hugs and kisses, and then we finally sat down again. I glanced across at Joe, and he looked back at me for a second. He smiled but I looked straight back at Dolly. Joe looked a lot better than the last time I had seen him. He had shaved, had his hair cut, and he was wearing a shirt and a smart pair of jeans. He was obviously making an effort, at least with his appearance.

'I can't believe I got three As,' said Dolly. 'I thought maybe two As and one B, but it doesn't matter because Durham, here I come!'

'The dream,' I said with a smile. 'I remember the day we did the tour and you were completely smitten from the moment we got there.'

'I remember that, too,' said Joe. 'That night at the hotel you said, I'm coming to university here, and that was it. Now you've made it happen!'

'So proud,' I gushed.

'Right, we should celebrate!' said Joe. 'Are you working today, Dolls?'

'Nope. I'm off.'

'Then what about dinner?' Joe looked across at me. 'Dinner is good, right?'

What else could I say? 'Of course. Wherever you want, love.'

'Just one thing,' said Dolly. 'Can I invite Elle?'

'The new girlfriend?' said Joe.

I had only heard fleetingly about Elle via text, and I was curious and excited to meet her.

'Not girlfriend, just, actually I don't know what she is. We haven't given it a label, exactly, yet, but yeah, casual girlfriend slash summer fling, maybe?'

'Invite her for dinner,' I said. 'I'd love to meet her.'

'I'll message her now,' said Dolly, getting up and slowly walking away, her fingers tapping at a hundred miles an hour on her phone.

With Dolly gone, Joe and I were suddenly alone. I barely wanted to look at him because, despite feeling calmer than I had the day of the argument, I was still so annoyed with him. I couldn't believe what he had done.

After the argument with Joe, when I was an emotional wreck, I called Sam and I arranged to meet him for a coffee. Obviously the moment we met, he could sense that something had happened, and after a quick coffee we went to his house for a proper chat. He put together a light lunch, and over tea and sandwiches I explained everything and he just listened. He was lovely, and looked so handsome in relaxed weekend clothes, in his gorgeous house in Hove – exactly how I had imagined it, so on-brand – and after everything with Joe, I did something spontaneous and so unlike me. I kissed him. We had finished talking, we both stood up at the same time, and suddenly we were so close to each other, and I leaned in and kissed him. The thing was, for a moment, he kissed me back, before we both pulled away at the same time.

'Freya, I...' said Sam. 'I'm sorry, but you're vulnerable, I'm your boss, and—'

'I'm sorry,' I replied quickly. 'Shit, sorry, Sam. You were just being so nice, and this house is gorgeous, and you, you're so handsome, and everything with Joe, it all—'

'You don't have to explain, although I appreciate the comment about my house, and... you think I'm handsome?'

He smiled at me, and I laughed. 'I think we both know the answer to that. I am sorry though. It wasn't fair to call you after my argument with Joe.'

'I'm glad you did. Despite everything that kiss was...'

We looked at each other, then both bashfully looked away after an intense second.

'It was, but I should probably go.'

'Right, yes, definitely,' said Sam.

I left, but after our kiss, which was a little more than pleasant and full of sexual tension, I was more confused than ever.

'I can't believe our little girl is off to university,' said Joe, his voice etched with nostalgia.

I looked across at him, and he smiled at me. He was obviously trying to have the sort of conversation the old us would have had in that situation. Perhaps by reminiscing about the past and lamenting that our little girl was *all grown up*, I might forget about the monumentally shitty thing he had done. He had obviously failed to realise just how pissed off I was.

'I'm not having this conversation right now,' I said, getting up and walking across towards the dishwasher. I downed the last dregs of my tea, opened the dishwasher, and put the mug inside. Joe got up and walked across, too.

'Freya, I am so sorry. I am. I was a fucking idiot. A complete and utter fuckwit, but I don't want this to come between us and ruin everything. Please, just talk to me,' pleaded Joe, and it was hard not to back down and have a conversation, but I didn't want to just forgive him. He needed to know how hurt I was, and that this wasn't just one of those conversations where he said how sorry he was, made a couple of glib jokes, and eventually I forgave him and let him off the hook. I had done that so many times before and I was tired of letting him off the fucking hook. He needed to know that his actions, his words, meant something.

'I don't want to have this conversation now, Joe.'

'But, Freya, we need to talk about it. You need to come home.'

'I don't need to do anything.'

'But you can't keep living at your mum's house. Marmalade must be driving you crazy. Seriously, how many times has he mentioned the air fryer?'

I looked at Joe and he smiled at me. He was doing what he always did. He was trying to dampen any sense of drama, of emotion, with comedy. It was, after all, what he was good at, and I felt myself soften slightly. It had always been so hard to stay angry at Joe.

'A few but that isn't the point. I'm still so angry at you for what you did.'

'I know, and I'm so sorry.'

'You said.'

There was a pause. A momentary silence. Joe took a step closer to me.

'Freya, when we had the argument, you said you'd thought about us and that maybe there was a chance of us giving it another try. I don't want this to get in the way of us.'

'There is no us, Joe. I had thought about it, was thinking about it, but then I found out about the show and now I know I can't trust you. First there was therapy and now this—'

'I'll go to marriage counselling together,' said Joe suddenly. He was looking at me with a serious expression, a determined look that gripped his entire face. 'I want to do that for you. For us. Freya, I want to give us another go.'

I couldn't believe what I was hearing. Joe was looking at me with an expression of hope and it was impossible to know what to think at that moment. For so long, I had begged him to see a marriage counsellor and he had always said no. The long conversations that had resulted in us sitting in Pelicano Coffee Co and putting together our 'Manifesto of Separation' had been one of the hardest things I had ever had to do. I didn't want our marriage to be over. I didn't want to start again, build a whole new life from scratch on my own, but I had realised it was the only solution left when we had tried and failed for eighteen long months to reignite the flame in our relationship. Now, when I had finally given up hope, when I had lost all faith in him, he turned to me and gave me the one thing I had wanted for so long. It was almost fucking cruel.

'No!' I said.

'What do you mean, no? Don't you think we can be saved?'

'It isn't about that, Joe. I asked you again and again to see a marriage counsellor and you said no. I tried everything to make our marriage work. I have shared this house with you since March and it's now the middle of August, and even when I thought we were making progress, and fuck, I did think we had a chance, you drop the bombshell that you had been lying to me for months! Now you want to see a marriage counsellor and give us another shot. What the fuck am I supposed to do with that?'

I couldn't help the tears that started to slide down my cheeks. I was so tired of crying.

'I know and I'm a fucking idiot, I am, but I'll do whatever it takes to make this work. I'll put in the effort, talk to a therapist together, and I promise no more lies. I have changed, Freya. The last four and a half months living together in this house has made me realise just how much I still want you and need you. I took you for granted, took us for granted, but having some space from our relationship but remaining together has changed everything for me. I still love you. Am still in love with you, Freya.'

I didn't know what to think, but I knew I couldn't have that conversation with him yet. I quickly dried my eyes, and then I looked at Joe, as Dolly was suddenly in the room again.

'Elle can make it at about seven, does that work?' said Dolly, who quickly sensed the tension between us, and probably saw my face. 'Oh, shit, sorry, I didn't mean to—'

'No, it's okay,' I said. 'Seven is fine.'

'Right, okay,' said Dolly uncertainly, and then she turned around and left.

'I'll see you at the restaurant,' I said to Joe, and then I left, walking quickly out of the kitchen and up the stairs to my bedroom. If there was one thing I needed at that moment, it was some peace and quiet. I flung myself down on my bed, and I lay there staring up at the ceiling, unable to comprehend the conversation I'd had with Joe. Did he really want to get back together or was he just freaking out because the reality of Dolly leaving and us selling the house was fast approaching? Did he really want to see a marriage counsellor, or was it just one final futile attempt to save our marriage because he was more scared of being alone than talking to a stranger about his feelings? The problem was that I just couldn't trust him any more. He had lied too much, too often, and it had left a hole in my heart I wasn't sure he could fill again.

Chapter Thirty-Five

Joe

I was standing outside the BBC on Langham Street plucking up the courage to go in. Carl was already inside waiting for me, and had texted me multiple times to make sure I was on time. We had a meeting with the head of comedy and drama, the head of output, the head of format, director of creativity and inclusivity, and someone else whose title I hadn't yet been made aware of. This was it. I'd had a meeting with Carl two weeks before where he had told me that the BBC loved the script, loved the idea of working with me again, and all I had to do was show up for a meeting to cross the t's and dot the i's. They were so worried about losing another sitcom to Channel 4, Netflix, Amazon, or basically anyone else who might be interested, that Carl was convinced everything was in my favour. I wasn't letting myself get carried away though because this was television and it was, if anything, fickle. One moment you were the flavour of the month and the next you were the flavour nobody ordered and had to get taken off the menu because they literally couldn't give it away.

I took a deep breath, then I started walking towards the building, ready to hopefully begin the next chapter of my life.

The last few weeks with Freya had been challenging to say the least. After our big argument we had barely spoken, but then we got together to celebrate Dolly's A-level results, and I laid everything on the line. I was ready to try again, I would see a marriage counsellor, and I told her I still loved her because I did. Perhaps it had taken losing her to realise just how much I wanted her, but I had been too late. She hadn't wanted to discuss it then, said she needed space and time, and I had given her nothing but space and time and still she hadn't said anything. She had moved home at least, and we had settled into patterns of uneasy communication around each other, which was somewhat unsettling. Obviously, I was too late with my big speech, and now it felt like we were just waiting for Dolly to move to Durham at the end of September. Freya was off to New York for a week with her Cold Water Club ladies, and I had this meeting. All talk of *us* had been postponed until an unknown time in the future. I had been trying not to think about it too much because I needed this meeting to go well. This felt like a tipping point.

I met Carl in reception, and we were greeted by a young girl called Lottie, who took us up to a meeting room where we were met by the BBC team, headed by the head of comedy and drama, Peter Darcy-Hopkins. He was fifty-something, tall and dressed in a navy suit.

'Joe, it's wonderful to finally put a name to a face,' said Peter, in a posh voice.

'You, too,' I replied.

'Carl, welcome. Right, Lottie, umm, coffee for everyone, and pastries,' said Peter, and then Lottie left the room. 'Right. Joe, this is Magda Blackman, head of output, Jacinda B, senior communications officer, Jasper

Hynes, head of format, director of creativity and inclusivity, and that was Lottie Whitehall, my personal PA.'

'It's lovely to meet you all,' I said, and we sat at a long wooden table in a trendy and contemporary meeting room. The energy of the BBC was just as I remembered it when I first met to discuss *The Mornings* all those years ago. The people had changed but the vibe was very much the same. It felt good to be back on the inside again, after years of feeling like I was in the wilderness.

'Right, let's start by talking about *The Mornings*,' said Peter.

'Loved it!' said Magda Blackman. 'I must have watched it at least ten times.'

'Yes, we all loved it,' said Peter. 'But that was very much then, and this is definitely now.'

Lottie opened the door to our room, and returned with a tray full of coffee, before she left and then returned with another tray of pastries. Everyone immediately started helping themselves. Carl was next to me, and he just had a coffee, while I grabbed an apple Danish and a coffee. After she was done, Lottie took a seat at the table.

'The thing is, Joe, that we love *House Shared*,' said Peter, a pain au chocolat in his hand. 'And it's exactly the sort of thing we want to add to our line-up.'

'Right, great,' I said, taking a sip of coffee, which had definitely improved over the years.

'Yes, it is rather great,' said Peter. 'The thing is, we had an idea, or rather Jasper had an idea, didn't you, Jasper?'

'I did,' said Jasper. Jasper was younger than Peter, perhaps early forties, dark hair, well groomed, with a colourful yellow tie, and he had a northern accent of some sort. Leeds? 'And this is the idea. Are you ready?'

I looked at Carl, who nodded at me.

'Ready,' I replied.

'What if, and this is very much a what-if scenario, but what if we took *House Shared* and expanded it, this way, that way, and perhaps if needed, another way?' said Jasper, using his hands to fully demonstrate all the ways in which *House Shared* could be expanded.

'Sorry, you've lost me,' I replied. 'What do you mean by expanded?'

'That's the exciting bit!' said Jasper. 'That's entirely up to you!'

'In many ways, what Jasper is trying to say,' chipped in Peter, when he could see the look of complete and utter bafflement that had moved onto my face, 'is that we love *House Shared* in its current format, but perhaps there is room to add to it, certainly in terms of content and perhaps also format.'

'I'm sorry, Peter,' said Carl. 'What is it that you're saying, exactly?'

'The thing is, we loved the show, but I also thought that maybe it could be more than just a sitcom in the literal sense of the term, "sitcom",' said Jasper, not really adding an awful lot of clarity.

'I think, and correct me if I'm wrong here,' said Jacinda B, senior communications officer. 'What we're trying to convey from a communications perspective is that we think *House Shared* has the potential to be a flagship programme for the BBC, and instead of the usual six episodes and a Christmas special format that historically most sitcoms tend to follow, we'd like to really expand it and take it further.'

'Exactly,' said Peter, still with a pain au chocolat in his hand. 'The idea of it, of two people trapped in a marriage, under the same roof, but clearly still in love, but not, separated but together, and the daughter, Cold Water Club… the whole thing felt, to me at least, like it was such a wonderful concept that we wanted to see what you thought about making it bigger.'

'Bigger?' I asked.

'Basically, in a nutshell, what we are suggesting is either to expand the number of episodes in a series, or, and I think this is really quite interesting, to make each episode longer,' said Peter.

'We'll need time to think about this,' said Carl. 'It will require more time, money, and Joe will need some specifics on what exactly it is you're after.'

'Right, yes, of course,' said Peter. 'But I think I can safely say without a shadow of a doubt that we have the time, the money, and the specificity required to make this happen.'

I was completely blown away by the meeting because they were clearly already on board with the show and wanted more of it. In my head, it was already six episodes long, but perhaps we could expand it and either write more episodes or make each episode longer if that's what they wanted. We spoke more about the specifics of the new expanded version of the script, and of what might actually happen, given it was now going to be bigger. There was talk of large amounts of money being offered to me to spend the next six months working with the BBC to develop the show. They were essentially offering me the keys to the BBC kingdom because they believed in the show and thought it could be something quite special.

I sat with Carl, who did his best to chip in with suggestions, and Carl and Peter were going to meet later in the week to discuss the details of the contract. All in all, the meeting was a triumph. Once all the coffee and pastries were gone, we wrapped up the meeting and it was time to leave, but Jasper had one last question for me.

'I'm intrigued,' said Jasper. 'Do you see Kate and Dan getting back together at some point?'

'I, umm, honestly don't know. Perhaps, but it would depend on the direction of the show. Why do you ask?'

'Because it seemed to me, reading the script, that the couple were still very much in love.'

'But the whole point was that they were separated and trapped in this now loveless marriage,' I replied. 'Surely that came across in the script, too?'

'I mean, yes, of course, but there was definitely still a lot of love,' said Jasper.

'I got the love, too,' said Jacinda B.

'Yes, me too!' said Magda.

'I mean obviously it's your script,' said Peter. 'But it seemed pretty clear they still had feelings for each other.'

'Deep-rooted feelings,' said Jasper. 'Hidden beneath the layers of resentment that had built up over the years, but yes, still very much there.'

'Right, okay,' I replied, confused and slightly bewildered that the love between the main protagonists was that clear. In my mind, I had made Dan and Kate – the fictional versions of Freya and myself – pretty much hate each other at the beginning, and then gradually over the arc of the first series, they began to have some feelings for each other again, but at no point did I think it was so overtly love. Had I added more love because that was how I really felt about Freya? Was I unloading all of my actual feelings for her into the script without even realising it? Was I that so fucking unaware of myself?

Outside the BBC with Carl, my mind was completely and utterly frazzled, and I had no idea what to think. Carl started talking about how wonderful it was, and that he would meet with Peter, and bash out the best possible deal for me, but it was definitely happening, and it was going to be really great. Finally, after years of professional failure and making no money, I was back in the game.

'Carl?' I said after he finished speaking.

'Yes, mate.'

'Do you think Dan and Kate are still in love?'

'In the script?'

'Yes, in the script.'

'Well, yes. It's obvious there's still quite a bit of love there. In the script.'

'And you didn't think to tell me this?'

'I mean, I thought you knew. You wrote the bloody thing.'

'Yes, I did, didn't I? The thing is, Carl, I think I was in love with Freya the whole time.'

'I'm sure you were. Freya is great. Too good for the likes of you.'

'Thanks, Carl.'

'You're welcome. Right, I have to dash. I have another meeting across town to get to, but this has been splendid. We'll circle back later in the week?' said Carl, already walking away, and looking down at his phone. 'Congrats again, this is going to be monumental!'

'Okay,' I said absently, but all I could think about was Freya, and whether what I had actually written was a sitcom about a loveless marriage or a show about a couple that still loved each other very much but had just drifted apart. Was the feeling I had when I told Freya how I felt and that I wanted to give us another go more than just a fleeting moment and had I felt the same way all the time, but I had been too stupid, too self-absorbed by my own work to see that, actually, all I really wanted was my wife back?

I stood outside the BBC, frozen by my own question. I wanted Freya back. It was the only thing that actually mattered, and I would do anything to make it happen, and that was when it came to me. The conversation I'd had with Karen and the question she had asked me: *What if Freya asked you not to make the show at all? To scrap it completely. Would you?* I knew I had to do something big to win her back, and surely nothing was bigger than giving up my career for her. It was a bold move, but when faced with the prospect of losing the only thing in the world you actually needed, it was a small price to pay. For so long, I thought I needed to be a successful writer to be happy, and I needed to be happy at work to be happy in life and with my marriage, but I'd been wrong the whole fucking time. What I needed to be happy was my wife. I took out my phone, dialled her number, and then I waited…

Chapter Thirty-Six

Freya

Lucy had booked a car to take us to Heathrow Airport, and it arrived at just after ten thirty in the morning. The plan was to get to the airport by midday, so we'd have time to eat and have a couple of drinks before boarding the flight to New York. Lucy, in classic Lucy style, had the whole week planned out, and we were all quite excited on the journey up. In the car, Lucy went over everything she had organised for us including a day visiting all the locations from her favourite television show, *Sex and the City*. She had personally curated an entire day of living like the girls from the show. She had also planned visits to all the top tourist destinations, and had a list of all the best places to eat and drink in Manhattan and Brooklyn. It was going to be a full-on five-day tour of New York's must-see places, and we were going to be absolutely exhausted on the flight home. Cold Water Club were officially on tour!

We got our bags from the back of the car, and walked into the terminal, ready to get checked in, go through security, and then we would find somewhere nice to have lunch and something to drink to get in the holiday spirit.

'I just need to pop for a wee,' said Lucy as soon as we walked into departures. 'I shouldn't have had that cup of tea before we left, but Stuart told me the tea in America is awful and if I didn't have one before I left, I'd regret it.'

'We're early, so take all the time you need,' said Caroline. 'We'll guard the bags.'

'Guard the bags?' I said as Lucy walked away. 'Do you think they're in danger?'

'You never know,' said Caroline, and I smiled and then looked around the airport terminal, while Debs started doing something on her phone, Amy wandered off to the toilet, too, and Helen was looking through her carry-on bag.

It felt strange to be there on my own without Joe and Dolly. Most of my other airport experiences for the last eighteen years had been with my family, which meant I had been in charge of their passports, all the travel documents, and making sure I knew where everything was and where we were going. Joe was generally rubbish at that sort of thing, and so it was always up to me, but I also never minded. Flying was generally a little more stressful with them in tow, but being on my own felt strange, too. Like I was missing something. All morning, I felt like I had forgotten something important, when all I didn't have was my family.

The airport was busy with people arriving, some stressfully trying to find their boarding documents, obviously a little late, and families with young children trying to keep everyone together like they were herding sheep. Couples and singletons breezed along, seemingly without a care in the world, and two young backpackers with giant backpacks, probably off on their gap year, were taking videos on their phones, perhaps posting on Instagram about having the time of their lives. The airport was always a good place for people-watching, and I loved nothing more than guessing where everyone was going and what their situations were. As we were waiting for Lucy, I got a text from Dolly:

> Safe flight. Text me when you get there. I want lots of photos! Love you!

I texted a reply, Lucy and Amy returned from the toilet, and then we made our way through check-in, and then security.

After browsing the airport shops, having a lovely lunch with a glass of wine, it was finally time to board the plane to New York. There was a genuine sense of excitement in the group at the prospect of the week ahead. The rest of the ladies were already discussing what they couldn't wait to do in New York. Caroline had been to New York with her husband Mark once before, and was eager to go to a few places she had been with him, and Amy couldn't wait to do the Friends Experience because it had been the show that had helped her get through chemotherapy.

As we walked along the passenger boarding bridge between the terminal gate and the plane, my phone started buzzing and, when I looked down, I saw that Joe was calling me. I couldn't answer at that moment, and would wait until I was seated to see if he called again or texted. Why was he even calling me when we had barely spoken in weeks? We showed our boarding passes to one of the flight staff, and then we turned right, passing the lucky business-class passengers, and found our seats. I was sitting next to Lucy and Caroline, with Lucy by the window and Caroline in the middle, and then behind us were Debs, Helen and Amy. We all got seated, stashing our carry-on bags away, and getting ready for the flight. I took out my phone, and saw that there was a voicemail from Joe. I was curious, and pressed play, putting my phone to my ear to listen.

'Freya, hi, hello, it's me. I, umm, just had a meeting at the BBC, and they want to commission the show. Everyone is very excited about it, and there's lots of money involved and they want to make it bigger. Anyway, I'm outside, and the only thing I can actually think about is you. It's you, Freya. It's always been you. I thought I needed this show, that I needed a programme on TV again, and that it would somehow magically fix us, fix me, but I was wrong. So, I'm going to give up the show, Freya. I'm going to tell Carl that I won't do the show if there's a chance it means I can get you back. So, that's it. That's what I wanted to say. I love you. Have a brilliant time in New York, and maybe we can talk when you get back. Okay, bye, bye, bye.'

Then he was gone, and I was sitting in my seat, completely and utterly gobsmacked, and I didn't know whether to laugh or cry. When he had told me he would see a marriage counsellor, that he still loved me, I said I needed time and space and he had given me that. The thing was, weeks had gone by, and I still wasn't sure what I wanted. Then there was Sam and the kiss. He had texted earlier, too, and said that when I got back from New York perhaps we could chat. I hadn't yet responded. I had two men chasing me, which felt surreal because it wasn't that long ago that I was facing a life alone. Joe still loved me, was prepared to give up his dream of having a show on television again, and it would be so easy to give him another chance, but could I trust him again? Then there was Sam, who was handsome, lovely, and we had so much in common, but was I even ready to start dating again?

'Everything all right?' said Caroline, while she fastened her seat belt. She could obviously see the look on my face, and the fact I was probably as white as a sheet.

'Umm, yeah, fine,' I said, putting my phone down and fastening my own seat belt. I wasn't ready to share the details of Joe's voicemail yet.

Lucy was busy looking out of the window, and I got my phone and listened to Joe's message back. Should I reply and, if so, what would I even say? I stared down at my phone, wondering how to respond – maybe a brief text that I had heard it with an appropriate emoji – when the captain was suddenly speaking and we were being reminded to put our phones on airplane mode, then Lucy and Caroline were talking, and I couldn't begin to think clearly, so I put my phone away. Joe would have to wait for a reply until I was firmly on American soil.

The plane took off through light clouds, and we were soon in the air, the green grass of England giving way to the blue of the sky, and speeding off towards New York. Lucy was excitedly telling us about a bar we had to visit that night, after we had checked into our hotel. A drinks service would start soon, then food, and Caroline and Lucy were looking through the media offerings. Lucy was excited because they had both *Sex and the City* films, and the television series. I settled in, and we soon had drinks in our hands, and we were talking about the next five days with genuine optimism.

It had been so long since I had been on holiday that I had forgotten what it was actually like, and I had never just been on holiday with the girls before. Lucy was soon off in the world of Carrie, Samantha, Miranda and Charlotte, while Caroline was listening to a podcast from her phone. I wasn't sure what to do because all I could think about was my marriage. It was strange getting away from Brighton, and having that space because, for some reason, being so far from Joe, from everything I knew, I did feel the need for him or, at least, the comfort of him. Joe and I had always shared these sorts of experiences together. I would miss his almost childlike joy in the smallest of things. He always made travelling fun, and his rose-tinted-glasses way of looking at the world, of finding the comedy in every moment, no matter how stressful, was something I would miss, and it was jarring because I had wanted to get away from him, but now having that distance was like a wake-up call that, actually, things weren't perhaps as black and white as I had thought when we were on the ground.

I put on my headphones, started listening to some music and closed my eyes, letting my mind drift away in the hope that perhaps some sort of answer might come to me while we were 35,000 feet in the air.

Chapter Thirty-Seven

Joe

I needed a plan and not just any plan but a really brilliant plan that would convince Freya I had changed, and that I was serious about saving our marriage. The problem was, as I was sitting in the living room with a cup of coffee, listening to the beginnings of a new day outside, nothing was coming to me. I had already told Freya I would see a marriage counsellor together, and that I would give up the show if it meant saving our marriage. I had confessed my love, put my heart on the line, but nothing had changed and she hadn't spoken to me about it since. All I had received from New York was a brief text that said:

> I still need time.

She had asked for time and space and I had given her both, but surely with her so far away I needed to use this time and space to do something big.

When I needed life advice, I would usually go to my friends, but Stuart wasn't really the romantic type, and Barney had had so little luck in love he was hardly the person to go to for guidance when it came to saving a marriage. Dolly was still working and spending all of her time with Elle, so was hardly about, and I couldn't imagine she wanted to give her dad advice about wooing her mum. Karen was my therapist, and she had made it quite clear what we could and couldn't discuss, which only left my father. It felt strange to go to him for advice, but since he had met Juliette, he was like a different person. He was a true renaissance man. I decided to give it a go because I was desperate and nothing was coming to me. I rang his number, and after a few rings he answered.

'All right, son?' said Dad.

'Hi, Dad. How's it going?'

'Yeah, not bad. The sale of my house is going through and that should be done soon, fingers crossed. The house in France is already ours, and Juliette is there now doing some work on it. It needs a lot done, and she's working with some local builders over there, and honestly, you think builders are unreliable here, you haven't been to the south of France. Sometimes they don't show up until lunchtime, if they show up at all. I can't wait to get down there, to be honest, and get cracking.'

'I bet.'

'It feels weird just waiting around in an empty house to sign some paperwork, but it's good to get all the loose ends tied up. I'm saying goodbye to friends, that sort of thing. What's happening with you?' said Dad, and this was the moment when I needed him. I hadn't had that thought often – maybe ever – in my life, but perhaps things were going to be different from now on.

'Actually, I need your help,' I said, and then I went on to explain everything that had happened recently from the show getting commissioned to telling Freya I was still in love with her. 'The thing is, Dad, since I told her, and she said she needed some time and space, we have barely spoken. It feels like there's time and space, and then there's, you know, time and space.'

'Right, yeah, I can see how that would be difficult. But how can I help you, exactly?'

'Right now Freya is in New York for the week with her Cold Water Club.'

'Very nice! I have always fancied going to New York. The Statue of Liberty, the Empire State Building, Central Park, getting one of those giant sandwiches—'

'Yes, Dad, but that isn't the point.'

'Sorry, Joe, got a bit lost there for a moment.'

'She's in New York and when she gets back, I want to do something big, show her just how much I love her. That I'm serious about us. I just don't know what to do, but I know it has to be spectacular. I need to blow her mind, Dad.'

'This is what you want me to help you with?'

'That's right.'

'You need something really big. A grand romantic gesture that will show Freya just how much you love her, that you've changed, and you'll do anything to make your marriage work again?'

'That's exactly it!' I said excitedly because he seemed to get it right away. Perhaps he had the perfect plan. There was nothing but silence down the phone and I waited, hoping Dad would suggest something ridiculously romantic.

After about a minute, Dad said, 'You could give the house a really good clean while she's gone, and make her something nice to eat? What's her favourite meal?'

'That's your enormous romantic gesture? A spring clean and steak dinner?'

'I mean, think about it, son. Who wouldn't love to come back from holiday to a clean house and a nice meal?'

'I know, Dad, but this has to be something huge, not a quick vacuum and a jacket potato.'

'Oh, right,' said Dad, sounding like someone way out of his depth, but then he said something that suddenly changed everything. 'What about your sitcom?'

'Sorry? What about it?'

'You said you wrote an entire television show about your marriage.'

'I did.'

'Maybe there is something you can do with that?'

'Like what?'

'I don't know, but you must have written some pretty nice stuff about her, about love, marriage, and all of that, right? Maybe you can use that in some way to show her exactly how much she means to you. What about that?' he suggested, still sounding rather unsure of himself, but it didn't matter because the wires in my brain that connected the dots and sparked ideas when I was writing were suddenly shooting off all over the place. It was like a firework show in my head. Why hadn't I thought of it before?

'Dad, you're a genius!'

'Yeah? Why's that?'

'Because you just gave me the most brilliant idea.'

'Right, well, you're welcome, son.'

'Thank you.'

'Do you need any help with it, or—'

'Not right now, but thank you, and Dad, am I going to see you before you leave for France?'

'Actually, now you mention it, I was hoping to stay with you for a few days once the house is sold, if that's all right?'

'Of course. Whenever you want. Just let me know the dates, and we'll sort it out. Okay, I have to go. I have a huge romantic gesture to plan!'

'Good luck,' said Dad before he added, 'and, you know, maybe give the house a spring clean, too, and that steak dinner will probably help. Just saying.'

'Will do, Dad,' I said, and then we hung up, and I had a lot of work to do.

The plan had come to me when Dad had mentioned the show. It was like the whole thing appeared to me in the way that sometimes ideas for shows would come to me while I was drifting off to sleep. This was a big, romantic idea and I would need some help, and I had no clue how long it would take to put it together, so I had to get going right away. I needed to call Carl because I would definitely need his assistance, and Dolly, too. I didn't know if this would be enough, but I had to try. My marriage was on the line and there was nothing I wouldn't do to make it work.

Chapter Thirty-Eight

Freya

It had been an incredible few days, and we had already seen and done so much. After a little bit of tiredness and jet lag when we had arrived, on the first full day in New York we had been to Central Park, eaten the best pizza of my life at John's Pizzeria in Greenwich Village, seen the *Friends* building, gone to the Friends Experience, taken the subway, which was nothing like the London Underground, had some delicious coffee, and then a great night out at a bar on the Upper East Side. On day two, we had taken the ferry to the Statue of Liberty, gone to see the 9/11 museum, which was difficult and emotional but well worth it, and we were spending the night at a rooftop bar in Midtown with sweeping views across the city skyline. It was a gorgeous evening, the views were to die for, and so were the drinks.

'My feet are literally dying,' said Debs. 'How far did we walk today?'

Caroline looked at her Apple Watch. 'Almost twenty-five thousand steps.'

'Which is how far in old money?' asked Debs. 'For the people without Apple Watches.'

'Almost twelve miles,' said Caroline.

'No wonder my feet feel like they've been attacked!' said Debs.

'Tomorrow is going to be even more walking,' said Lucy. 'Sorry.'

'It's okay,' said Debs. 'I need to walk twelve miles just to walk off all the food!'

It was true that our New York diet had been quite carbohydrate heavy. Most days we had bagels for breakfast, pizza for lunch and sometimes dinner, and also lots of dessert. If we didn't all want to return to Cold Water Club a good stone heavier, we needed to keep walking. As we sat there, Lucy's phone buzzed with a text. She looked down at it, smiled, quickly texted something back, and then put her phone back on the table.

'Who was that?' I asked.

'Stuart,' said Lucy. 'He couldn't find something for George, needed help logging into the online banking because he had somehow locked himself out, and he loved me.'

'Men. Bloody useless without us,' said Helen.

'Totally true,' said Caroline. 'I've had over fifteen texts from Mark in the last day alone, asking how to do things. I just replied, figure it out! Honestly, if something happened to me, I'd give them a month before they were basically savages.'

'Oh my God,' said Lucy. 'If something happened to me, Stuart wouldn't know how to do anything. He's great at work, but essentially just another child at home. Actually, now that I think about it, George is probably more useful.'

'Do you think they do it on purpose?' asked Amy. 'Fergus and I don't have any children, so he doesn't have that excuse, but the man can't even put on bed sheets properly!'

'I believe it's called weaponised incompetence,' said Lucy. 'I know for a fact Stuart intentionally does things badly, just so I'll do them instead.'

'Mark, too! I mean, how hard is it to unload the dishwasher? He will go into the dishwasher in the morning, take out what he needs, and leave the rest!' said Caroline.

'Now that is lazy!' said Helen, as our food arrived, and we ordered more drinks.

I had been having such a great time in New York, and being with my Cold Water Club ladies had been incredible, but I couldn't stop thinking about Joe the whole bloody time. Hearing the other ladies complaining about how useless their husbands were without them, it did make me think about Joe and that, despite his shortcomings, he was good around the house, and our marriage was for the most parts an equal partnership. At least it had been for so long. All I wanted to do was enjoy the sights and sounds of New York, the incredible food and energy of the city, but I couldn't stop my mind from wandering back to Joe and wondering whether, after everything that had happened, could we save our marriage?

I had been in my head about it since take-off from London, perhaps it was time to share it with the group and get their perspectives. They were, after all, my closest friends and I trusted them and valued their opinions. Once everyone was settled with food and drinks, I decided to bring it up. We were at a rooftop bar in New York with the most incredible views. What better place to try and decide the rest of my life? This was real-life *Sex and the City*!

'I need some advice,' I said, looking around at the group.

'We're listening,' said Lucy.

I took a moment to compose myself and collect my thoughts before I started speaking.

'I think I mentioned before we left that Joe and I had a huge fight. What I didn't tell you was why. He's written a new show, and it's getting commissioned by the BBC—'

'That's great news!' said Caroline excitedly before her face slipped into a frown. 'Right?'

'It is. Joe's spent so many years trying to get a show on TV again, and he's achieved it and it's great for him. The thing is, the show is entirely about the break-up of our marriage, and he never told me he was writing it. He never asked for permission to use our pain, our heartbreak for a show, and when I found out I was so angry with him—'

'Rightfully so!' said Debs. 'That's disgraceful behaviour.'

'It is,' I replied.

'I can't believe Joe would do that to you,' said Lucy.

'Me either,' said Caroline. 'I hope you told him exactly what you thought of him.'

'I did. I was so angry, still am, but he also told me he's still in love with me, will even see a marriage counsellor together, and just before we took off, he left me a voicemail and said he'd even give up the show for me.'

'Wow!' said Lucy. 'I mean, obviously what he did was totally shit, and I understand the trust issues, but it sounds like he's prepared to give up a lot for you.'

'I know, but he still lied about seeing a therapist, he lied about the show he was writing, and the last eighteen months of our marriage were pure dog shit, if I'm honest. But the thing is, living together these past six months but not married, it's, I don't know, made me see him in a different light. I was actually thinking about us getting back together again before I found out about the show.'

'So now you're conflicted and want our advice?' said Debs.

I looked around at my group of ladies and smiled. 'I do. Although there's something else, too. After I had that huge argument with Joe, I went to see Sam—'

'Sam-from-work Sam?' said Lucy.

'Sexy Sam?' said Amy with a salacious smile.

'The very same, and we kissed.'

'OMG!' said Lucy. 'You and Sam kissed? What was it like?'

'It was great,' I replied. 'Really great, actually, but it's just, I can't even think about Sam until I know how I feel about Joe. Which is why I need your advice.'

'Can I go first?' said Caroline, and everyone, including me, nodded. 'What he did was fucking awful. He lied to you and used your pain and suffering to write a television show without asking if it was okay. I'd be so angry with Mark if he lied to me like that. He'd be getting nothing in the sack for a good six months, and he'd need to cook me a lot of dinners, but ultimately the idiot made a mistake and if you think there's even the smallest chance of it working out, I'd give him another go.'

'Thanks,' I replied before Debs jumped in.

'I wouldn't,' said Debs with steely determination. 'I think once the trust is gone that's it. If Steve did something like that, I'd kick his ass to the ground faster than Usain Bolt with the wind behind his back. I'm sorry, Freya, but it's a no from me.'

'Even though he said he'd give up the show for me?' I asked.

'It's a nice gesture, but you said it yourself, your marriage wasn't good for eighteen months, and he's lied to you twice in the last six months. How will you ever trust him again?' said Debs.

'I'm torn,' said Helen, the only divorced woman in the group. 'On one hand, I can see where Debs is coming from. Trust is so important in a marriage, and once you lose that trust, it's hard to get it back again. On the other hand, being divorced and single in midlife is completely rubbish and I wouldn't want that for you either. I suppose if I had to lean one way, I'd say, if you think you can trust him again, and if you still love him, then give it another go. Plus, I think him offering to go to counselling and giving up his dream shows that maybe he's changed.'

We all looked towards Amy, the person in the group who had probably been through the most difficult of times, surviving cancer, and we all knew how much her husband, Ferguson, had helped her. Of all of us, she perhaps knew the most about the importance of a strong relationship.

'I think I'm with Caroline,' said Amy. 'A swift kick in the balls and then you move on!'

I think we were all taken aback by Amy's blunt reply, and after a second we all laughed.

'Okay, fine, I'm good with that,' added Debs. 'If Joe accepts a good kick in the balls then maybe take him back! But only on your terms and make them bloody good ones!'

We all took sips of our cocktails, and ate our food for a moment until I looked towards Lucy, who had yet to venture an answer.

'Luce?' I said. 'What do you think?'

'I think, I can't really give you a good answer because I know Joe well, too, and he's friends with Stuart, so it all feels a little weird. Plus, everyone else has given such good answers. I will, however, ask you this. Regardless of what he's done, the trust issues, etcetera, are you still in love with him?'

This was perhaps the most difficult question to answer, and the one I had been rolling around my head for the past month. One of the reasons I had asked Joe for time and space was that I needed time to really think without being around him. I wanted to feel what it would be like to miss him because then maybe I would know if I was still in love with him or not. Could I imagine a life without him? Would absence make my heart grow fonder?

'The honest answer,' I said to Lucy, 'is that I don't know. I think I'm so afraid of making the wrong decision that I'm afraid to make any decision. At our age, everything feels so fucking hard, like if I mess this up, then I'm going to be back in the same place in another year when I'm another year older, with another year of wrinkles, more baggage, and another year of being sad. But then I think, what if it's the best decision of my life? What if we're happier than ever? Then there's the possibility of Sam, or at least someone else different down the tracks, too, and it's like, how am I supposed to know?'

'I think that's the thing about life,' said Caroline. 'Is that we never know. Whether it's a wee decision or a huge one, we never know how it will turn out until it does. I say trust your gut.'

'Hear, hear to that,' said Helen. 'Always listen to your gut.'

'Thank you, ladies,' I said, and I knew they were right.

'Well,' said Lucy. 'With that, let's toast to Cold Water Club, being here together in New York, and whatever happens with you and Joe, whenever I end up moving away with Stuart, and whatever happens with all of us, I just wanted to say thank you. Thanks for all the early mornings, the great chats, and just being there for each other. To Cold Water Club!'

'Cold Water Club!' we all said in unison, chinking our glasses together over the table, and then I looked at the view of New York, and it felt surreal to be there at that moment with those women. My life for the past six months since Joe and I had decided to separate had felt surreal. Almost as if I was watching it like a film rather than actually living it, and this was the same. Perhaps it was why I was having such a hard time making a decision. I knew when we landed back in London, when my feet were firmly back on British soil, I couldn't keep avoiding it. Time and space only worked for so long, and so I needed to find out what that last piece of the jigsaw puzzle was. What was the thing that was holding me back from making a decision and would I find out over the course of the next few days in New York?

Chapter Thirty-Nine

Joe

'Do you really think the sign is a good idea?' said Dolly.

'Yes, Dolly. It took me ages to make,' I said, taking the rolled-up paper that contained the sign, and laying it out on the hallway floor.

'And you don't think it's a bit shit?'

'Clearly you do.'

'No, I think the sentiment is fine, Dad, I do, it's just… Do I really have to hold it up in front of the house where everyone can see us? Like neighbours, people passing by, and drones?'

'I can't exactly hold the sign on my own, can I, and drones, really?'

'I literally saw a drone just the other day,' said Dolly with a sarcastic smile. 'I'm just not sure a big gesture is the way to go.'

I stopped for a moment and looked at my daughter. She was leaving for university in a week, and it felt like the moment to impart an important life lesson to her. All my years of experience and of writing about love, and she was going to get all of that knowledge in a single, succinct sound bite.

'Dolly, when it comes to love, a big gesture is always the way to go,' I said, and Dolly looked at me, shrugged her shoulders, then walked off to make herself something to eat.

The last five days had been absolute hell. I had wanted to call Freya, text Freya, and explain exactly how I was feeling, but I knew I couldn't. She'd said she needed time and space and I had to give it to her. After days of ploughing through the turgid workings of my mind, I had come up with The Plan, thanks to my chat with Dad, and now I had everything in place. It had meant calling Carl, and asking for a huge favour from him, but he had come through in a big way and I hoped it was enough. The sign was just the opening gambit in my attempt to win Freya back, but the real surprise, the bit that had taken me all week to do and that I had only finished last night, was what would hopefully convince her I was serious. I had spoken with Dolly and explained everything, and she had been instantly on board with 'The Plan' – all except the idea of the sign, apparently – and so, there we were, waiting to greet Freya after five days in New York. The thing was, with almost a month of time and space and five days in New York with her friends, I literally had no idea where her mind was. Perhaps she had already decided that we were done, and nothing I could do or say would make a jot of difference – even offering to give up working on *House Shared*.

On the day before Freya was due to return, I had a Zoom call with Carl, and we spoke for an hour. He'd had a meeting at the BBC and they were willing to offer me a very generous financial package, and initially they wanted ten thirty-minute episodes of *House Shared*, although, depending on viewing figures, it could be more. I would need to go up to London soon for meetings. Obviously, I hadn't mentioned to Carl or the BBC that I had offered to scrap the whole project if it meant saving my marriage. If Freya did want to go down that route, I would, but I wasn't looking forward to the conversation with Carl if that was the final outcome. I wasn't thinking that far ahead though because I couldn't. I had to just focus on today.

After a bowl of cereal, Dolly returned to the hallway with a cup of coffee for her and one for me. Freya had sent me her flight information before she had left, and so I had checked they had landed on time. Freya was officially back on British soil! I knew Lucy had booked a car to bring them all home, so fingers crossed she would be walking in the front door soon.

'Thanks for the coffee,' I said.

'You're welcome. It looked like you needed it. How much longer until she arrives?'

'Best guess,' I said, looking down at my watch for some reason, 'the next thirty minutes.'

'Right,' said Dolly, taking a sip of her coffee, and I had to admit I was bloody nervous. No, I was more than nervous, I was absolutely terrified. Not just about the sign because it was, in no uncertain terms, a bit of a gamble, but because this was the rest of my life. I wanted to tell Freya how I felt and what I wanted, but if she felt differently that was it. We would be getting separated, divorced, and I would be alone. My life and dreams of us getting old together in tatters.

Dolly stationed herself by the front window so she could see when Freya pulled up outside, while I waited in the hallway with the sign. I imagined Freya arriving at Heathrow, and walking through the arrivals gate where they had filmed the opening scene from *Love Actually*. That montage of families and lovers reuniting to the voiceover of Hugh Grant telling us that love actually is all around. It was beautiful, and Richard Curtis had been right the whole bloody time. Was he ever wrong?

'She's here!' Dolly suddenly exclaimed from the living room. 'Mum's home!'

The next second I heard Dolly running from the living room and into the hallway.

'Right, I'm ready to hold the world's lamest sign and completely embarrass myself,' said Dolly. 'You do know that someone might film it on their phone, and if Mum says no, and you start crying like a baby, it will be all over the internet in like five minutes. Hashtag not love actually.'

'Hilarious. Now, grab your end of the sign and let's go!'

I opened the front door, and then we picked up the sign and walked outside. Luckily it was a gloriously sunny day, and not pissing down with rain. I had decided on the sign yesterday morning, and I had gone out, bought the necessary materials and made it last night. The occasion felt like it needed a big gesture and this was definitely a big gesture. We shuffled outside and stood across the front of the house, holding the sign out wide so Freya could read it as soon as she arrived. A black Mercedes van was parked outside, and then the sliding door opened, and Freya got out. She stood on the pavement, and turned towards us.

She was looking directly at the huge sign that said in large, hand-painted letters:

FREYA JANE WALLACE, WILL YOU MARRY ME… AGAIN?

The moment she saw it, Freya's hand went to her mouth, and then she slowly walked towards us. At the same time, Lucy got out of the van, dashed past Freya and then towards us.

'Sorry, Joe, I really need a wee!' said Lucy quickly. 'Oh, nice sign.'

Lucy ran past us and into the house, as Freya slowly walked towards us. Other people were walking past the house and looking on with interest. I did see someone with their phone pointed at us. Was Dolly going to be proved correct, and if Freya rejected me, would I be all over social media in a matter of hours with some unfortunate romantic-comedy-based hashtag?

'Joe, what's this? Will I marry you? Again?' said Freya, standing in front of me looking completely flabbergasted. Slowly, from the black van, other members of Cold Water Club emerged. I hadn't met any of them yet, and so this was definitely going to be a talking point if Freya and I worked things out and they became a part of my life, too.

'Hi, Mum!' said Dolly, still holding up her end of the sign.

'Hello, love,' said Freya, still visibly shocked.

I took a deep breath, as time seemed to slow, and then I began to speak. Five days of thinking, planning and knowing exactly what I wanted to say to my wife.

'Freya, when I was at the meeting at the BBC, they all asked me whether I thought the couple in the show would ultimately get back together, and I said I didn't know. Honestly, I wasn't sure, but then literally everyone in the meeting, including Carl as it turned out, said that they were clearly still in love, and it got me thinking. Everything that has happened to us over the last six months, the good and the bad, it's all because I still love you. I probably wouldn't have written a whole show about us, which turns out to be nothing more than a love letter to you, if I wasn't still in love with you. I know I fucked up, have spent far too long taking you for granted, making mistakes, but if there is one thing I have learnt over the past six months, it's that I don't want to share a house with anyone else for the rest of my life but you.'

'Oh, Joe,' said Freya with tears pooling in her eyes.

'I want to be unseparated from you, Freya, and I know it's not going to be easy, and will require work, but I *want* to do the work. I want to grow old together and make our life exactly the way we had always dreamed about. I also know it will take a lot more than just a sign to show how much I love you, so if you'd like to come inside, I have something to show you.'

The other members of Cold Water Club were awkwardly hanging around on the pavement and then Lucy reappeared from using the toilet.

'Can everyone come inside?' said Freya.

'Umm, well, what I made is quite—'

'Dad,' said Dolly. 'I think everyone should see what you made. Plus, it's probably a lot better than this sign. It is better, right?'

'Yes, it's better. Fine, everyone come inside!' I said loudly so everyone could hear. It wasn't in 'The Plan', but then again, none of this was in my life plan, was it?

We all marched inside the house and they all followed me into the kitchen diner. The room was completely dark, and I had set up the computer, which I had managed, with Dolly's help, to connect to the television and I had it all ready to go.

'Come in and sit down,' I said nervously.

Everyone came in and found a seat.

'What's going on, Joe?' said Freya.

'Just watch,' I said, going to my computer and starting the video.

The idea had come to me when Dad had mentioned the show. Somehow my mind connected the show to me creating a short film of our marriage – the story of us. Luckily, we had plenty of footage from our wedding, and then a little later, lots of videos of us on our phones we had taken over the years. What I needed from Carl was someone with the technical know-how to take all the footage I could find, edit it together, and put some music over the top. Fortunately, Carl knew exactly the person who was willing to help, and so we spent the next few days creating this film. The film Freya, Dolly, Lucy, the rest of Cold Water Club and myself had just settled in to watch.

After I had watched it for the first time, already with tears in my eyes, I had decided on the Snow Patrol song 'You Could Be Happy'. Three minutes and two seconds of Snow Patrol brilliance would say everything I needed to say to Freya, and it had a wonderful poignancy to it that along with the film had me in floods. The film opened with footage from our wedding, and then some rather rough footage from our honeymoon, and then gradually over the years as technology improved and film quality got considerably better, shots of me and Freya together. Dancing at a wedding in Edinburgh, walking along a beach, playing with a very young Dolly, holidays abroad, simple moments at home we had caught on our phones, laughing and walking along the South Bank in London, on the beach in Brighton, ice cream and cocktails, and every moment I could find when we were so happy, and I hoped it showed Freya how happy we could be again.

I stood next to Freya through the whole thing, and slowly as we watched the film, I heard sobbing, and then I saw that Freya was crying. Lucy was in tears, too, and every other person in that room was also weeping. Eventually the film finished along with the music, and there was a black screen and the words came up:

> I want to make you that happy again. Love
> you always. Joe x

Then it finished, I stopped the computer, and all I could hear was sniffling.

'That was really lovely,' said Lucy between tears.

'It really was beautiful,' said one of the Cold Water ladies in a Scottish accent, and then Freya stood up and turned to me. I looked at her, and she was obviously tired after a long flight, shocked, but the main thing she looked, above everything else, was beautiful.

'What do you say, Freya? Will you marry me again?' I said hopefully, and I waited with bated breath, until finally she spoke.

'Firstly, Joe, that really was a lovely film, and secondly, I don't know what I think. We separated for a reason, and I agree that there are reasons why we slept together again, and why despite everything, you still drive me crazy, but I don't know if it means we belong together. Whether you and I can ever be that happy again.'

I had the sudden terrifying thought that I just wasn't enough. My big gesture, my words, the film and all the years we had been married weren't enough, and Freya was going to say no.

'I've spent the last five days in New York having the time of my life. We ate incredible food, visited some amazing places, toured every location from *Sex and the City*, and saw the view at sunset from the top of the Empire State Building. And yet, every moment of the last five days has also been me thinking about you. Every day I woke up and we walked around New York, and I thought about you. When we were eating the most incredible pizza at John's of Bleecker Street or drinking cocktails at a jazz bar on the Upper East Side, I was thinking about us, and yet I still couldn't decide. It only occurred to me when we were coming in to land today that I had spent five days in one of the greatest cities in the world, with my best friends, and all the while, I had been thinking about you and me, and surely that meant that I still loved you because, otherwise, I probably wouldn't have been thinking about you while I ate one of the best bagels ever at Tompkins Square Bagels, and it was so good, but do you know what I thought? I wish Joe could taste how good this was.

'So, Joe, I couldn't make a decision about us, but what I came to realise is that you and I aren't as simple as a decision. We are a part of each other. But before I answer your question, there is something I have to tell you.'

'Okay,' I said somewhat nervously.

'The day we had the argument, when you told me about the show, I was so angry with you and I kissed Sam later that day.'

'Mum!' said Dolly, and everyone in the room looked towards her. 'Sorry.'

'I wanted you to know before I said anything else,' said Freya, and I just looked at her and then I smiled.

'I don't care about that, Freya, it's in the past. The only thing I care about now is the future,' I said, and then I found myself getting down on one knee in front of her. 'Freya Jane Wallace, will you do me the honour of becoming my wife again? In sickness and health, through good times and bad, and even when I'm being a bit of a knob, till death do us part?'

Freya looked down at me with tears in her eyes, and said, 'Of course I will, you daft bugger, now stand up and kiss me!'

I stood up, took Freya in my arms, and our lips came together, and from all around us, all I could hear were whoops, cheers, and all I could feel were Freya's lips on mine, and I knew I didn't want to ever stop kissing her. Not now. Not ever.

Chapter Forty

Freya

I didn't know at what point I would completely lose it. Obviously dropping Dolly at university was going to be tough, and at some point I would have to let all the tears go, and cry like a baby. I had been on the verge of tears all week, ever since I got back from New York. Partly because of what had happened with Joe, and all the tears of joy I had shed over that, and now all the tears of sadness I was crying over Dolly. I had basically been a fucking emotional mess, and you would think I had no tears left, but as we stood in her small room in the halls of residence, and we knew it was time to say goodbye, I could feel a barrage of tears just waiting to escape and explode down my face. How do you say goodbye to your child without completely losing your shit?

It had all started at five o'clock that morning, when we had put the last of Dolly's bags in the car. It was a six-hour drive to Durham, and we had planned a one-hour stop for lunch in Nottingham, and perhaps another stop at a service station for coffee and snacks. How had it come around so quickly? It only felt like five minutes since Dolly was starting primary school. At times her life felt like it had been so long, and the years when she was little seemed to take an eternity, but now she was leaving us, I wanted to go back and do it all again. I wanted to savour every second once more and cherish each moment with a greater degree of appreciation. I wasn't ready to say goodbye to my daughter.

'So,' said Dolly, standing in the middle of her small room.

It really was a very tiny space, and it seemed like she might struggle to fit all her stuff in, but it didn't seem to be bothering Dolly. To be fair, my memories of freshers' week were mainly being drunk, not sleeping, and signing up for clubs I probably, almost definitely, didn't attend, and I'm fairly sure I didn't care once about the aesthetics of my room.

'So,' I replied. 'We should probably—'

'Yes,' said Joe. 'Give you some space.'

'Okay, well, thank you, and I love you,' said Dolly, and I could feel myself beginning to crumble. She walked forwards into my arms, and I held her, and I didn't ever want to let her go. She might feel like a woman now, the curves of her body were definitely feeling more grown-up, but she would always be my little girl.

'Okay, Freya, I think you can let go now,' said Joe after about a minute.

I slowly let Dolly go, and she sank into her father and gave him a hug, and then after another few minutes of us dithering we decided it was actually time to go. It was clear Dolly just needed us gone because she wanted to get on with the rest of her life. There were other slightly lost, nervous-looking teenagers in other rooms with other sad, terrified-looking parents saying goodbye. Everyone just had to let go. Joe and I both gave Dolly one final hug each, one last kiss, and then eventually we left her room.

Joe and I walked to our car in silence, and I was doing my best to hold in the tears for as long as I could. We found our car, got in, and I was about to let my tears go, when there was suddenly an almighty sob from next to me. I looked across and, much to my surprise, I saw Joe crying his heart out, and making the loudest racket.

'Oh my God, Joe,' I said, my own tears suddenly on hold. 'Are you okay?'

'She's gone, Freya. Our baby girl is gone, and she might not ever come back again, and I'm going to miss her so much.'

'I know, Joe, I know,' I said, placing a hand on his back and rubbing it.

'I'm just… I'm just so sad.'

'Me, too,' I said, and Joe looked at me, stopped crying for a moment, and then he fell into me and cried even harder into my shoulder. Apparently, it was going to be me who had to keep themselves together today.

We sat like that for about fifteen minutes until eventually he relented and stopped sobbing. We had a hotel booked for the night in York because it was only a short drive away, and it was supposed to be a beautiful city, full of lovely old buildings and, of course, the thirteenth-century Gothic cathedral. We were going to spend the night in York, and then drive back to Brighton in the morning. When it was clear Joe had finished crying, but was in no fit state to drive, we switched seats so I could drive, and we started off towards York.

The last week since I had got home from New York had been a bit of a blur. After watching Joe's incredible film, everyone made themselves scarce, and we sat in bed and just talked. We spoke about all the things that had gone wrong in our marriage, and all the things we wanted to fix going forwards. We agreed to see a marriage counsellor together for as long as it took, and perhaps beyond that. I had told Joe he definitely needed to continue making *House Shared* with the BBC, and how it could be something of a historical document of our marriage, and also perhaps a warning sign for the future. We were one hundred per cent open and honest with each other, and we told each other everything – the good, the bad and decidedly fucking ugly – and then after about three hours of that, we had sex, and it was by far the best sex we'd had in many years.

Since then it felt like we were back in the honeymoon period of our relationship, although overshadowed slightly by Dolly packing up her room and leaving for university. Now she was gone, and after we had picked ourselves up, it was time for us to begin the next chapter of our lives together. Act two was officially underway.

I met with Sam over coffee and explained everything. I felt awful for him, but he had taken my news with genuine good grace and been nothing but kind and supportive. He had said that despite being sad for himself, he was happy we had managed to work things out. Somewhere out there was a very lucky lady, who was going to get a brilliant boyfriend one day.

With Joe getting his show commissioned at the BBC, we had decided to splurge, and we were staying at The Grand hotel in York, which was sumptuous and lovely. Over a full English breakfast at the hotel the following morning, we both spoke about what we wanted to do next.

'I'm in no rush to get back,' said Joe. 'Carl said it will be at least another few weeks before we get into meetings with the BBC.'

'I could take a few days off work. I mean, I only just had a week off for New York, but they won't miss me for a couple of days.'

'Right then,' said Joe. 'Where do you fancy going?'

'Anywhere?'

'Within reason. Anywhere in England.'

'Or Wales?'

'Or Wales.'

'Let me think,' I said, and then I took a sip of my coffee and a bite of toast. 'You know somewhere I've never been?'

'Hull? Bradford? Aberystwyth?'

'Yes, I mean, I haven't been to any of those places, but also, I've never been to Liverpool.'

'Liverpool? That's where you want to go?'

'Why not? The birthplace of The Beatles. I think at least once in your life, you should probably go to Liverpool, and then maybe Stratford-upon-Avon to see where William Shakespeare was born. Have you ever been?'

'Actually, I haven't.'

'That's settled then. Liverpool and then Stratford-upon-Avon.'

'Okay,' said Joe with a smile, popping some bacon in his mouth.

After breakfast we wandered around York, which was lovely, spoke with Dolly on the phone to see how her first night had gone, and she was fine, if not slightly hungover. After seeing the sights, we returned to our hotel and had sex because it was such a lovely room, and it felt wrong not to, before we packed up the car, and got ready to hit the road to Liverpool. It was about a two-and-a-half-hour drive to Liverpool, and while Joe was driving, I booked us into the Hard Day's Night Beatles-themed hotel.

'Right, all booked in,' I said, putting my phone down.

Joe reached a hand across and placed it on my leg.

'Love you, Mrs Wallace.'

'Love you, too, Mr Wallace. So, when is the big day?'

'Our re-wedding?'

'Exactly. You asked me to marry you again, and now I'm expecting a wedding.'

Joe laughed, before he looked across the car at me and said, 'Actually, I was thinking about this Christmas.'

'Won't it be a bit chilly for a wedding?'

'In England, yes, but in the Maldives, I think it's looking quite pleasant.'

'The Maldives! How much are the BBC paying you again?'

'Enough. Plus, I was thinking about keeping it small. Just you, me and Dolly. How does that sound?'

'I think, it sounds fucking amazing!'

'Right then, let's get it booked up. I've always wanted to stay in one of those little villas over the water.'

'Oh, me too!'

Joe kept driving, and I started looking at resorts in the Maldives on my phone, and as we got nearer to Liverpool, I couldn't help but think back to that day when Joe and I met at Pelicano Coffee Co in The Lanes and decided to separate. That felt like a million years ago now, a different lifetime, and yet it was only just over six months ago. Sometimes years passed by, and you really felt like nothing had changed, and it was true because some years not much happened, but then years like this happened when you felt like you had really lived. We had been through something and came out the other side still intact. It did make me appreciate that life changed and evolved, and if so much had happened in the last six months, why couldn't the next six months or year be just as turbulent? Joe had his show with the BBC that would no doubt take up much of his time, and he would be going backwards and forwards to London, and who knew what would happen with that? Maybe it would become a runaway success, his career could take off again, and maybe in a year, we'd be living in Los Angeles, Joe working on a film or a huge American television show. I still wanted to become a solicitor, and who knew where that would take me, and then there was Dolly to think about, too. Life was unpredictable even when you thought it couldn't surprise you any more. The only thing I knew at that moment, as we drove towards Liverpool, was that I loved Joe and Joe loved me, and that was enough.

Chapter Forty-One

Joe

One year later

Everyone was at the house, and we were all waiting for the first episode of *House Shared* to come on the telly. It was Freya's idea to have a big premiere party at our house to celebrate, and she had literally invited everyone we knew. We had even, for the big night, bought a much larger television set, which we'd had a man put up on the wall in the kitchen diner. It felt like a huge moment because when *The Mornings* had aired in 2005, Freya and I celebrated with Carl at a pub in Soho, but this felt even better and perhaps more significant. Then I was just a kid, and it was impossible to really appreciate what a huge moment it was. Also, then I hadn't gone through the wasteland of failure, and so my comeback felt so much sweeter.

'Where's the champagne?' said Freya eagerly.

'In the mini fridge in the garden,' I replied, as the clock ticked down to nine o'clock, when the very first episode of *House Shared* was going to air. Dolly was next to me with her girlfriend, Elle.

'Are you so excited?' said Dolly.

'I'm ninety-nine per cent nerves,' I replied.

'He's always like this before anything,' said Freya, who had returned with two bottles of champagne. 'He puked in the toilets at the pub before *The Mornings* premiered.'

'Thanks for that historical nugget,' I said to Freya. 'I just want people to love it.'

'And they totally will,' replied Dolly with a smile.

'Right, five minutes to go,' said Freya. 'Let's get these bottles open!'

'Need a hand?' said Stuart, who had come back to Brighton with Lucy and the boys especially for tonight. They had moved to Rugby at the beginning of the year, and we missed them terribly, but Stuart's new language school was going from strength to strength, and they all seemed happy. 'I did a course once, and we were shown how to correctly open a bottle of champagne.'

'Of course you did,' I said. 'Anything you can't do, mate?'

'Umm, let me think,' said Stuart, and we all looked at him, before Lucy gave him a nudge.

'Tell them about the dance class we took last month,' said Lucy, with a delicious grin. 'What did the instructor call you?'

We all looked towards Stuart, who said slowly and quite despondently, 'The worst dancer with the least amount of rhythm she had ever seen.'

'Sorry, mate,' I said, clapping Stuart on the back. 'But could you still open the champagne?'

Stuart smiled then opened the bottles of champagne we had bought for the occasion. There must have been about forty people in our kitchen. Freya's mum and Marmalade were there, and Marmalade was very excited about the prospect of meeting someone famous. Unfortunately, none of the stars of the show could make it, and so he just had to make do with me. Dad and Juliette had come across from France, and it was great to see Dad so happy and, probably for the first time in his entire life, tanned. He had lost weight, too, and looked like a different man.

Barney was there with Phoebe from Bristol, who was now Phoebe who formerly lived in Bristol but now lived with Barney in Brighton, and they seemed to be really happy together – there were even rumours of an impending engagement. Carl had come alone because his girlfriend had caught him cheating, and so another relationship seemed to be over for him. We had invited other friends, and some of the BBC team. All the members of the expanded Cold Water Club were there, and there were twelve in total now. I had gone along once, but never again. I would leave the freezing cold water to Freya and her ladies. My testicles still hadn't forgiven me!

Freya lined up all the plastic champagne flutes on the kitchen island and filled each one with champagne as we got ready for the show.

'Everyone get a glass of champagne!' said Freya. 'Dolly hit the lights.'

'Righto,' said Dolly, who turned off the lights, and the room was suddenly almost dark except for the light from the television.

There were about four minutes to go, and I just wanted to say a few words before the show began. Once everyone had a glass of champagne, I walked to the front of the room, and looked out at everyone.

'I just wanted to say a big thank you to everyone for coming tonight. We've worked so hard on this show, and it's taken us a long time, but we're finally here and I'm so proud of it. Thank you to my wonderful daughter Dolly, for all her support and help, to Carl, my erstwhile agent, for always believing in me when many others wouldn't, and lastly, to my beautiful wife, Freya, who made this all possible. We had some pretty dark times there for a while, but we came through them, and I can say now, without a shadow of a doubt, that we're happier and more in love than ever. So, here's to marriage, and to sharing a house even when you think it might be over!'

Everyone raised their glasses, and we toasted, just as the show before *House Shared* ended, and then the continuity announcer started speaking.

'Turn it up!' Dad shouted, and Freya turned the volume up as everyone went quiet and looked towards the television.

'And now on BBC One, we have a brand-new comedy about love, marriage and parenting that asks the question... is it possible to move on when you haven't even moved out? This is *House Shared*.'

Everyone in the room clapped and cheered, and then the opening credits rolled with the music they had written for the show along with a montage of old family videos. As I watched, I felt a huge wave of emotion grab me, and I reached out and held Freya's hand on one side of me, and I put my arm around Dolly on the other. I thought briefly of our remarriage in the Maldives that Christmas. It had been incredible and so beautiful; it was impossible to put into words. We had fortunately managed to squeeze it in between breaks from writing the show and with Freya's busy new schedule as she trained to be a solicitor. There had been points over the last ten years when I thought this would never happen again. There had been moments over the last couple of years when I wasn't sure Freya and I would still be together. I couldn't help the tears that leaked out of my eyes and down my face. Somehow we had made it, and staying in this house, sharing these moments, had not only saved our marriage but given me the chance to have another show on television. I had everyone and everything I needed in that room. For a second I looked towards Freya, her face lit up from the light from the television, and then I looked at Dolly, and I smiled to myself, before I turned back to the television, where the opening scene in a coffee shop in Brighton had just started.

'I see a table back there,' said Kate.

'Right, I'll get the coffees. The usual?' said Dan.

A Letter from Jon

I would imagine that if you've got this far you have already read the book, so I really hope you enjoyed it. However, if you are somehow reading this and you haven't read the book, this is my pitch to you. Although now that I think about it, if you have read the book then you might find this interesting too. Either way, this is my letter to you about how I wrote *Not Moving Out*.

A few years ago I read an article about the rise of parents who were being forced to either cohabit after breaking up, or they would rent an extra property and they would switch out living there while the children stayed in the family home. I believe it's called 'birdnest' parenting; look it up, it's very interesting. After reading this article and a few other things around the subject, I knew it would make for an interesting romantic comedy. The idea of two people separated but forced to keep living together, for me at least, had all the hallmarks of a great love story. I just wondered whether perhaps staying in each other's lives when the love was gone, would ultimately bring them back together again. It was an intriguing concept.

For me, the whole idea clicked into place when I decided to make Joe, the husband, a failed television writer. There had to be a reason why the couple had fallen out of love that wasn't so bad, so utterly awful, that they couldn't come back from it. In so many novels and television shows they tend to focus on people cheating and I knew I didn't want either of my characters to do that. So once I had one of the couple be the sort of 'loser' in the marriage, while the other character becomes the successful one, it was easy to see how they could drift apart. I also had to make sure that the very thing that had torn them apart was also the thing that brought them back together again.

Not Moving Out is a romantic comedy about love when you are older, about marriage, parenting, parents, friends and lovers. As most of my books do, it features an eclectic cast of characters like the daughter, who has a secret she hasn't been able to tell her parents, a slightly overbearing but well-meaning mother, her partner Marmalade – if you've read the book you'll know – a friend of Joe who just can't seem to find love, Joe's agent, who can't seem to keep it, and Freya's Cold Water Club – a group of women who take a dip in the sea most morning – who help Freya make the most important decision of her life.

There is a lot more to this story than just two people who have fallen out of love but because of money and circumstance are forced to live together for six months. At its heart it's a love story, but underneath it's a story about a group of people all trying to be happy. As I approach fifty myself, I find it increasingly harder to write love stories about people in their twenties – unless like in *One Hundred Moments of Us*, I set it back in time – and so writing about people in their forties, still trying to hold onto love, was something I found far more rewarding. I think if, like me, you are firmly into middle-age or perhaps older, you will definitely be able to relate to this book, and if you're younger, perhaps you'll learn a thing or two about what's coming!

I hope you love this book as much as I enjoyed writing it. Of all the books I've written, I think I enjoyed writing this one the most. The characters felt so authentic to me and I loved the Brighton and Hove setting. Lastly, thank you for buying this book and reading Joe and Freya's story – I think it's a good one.

Acknowledgements

Firstly, a huge thank you to my publisher Hera and to their brilliant team who helped shape and inspire this book. A special thank you to Jennie for really pushing me to make this book so much better than it was when I first handed it over. It's sometimes difficult as a writer to see where the story you have spent months working on can be improved and this is why you need people you can trust to help guide you. Also a shout-out to the wonderful editors for their suggestions, ridiculous eye for detail, and for some funny little notes.

Thank you to all my readers who purchased my previous book, *One Hundred Moments Of Us*, wrote reviews and messaged me with such lovely messages. Writing a novel is such an enormous endeavour and it requires a village of people to make it happen, and so when all of that work pays off and people love what you have created, it makes it all worthwhile.

I want to thank Brighton and Hove for this book – I know, it's a strange one, so stay with me. I lived in Brighton and Hove for a short time, but it had a real impact on me and it's a key part of this book. Most of my novels have been set in London, another place I lived for a few years, but when I started writing this book I knew I wanted to set it in Brighton and Hove. It's such a beautiful, special place, and I think it really enhances the story. So thank you Brighton and Hove for all the memories.

As always, I need to thank my family, who are often forced to deal with my 'writer brain' which means I am usually off in my own world, and even when I'm not, I do have to occasionally dash off and write something down. They are awfully patient with me. I also use the term 'writer brain' as an excuse for my 'middle-aged, rapidly approaching fifty brain', which seems to be quite similar – confused, distracted, and often muddled. Sorry.

I want to say thank you to my parents, who without I wouldn't even be writing this sentence. Sadly, I lost my mother a few years ago, but she's still with me in spirit and I think of her often. My father is still going strong, running park runs every week in his seventies, which I hope to be doing myself one day. The role of parents and parenting is an important theme that runs throughout this book because I think it's integral to who we become as adults. Everything we go through and become is shaped, in some way, by our parents, so thank you Mum and Dad. When as a young man I said I wanted to an author they only supported that dream, and without them, I probably wouldn't have made it – and thank you for always sending me money when I was a poor struggling student. Lastly, as always, to my wife, for everything.